JUST ONE KISS

(Pine Grove Novel, #5)

Jean C. Joachim

Moonlight Books

Dedication

To My Readers. Thank you for your love and support.

Acknowledgment

THANK YOU TO MY EDITOR, Sherri Good, and my proofreader, Renee Waring. A special "thank you" to Vicki Locey, and Roz Lee whose encouragement keeps me on track. Thank you to the Joachim men, Larry, David & Steve, and the newest member of our family, Pam, for keeping me grounded and believing in me.

Just One Kiss
Copyright © 2019 Jean C. Joachim
Edited by Sherri Good
Proofreader: Renee Waring
Cover design – Dawne Dominique, Dusk to Dawn designs

PUBLISHER
Moonlight Books

Just One Kiss
(Pine Grove Novel, #5)
Jean C. Joachim
Chapter One

RUSTY SHIFTED IN HIS seat across the desk from the school social worker.

"Mr. Reisse, your son needs you," said Sylvia Kaplan.

"He's got me."

She shook her head. "He's acting out in the classroom, and at recess. If you don't take some action, I'll be forced to recommend services for him."

"Services? Like putting him in foster care?" Rusty rose halfway out of his chair.

"Like sending him to spend time with me and the district psychiatrist. I'm sure you'd rather give him private care."

"He doesn't need a shrink. He's just a normal boy."

Again, she shook her head.

"Not exactly. Tommy's good at heart—but he needs attention. With your wife gone to make films in Europe..."

"My ex-wife."

"And you working twenty-four seven, the boy's lonely. Do you read to him every night at bedtime, Mr. Reisse?"

"After the game, it's too late. He's asleep."

"Who takes care of him while you're away?"

"His aunt. Sometimes a babysitter."

"He needs you, Mr. Reisse. His father."

"I have to work."

"I suggest you take time off."

"How much time?"

"As much as possible. You're not a poor man. Could you manage the summer?"

He raised his eyebrows.

"The whole summer off?"

"That's right. Get a cabin in the woods. Away from the television and video games. Just the two of you. Read to him. Fish. Hunt, if you must. Teach him baseball. Anything. Just spend time with him."

"What about my job?"

Mrs. Kaplan smiled at him. "Come now. You're telling me the famous Rusty Reisse, two- time World Series MVP, can't get a couple of months hiatus or sabbatical, or whatever you'd call it from your broadcasting job?"

Rusty swallowed. This woman was a ballbuster. She could take on any pitcher and hit it out of the park. What chance did he stand?

"Do you love your son, Mr. Reisse?" Her gentle tone turned harsh.

"Of course, I love my son."

"Then try putting him first." She pushed to her feet.

"But I—"

"The boy is not beyond help. But he needs it now. If you let this summer go by, I will take action in the fall."

Rusty stood up. "And where do you suggest I find such a place?"

"You have many resources, I'm sure. You're well off, you must know thousands of people. Find a place. Do it for Tommy."

"And? If I do?"

"Let me know. I'll expect weekly emails from you reporting on your progress. His progress, really."

"Weekly?"

She bent over the desk and made direct eye contact. "Don't you get it, Mr. Reisse? Your son is slipping away—heading to a bad place. I'm trying to save him."

"Okay, okay. I admit he's been a little difficult lately."

She raised her eyebrows. "A little difficult?" She picked up a small stack of papers. "Do you know exactly how many times he's been sent to the principal's office?"

Rusty cringed.

"Of course, you don't want to know. He's only eight, Mr. Reisse. If you don't pay attention to him now, those could be trips to juvenile detention by the time he's thirteen."

Fear spiked through Rusty. "Okay. I got it. Cabin in the woods. Weekly email."

Mrs. Kaplan smiled at him. "Good. I know you can do anything you set your mind to."

"Thanks for the vote of confidence." He attempted to smile, failed, and left her office.

Rusty made his way to his office, near Tommy's private school on the Upper East Side of Manhattan. He plopped down at his desk. Turning to face the huge windows behind him, he simply stared, trying to take in what Mrs. Kaplan had said.

His secretary, Bernadette, rattled off Rusty's obligations for the week. "Here are your messages. And the schedule for next week. Five interviews. Also your schedule for training camp. Harry wants to see you."

"Thanks." Feeling numb, Rusty made his way into the head of the network's office.

"Rusty. It's about time. Where have you been?"

"At school."

"What?"

As if someone had lit a match to his foot, Rusty jumped to life. "Harry! My kid's in trouble. He's failing. He's losing it. I need to take off July and August."

"July and August? What about training camp? What about the new season?"

"Get someone else to cover it."

"But you're Rusty Reisse."

Rusty pounded his fist once on Harry's enormous desk. "Didn't you hear me, Harry. I said Tommy's in trouble. I'm taking time off. He needs me. Fire me, if you want to. But I'm leaving now. I'll be back in September."

Harry leaped to his feet.

"Why you can't do that! You have a contract with us."

"Then sue me. It's my kid, Harry. Nothing's more important than Tommy."

"You son-of-a-bitch."

"Are you kiddin' me? My son. My kid. I thought you'd understand."

Harry sank down in his chair. "Really? You're not shittin' me? Tommy?"

"Yeah. I didn't see it. But the social worker read me the riot act. So I'm taking time for him. That's it. No compromise. No discussion. You're a father. Don't you get it?"

Harry's tone softened. "I do. I do get it. I'm sorry to hear that."

"I'm gonna take him away for a while. Just the two of us."

"Okay. Keep in touch. We'll cover for you. We'll figure something out."

"Talk to Bernadette. She knows everything and everyone. Thanks, Harry. I appreciate it."

"You'll be back in September?" Harry stood up.

"I will."

"Good luck." The men shook hands

Rusty returned to his office, packed up, and stopped at his secretary's desk.

"You can reach me by cell phone or email. But only if it's a dire emergency. I'll be gone until September."

"September?" Her eyebrows rose.

"Yeah. Don't ask. Keep it together for me," he said, patting her cheek.

"I'll try."

Rusty headed for his favorite restaurant, "The Goal Line." He sat at the bar and ordered Chivas Regal on the rocks and a burger. After knocking off one drink, he nursed a second, waiting for his food. A slap on the back drew his attention. It was Fred Carter, his old college buddy. The two men had gone through divorces together.

"Hey, Rusty. You're here early."

"Got some bad news."

"What happened?"

Rusty explained his predicament. "It's June fifteenth. Where the hell am I going to find a cabin in the country now?" He took a sip.

"I just might be able to help you."

"You?"

"Roberta and I bought a little place in Pine Grove, years ago. It was supposed to be our weekend getaway. Yeah, back when we were still talking. Anyway. We're still talking settlement, and she forgot about it. It's community property. I have the right to rent it out, if I want to. And I'll give it to you cheap."

"How big is it?"

"It's two bedrooms, fully furnished, and two grand for the whole summer."

"Really?"

"Yep. For an old buddy."

"That's great. I'll take it. Do you want a check now?"

"Why not?"

Rusty whipped out his checkbook and scratched out the rent. He handed it to Fred.

"Roberta can't throw us out, can she?"

Fred shook his head. "Nope. Now you're set. Hope you and Tommy have a great time."

"Me, too." Rusty rubbed the back of his neck.

ACROSS TOWN, MEG GUNDERSON, second-grade teacher, sent her class out to recess. She busied herself putting away supplies, hanging up smocks, and tidying up her classroom. She had the neatest one in her grade. Smiling with pride as she put things away, she answered a knock.

"Roberta, come in."

"I have the plans for the end-of-year party. Just wanted to run them by you," Roberta Carter said, entering the room.

The two women huddled together by the teacher's desk, examining papers. When they were finished, Meg sighed. "Looks great."

Roberta stuffed the plans back in her shoulder bag. "How are you?"

"I'm okay. But summer is a big question mark."

"I thought you were going to take a group of kids to the Adirondacks."

"It fell through."

"Weren't you talking about going away with your boyfriend?"

"Changed my mind. Charlie doesn't like him. It wouldn't work."

"Hmm. How about spending the summer in my cabin in Pine Grove?"

"You have a cabin?"

"Fred doesn't know, but I'm getting custody of it in the divorce. It's a lovely place. Two large bedrooms. Fully furnished. You know my taste."

"I can give it to you for a bargain price. Twelve hundred for the whole summer."

"Twelve hundred? That's cheap."

"You deserve a break. You're the best teacher the twins have ever had."

"Thank you."

"It's the least I can do."

"It's very kind of you. I'll take it. Charlie'll love being in the country."

"And you, too."

"Where is Pine Grove."

"About two hours northwest of the City. Rural. Quiet."

"Perfect. After this crazy year, I need the rest."

"I'll show you on a map."

Roberta whipped out her phone and Googled a map of western New York state. The two women pored over the picture while Roberta filled Meg in on things to do in Pine Grove.

"Sounds ideal. Charlie and I need some down time."

Roberta patted Meg's arm. "It's been hard for you, losing John. Raising Charlie alone."

Meg sighed. Her eyes filled. "I miss him so much. So does Charlie."

The children returned to the classroom, ending the conversation between the women. Meg couldn't wait to tell her young son about their summer adventure.

She picked him up from his classroom, and they headed for home. On their walk, her mind conjured up projects and experiments they could do over the summer.

"And you're going to love being in the country. We can test the water for bacteria. We can catch frogs to keep for the summer. Maybe even a snake."

"A snake? Mom, how come you're the only mother who isn't afraid of snakes?"

She'd laughed. "Maybe because I grew up studying them. They're really cool. You'll see."

Charlie asked a million questions on their way home. His interest in their new home for the summer lifted Meg's spirits. Being a mother and father to her son weighed her down from time to time. This trip would be a relief.

Meg, a former high school science teacher, now taught elementary school. After her husband died in a car crash, she took time off to take courses in early childhood education. She went back to work in a public school where Charlie was enrolled.

Charlie watched "Bill Nye, the Science Guy" while she fixed dinner. While she stirred spaghetti sauce, she created a mental list of books and equipment to bring.

"Mom, can we get a dog?"

"A dog? Charlie, I have enough to handle as it is."

The boy frowned.

"Maybe someday. But not now. Besides, you'll have plenty of animals around when we get to the country."

"When are we going?" He twirled some pasta with his fork.

"As soon as school is over."

"How much longer?"

"Two weeks."

He hung his head. Meg leaned over to hug him. "I know. But it'll go fast."

He looked up into her eyes and she smiled. For the first time since John's death, she had something to look forward to.

"We're gonna have a great time."

"Promise?"

"Promise."

MEG GLANCED AT THE GPS, then steered the car through the dark country roads toward their destination while Charlie slept soundly in the backseat. She smiled. At eleven, there was no traffic. She lifted her shoulders, then pushed them down, and took a deep breath. Meg loved driving on empty rural roads and adored the countryside.

She'd grown up in a small town in Ohio and then met John in college. After she married him, they'd moved to the City. He had a lucrative career on Wall Street.

He'd provided a large apartment on the Upper West Side—entire second and third floors of a townhouse. Meg had everything, except grass and trees. When Charlie came along, she'd stayed home and spent days in Central Park with their son.

After John died, she froze.

Meg's sister had been urging her to make a change, but she couldn't. Maybe taking this summer away would bring her back to life, emotionally.

The GPS put her within two miles of her destination. Her pulse kicked up. Impatience pushed her foot down a little harder on the accelerator. Picking her gaze up from the road, she eased down on the brake as a sleepy little house emerged from the darkness.

How thoughtful of Roberta to leave the light over the front door on. As she signaled for a turn, she frowned to see another car in the driveway. Maybe Roberta had a spare car? Could she have forgotten about Meg's arrival date?

She pulled up next to a silver BMW SUV. Hmm, maybe Roberta had custody of the house already?

Meg opened the trunk and took out two bags. The rest could wait until the morning.

She jostled Charlie. "Sweetheart. Charlie. Dear. We're here. Can you get up long enough to get into bed?"

Meg prayed the beds were made up already. Charlie mumbled something, rubbed his face and slid out the door. He stumbled his way up the cement path with his mother toting the bags right behind him. Meg fished the key from her purse. She put it in the lock and swung the door wide open.

As Charlie tripped up the step into the house, the sound of barking, once faint grew louder. As the boy moved inside, the hound from Hell, snarling, teeth bared bounded into the room. Charlie and his mother screamed at the same time!

Seeking escape, Meg fled to the dining room, dragging Charlie behind her. The dog nipped at the boy. Using all her strength, Meg grabbed him by the waist and vaulted him onto the table. Then she scrambled onto a chair, then the table with the black dog close behind.

She and Charlie clung to each other screaming. The dog jumped, but Meg raised her foot and kicked its snout. The dog yelped.

"Hey! Don't kick my dog!" came a masculine voice.

Meg looked up. "Call off your dog!"

"Come here, Coco. Did the bad lady hurt you?" A man dressed only in boxers, followed by a young boy in pajamas fussed about the dog. The animal calmed down for a moment before it snarled again at Meg and Charlie.

"It's okay, Coco. I don't think she's armed."

"Call off your dog!" she repeated, only louder.

"I will, if you tell me what you're doing breaking into my house." Despite his words, the man grasped the dog's collar and held her at bay.

Slowly, Meg let go of her son. "You okay? Did the dog bite you?"

Charlie nodded. "I don't think so. She ripped my pants."

Meg examined the boy's leg. "Damn. She did. You'll pay for new pants, mister. And by the way, what are you doing squatting in my house?"

"Your house?" His eyebrows rose.

"You heard me. Keep that beast away from me," she said, easing her way down from the table.

"I paid to rent this house for the entire summer! So get out before I call the cops." Rusty frowned.

"Cops? Please do! I paid to rent this house for the entire summer. This is thirty-five Pond Road, isn't it?"

The man yanked open the front door and checked the number nailed there. "It is. I have paperwork."

"You? I have paperwork, too!"

"I'm calling the cops," he said, leaving the room.

"Fine with me." Meg folded her arms across her chest. "And take the beast with you."

"Come on, Coco. You don't have to stay here and be insulted."

"What kind of dog is it?" Charlie asked.

"Rottweiler," the other boy replied.

"I'm Charlie."

"Tommy. Wanna see my room?"

"Don't leave my sight. The dog isn't safe!"

"Aw, Coco won't hurt you. You're with me."

Despite his mother's words, Charlie went off with Tommy.

The man returned with his cell phone in hand.

"Come on, Coco," the boy called, and the Rottie obeyed, following the boys into the back of the house.

"I'd like to report an intruder," Rusty said into his cell.

Meg wound her arms around her middle and took a deep breath. She'd stopped shaking and turned her attention to the man in front of her. He was tall, and his mussed hair and scruffy face gave him an attractive bedroom look. She dropped her gaze to his chest. Impressive. The guy obviously worked out. In the dim light, she saw the planes of his pecs and the dusting of brown hair covering them. He even had a shadow of abs.

Remembering he stood in her house, Meg's anger and hostility returned.

"They're on the way."

"You say you have paperwork? Good. Get it. Show it to the cops."

The sound of a siren in the distance soothed Meg. She'd soon have her house back and this interloper would be tossed out on his, sexy, pushy behind.

Chapter Two

Rusty stood with his phone in hand and glanced down. He was practically naked. *Sure won't look too good when the cops get here.* He hustled back to his room and thrust his legs into his jeans. He grabbed a tank top and yanked it on. After he zipped his fly, he returned to the front of the house.

Little Miss Cat Burglar shifted her weight. He studied her. *What's a hot chick like her doing breaking into houses? And with her kid, too? Some people have no standards. No morals.* Still, he noticed how her short blonde hair caught the dim light in the room just so. And her body? Nice. He stared at her chest, imagining his hands on her breasts. Geez, exactly the right size. Although he couldn't see her butt, he imagined her slender legs led to a nicely-shaped rear end.

Breaking and entering, theft, and lying—remember who she is! Bad chicks can be hot, too, he reminded himself.

The siren went off and two uniformed state troopers, guns on hips, came up the path. The boys ran to the front, followed by the barking Coco. Tommy opened the door.

"Your dog? Control him." The officer waited.

Rusty grabbed Coco by the collar. "Yes, sir." Rusty noticed the man's nametag.

"Now what's the problem?" the officer said.

Rusty and the woman started speaking at the same time. Voices escalated and Coco barked. The officer raised his hands.

"Wait a minute! Wait! Slow down. Either put the dog on a leash or in another room. Then, one at a time." Officer Bolton said. "Ladies first."

"Thank you," the woman replied.

"Just my luck. An unliberated cat burglar," Rusty muttered.

"I'm not a cat burglar!"

"Your name, miss?" the officer asked.

"Meg Gunderson. My son, Charlie."

While Meg whipped out her papers, Rusty shifted his weight. Surely hers were a forgery.

The trooper looked them over.

"And you, Mr...? Reisse, isn't it? Rusty Reisse? You played for the New York Nighthawks, didn't you?"

"Shortstop. Seventeen years." Rusty tried to look modest but failed.

"You're a baseball player? Explains the lack of brains," Meg said, staring at him.

"Why you...lady, you've got a lotta balls."

"Please! There are children here." Meg folded her arms across her chest.

"Yeah. And they both know what balls are." Rusty grinned.

"Mr. Reisse, would you give me an autograph?" The trooper whisked out a piece of paper and a pen. "Just make it out to Roger, my son."

"Sure thing, Officer Bolton. Happy to." Rusty smiled as he scratched out a phrase and his signature.

While he signed, the trooper examined his papers. He folded up each set and handed them back to the proper person. He shook his head.

"I'm sorry to tell you, folks, you both rented this place."

"What?" Rusty and Meg said in unison.

"Right. Go ahead look at each other's leases and checks. Either someone was scamming you or playing a nasty joke. But you both contracted for this house. You both have equal rights to be here."

"But he can't. I mean. It's ours. I don't want him here."

"Nothing I can do, ma'am. I suggest you exchange papers, and you'll see what I mean. Toss a coin or something. You'll have to figure it out on your own." Officer T. Bolton folded up the autograph and slipped it in his pocket. "Goodnight."

"This is my house."

"No, it isn't," Rusty said, unfolding her papers. They each studied the other's lease and shook their heads. Meg burst into tears.

"Just like a woman. Cry to get your way," he said to himself. "You can blubber all you want to; Tommy and I are not moving out. But I will help you carry your bags back to your car."

"We don't have any place to go," she said.

"Back to the city?"

She shook her head. Fishing around her purse, she finally pulled out a tissue. "I promised Charlie summer in the country."

"Yeah? Well, the guidance counselor told me if I didn't get Tommy away for a while, bad things were going to happen." No way would Rusty reveal how desperate his situation was to this total stranger.

Meg sank down on the dining room chair. "It's all Roberta's fault."

"Roberta? Yeah. And Fred, too. Bastards."

"Please don't use bad language in front of my son."

"Sorry." Rusty rubbed his face, then the back of his neck. "Look. Why don't you and your son stay here tonight? It's late. We'll sort this out tomorrow."

"Where will we sleep."

As chivalrous as he was feeling there was no way Rusty was giving up his bed. "I think the sofa is a sleeper. Let's see."

"Charlie, there's an extra bed in my room. Come on."

Charlie picked up his bag and followed Tommy. Coco trotted along behind. Sure enough, Rusty had been right. He tossed the cushions and opened the bed.

"We're in luck. It's already made up."

"Thank you."

While she showed some appreciation, it had been forced, reluctant. Since she wasn't a cat burglar, he couldn't justify tossing her into the street. Besides, she had a son about Tommy's age.

"Where's the bathroom?"

"First door on the left. Boys' room is on the right. Mine is on the left."

"Fine. Excuse me." She opened her bag and rummaged around. Rusty retreated. At least he knew when to leave. Stopping by the boys' room, he found each one in a bed.

"Thanks, Mr. Reisse," Charlie said, turning an angelic face to Rusty.

"You're welcome. We'll get this straightened out tomorrow. Goodnight."

The boys returned his goodnight. He turned out the light and climbed back into bed. By now, he was beyond tired. Still, the solution for the situation escaped him. Annoyed, he closed his eyes and prayed it had all been a dream. And when he awoke, Miss Meg Gunderson and her cute tow-headed son would be gone, having been nothing more than a figment of his imagination.

IN THE BATHROOM, MUMBLING to herself, Meg changed into her nightgown.

"The police know I'm here. And if he's a rapist murderer, they'll know he did it." She wondered if he'd knock her off just to get the house. What would he do with Charlie? No way. An ex-pro baseball player wouldn't. If he was proven guilty, he'd never get into the Baseball Hall of Fame. Isn't it what every player wanted?

She chastised herself for being paranoid and brushed her teeth. When she finished, she padded into the boys' room and kissed Charlie goodnight.

"Goodnight, Tommy. Thank you for letting Charlie stay in your room."

"It's like having a brother without the annoying little kid part," the boy said.

Meg had miscarried a month before John's accident. Seeing her son happy with Tommy, she wondered if he would have been happy with a sibling. Maybe, someday.

Back in the living room, she pulled down the covers on the sofabed and climbed in. The room had cooled with the mid-June country night air, so she hauled her ass out of bed to slip on leggings and a sweatshirt. Not a good idea to go looking for an extra blanket at this hour. The hound from Hell might trap her in the linen closet. If there even was a linen closet in the place. She returned to bed.

Once she warmed up, sleep came quickly. Since John's death, she'd learned to shove unpleasant or disturbing thoughts from her mind. Now she needed sleep to be fresh to tackle their unpleasant situation in the morning. She needed to prevail, convince the arrogant asshole he was wrong and send him packing. But how? One more yawn and the next thing she knew, morning sun crept through the living room curtains and poked her right in the eye.

She cracked an eyelid open. Her phone said five thirty. Oh, Lord! No way would she be getting up at this hour. Startled by a snorting sound, she rolled over, coming face-to-snout with the behemoth the jock called a dog.

"Nice, Coco. Nice doggie. Go play, eat a bear or something." She attempted to shoo the pooch away, but the monster didn't budge.

Coco stared at Meg, then licked her face.

"Ewww. Yuck. Yucky, yucky, yuck!" She wiped her face with her fingers as she bounded out of bed and into the bathroom. After scrubbing her cheeks, she returned to bed. Coco was still there.

"You can't want breakfast at this hour?" Meg shook her head. "Walk? So early?"

A low woof emanated from the giant beast.

Meg searched the living room, picking up newspapers on the end table and jackets slung on chairs. "Where's your leash?"

The mighty Coco lumbered away, returning two minutes later carrying the missing leash in her mouth.

"Oh. I see. Fetch really means something. Okay." Gingerly, she approached the massive dog. "How the hell?" Meg tried the harness one way, then another with no success. "Why can't they have a stupid collar and leash. What is this? A harness or a torture device? Oh, yeah. A harness. Like a collar could hurt this thing. She's the size of a baby elephant."

After five minutes, she got the hang of it and clicked the ends together. She slipped on flipflops and padded to the kitchen.

"Bags. Bags. Can't go out without a bag," she muttered, rummaging through drawers. After she opened a large cabinet, she spied a bag of bags hanging on the door. Meg stuffed two in the pocket of her sweatshirt and unlocked the back door.

Coco took off, lumbering down the steps and onto the lawn, yanking the leash from Meg's hand. "Stop! Coco! Come back!" She ran after the dog, who stopped at a tree to sniff. Meg grabbed the leash.

"Rules. We need some rules here. I'm not doing this every morning. Just so you know. And when you come out with me, you'll walk like a lady. No taking off. Okay?"

The dog squatted.

"There. Good. Now can we go back inside?"

Obviously, Coco was better at pulling than listening as she continued on her way, trotting along at a good clip, dragging Meg behind her.

Fifteen minutes later, Meg opened the back door. The dog pushed ahead and made a beeline straight to her food bowl, which she nudged toward Meg.

"Breakfast now, huh?" The dog pulled her lips back into a grin. "I don't know what they feed you. Let's see..." She opened the pantry and found a big bag of dry dog food, filled the dish, and gave her water.

Meg put the bed together, then headed back to the kitchen. After taking a peek in the fridge, she inspected the pantry. It wasn't exactly well-stocked, but it had the basics.

She pulled a mixing bowl down from a shelf and went to work. The familiar aroma of melting butter pleased her nose. Still wearing her nightgown, sweatshirt, and leggings, Meg hummed a favorite tune and danced a little as she poured fresh pancake batter in the pan.

"Well, well, well, she sings, she dances, and she cooks, too."

The deep, masculine voice startled Meg. She whipped around to face a half-naked Rusty lounging against the doorway. She eyed his smokin' hot body clad only in boxers. Damn, the man was fit. Staring at his chest started sensations in her private places. She swallowed. Gradually her gaze made its way to his face.

His eyes laughed at her. Anger ignited. "Do you always come undressed to breakfast?"

"Do you always wear a nightgown, sweatshirt, and leggings to bed? Isn't it overkill? Of course, you're probably used to sleeping alone."

She flipped the pancakes onto her plate and pursed her lips. "At least I'm decent." She dropped her gaze to his fly. "I hope Mr. Winkie isn't going to pay us a visit."

Rusty's eyes widened. He looked down, then covered his crotch with his hands. "Oh, shit. Sorry." He ran from the room.

Meg's anger dissolved into laughter. She opened the maple syrup, applied some to her food, and sat down to eat.

Before she'd finished half of the short stack, Rusty was back, fastening his bathrobe.

"Mr. Winkie?" He cocked an eyebrow. "I hope you're not teaching your son to call it that."

Meg raised her eyes to his. With a steady voice, she replied. "Actually, I'm teaching him to call it his penis. Because that's what it is. Not a dick, not junk, nor a Johnson, not the little fellow, not cock, not his equipment, not the other head, and not Mr. Winkie. What are you teaching your son?"

"All of the above. And a few others you didn't mention. Got any more of those?"

She made a face. "Do you mean you'd like me to make you some pancakes?"

"Yeah. Isn't cooking woman's work?"

Anger boiled up in her chest. Unable to hide it, her voice took on a tone so cold it could freeze meat. "For your snide comment, you can cook it yourself. I'll be nice enough to let you use some of the batter I made. I said *some*. Save most of it for the boys."

He grinned and shook his head. "At least you didn't throw it at me. It's so easy to get your goat. Looks like you're going to be the entertainment around here."

"Uh, no. Because you're leaving. I'll help you pack."

"Oh, yeah? Fuck that shit. We were here first. And we're staying." Rusty approached the stove. He picked up the handle of the pan and yowled in pain, throwing the pan back on the burner.

"Oops. Guess I forgot to tell you the pan was hot. I'm so sorry." She smiled sweetly at him.

Clutching his hand, he headed for the freezer where he grabbed a couple of ice cubes.

"I'm not used to cooking."

"Who feeds your son?"

"I have a housekeeper. And she's a darn good cook, too."

Her ears got hot, though, she had no clue why this information burned her up. "You need a housekeeper?"

"When you've hit it big in baseball, you don't have to do any menial shit anymore."

"Menial? I consider cooking for my son an important part of parenting."

"Yeah? Well, count me out. I consider playing baseball with my son an important part of parenting. Do you play ball with Charlie?"

She shook her head. Anger flared higher. "Baseball is a waste of time. I'm teaching my son about science. Nature. He can already identify twenty different species of bird, snakes, and lizards. And he recognizes many bird calls."

"Snakes? The only snakes my kid will learn about are the kind who wear spiked heels and tight skirts."

"You give chauvinist a bad name." She finished her food and dumped her plate in the sink.

"Aren't you going to help me?" He turned toward her.

"It's pancake batter, butter, and a hot pan. Figure it out. He who doesn't prepare batter does the dishes," she said, sticking her nose in the air and heading for the door.

"And stop trying to seduce me with your sweatshirt and leggings get-up, will you? There are children in this house." He laughed.

She uttered a grunt of frustration and strode into the living room.

WHILE HE POURED HIMSELF a cup of coffee, Rusty watched her walk away. Her bulky clothing didn't totally cover up her cute body. Slim legs, small breasts—maybe a B cup? And the cutest damn butt he'd seen in ages. The short blonde hair was distinctive. He'd tired of all the long hair everywhere. Couldn't tell one chick from another in a bar. It just got in the way in the bedroom, anyway.

Her huge blue eyes, chic haircut, perky nose, and perfect lips commanded his attention. Hell, if they'd met at a bar, they'd already be sharing a tube of toothpaste. But the mouth on her. And her attitude?

She could shove it if she thought she'd be running him and Tommy out of this house. He found it first, paid for it first, and they were staying.

Besides, he needed to repair things with his son. Angela, his ex, made it clear she'd rather be acting or dancing, or whatever the fuck she was doing in Europe, than taking care of their son. But what did he know about parenting? Nothing. Still, the school had convinced him spending more time with Tommy would help him in school.

Rusty didn't mind. He loved the City, but country life had its merit, too. And the cute little chick sharing his house might end up sharing his bed. Nothing he liked more than a challenge.

Turning his thoughts to food, he eyed the pan, butter, and bowl of batter with suspicion. Behind him, a voice piped up.

"First you put the pan on the stove. Turn on the flame, then put some butter in. Like one pat. When it melts, you pour in some pancake batter." Tommy grinned at his father.

"How do you know so much about cooking?

"Mrs. MacDougal taught me."

"When? When does she teach you about cooking?"

"After school."

"She makes pancakes?"

"Sometimes she makes them for dinner."

"Crepes?"

"Yeah, yeah. That's what she calls them. I call them pancakes." Tommy went to the fridge and took out a carton of milk. Rusty took his son's advice.

Charlie and Meg joined them. She wore a tunic, the same leggings, and a little makeup.

"Figured it out?" She raised her eyebrows.

"I told him," Tommy piped up.

"Learning to cook from your eight-year-old son?" Again, she raised an eyebrow at him. Rusty sensed heat traveling to his face.

"He had advice."

"Oh, I see. But he's a boy. And he knows how to cook? Tsk tsk, you're falling down on the job, Rusty."

"Mrs. MacDougal and I cook a lot. She makes my lunch and dinner. Sometimes she lets me help in the kitchen." Tommy beamed with pride.

"I think it's wonderful, Tommy. Charlie helps me cook, too."

"Hot dogs, hamburgers, and salad are my specialties," Charlie said, stumbling over the last word.

Meg watched over the pancakes, giving Rusty instructions. He bristled at her condescending attitude but did what he was told. They turned out perfect.

After breakfast, Rusty harnessed Coco.

"I took her out already. And fed her, too."

"Aren't you just the handiest person to have around?" Rusty shot her a nasty look. Tommy tugged on his father's robe. In a loud whisper, he said, "Dad, be nice."

Meg hid a smile behind her hand. "Get dressed, Charlie. Long pants. We're going to look for birds."

"Mom, can Tommy come, too?"

"If his father says so. Sure."

"Can I, Dad?"

"Bird watching?" Rusty made another face.

"A little intellectual stimulation won't hurt him."

"Can Dad come, too?" Tommy asked.

Meg's eyes widened. "I doubt he wants to."

"I have to work, Tommy. You go ahead. Don't do anything dangerous, Ms. Gunderson."

The boys raced to their room.

"Just don't turn him into some kind of nerdy freak, okay?"

"Oh, you mean like me?" She stood, hands on hips.

He gave her a long look. "Yeah. Like you."

"Don't worry about it. I'm sure you can buy a guidebook to translate what he talks about when he gets home. Who thought such a young lad could leave his father in the dust intellectually?" She pretended to yawn.

Steam boiled up inside Rusty. She'd touched a nerve. He wasn't proud of his lack of learning. She must have at least two degrees, he figured, if she's a teacher. And Rusty had none.

"Okay, okay. I'm coming." He frowned at her.

"I don't remember inviting you."

"If Tommy goes, I go."

"Well, then. I guess you've invited yourself."

"Damn straight. Don't get so fucking superior, little Miss School Teacher."

"Watch your language."

"Why? Your son'll pick it up in middle school anyway."

"At least he can wait until then."

"Hasn't he ever heard the eff word?"

She shook her head. "Not from me."

"Oh my God. You're really a little prig, aren't you?"

"Don't call me names. I use proper English."

"Well fuck it." He escaped to his room, leaving her open-mouthed. Chuckling to himself, he dressed quickly. He left two buttons of his golf shirt unbuttoned. *Give the woman a thrill.* Rusty shook his head. This wasn't going as planned at all. She was supposed to do all the cooking, sleep with him, and keep her high-flying ideas to herself. Hah! Like that was gonna happen. He shook his head. What the hell had he agreed to last night? Bird watching? Next best thing to being dead.

Chapter Three

Meg dragged her suitcase into the dining room, fished out jeans, a long-sleeved shirt, and then dressed in the bathroom. If she had to use the bathroom every time she changed clothes, this was going to be a long summer. She needed that jerk, Rusty, to give her the master bedroom. Damn it. Whatever happened to chivalry?

When the boys had assembled by the front door, Meg cleared her throat.

"I have an announcement. Until we get this worked out, I'm taking over the dining room. I'll hang a shower curtain over the doorway and no one is to come in unless they knock first. Got it?"

Charlie and Tommy nodded. Rusty shook his head. "Really?"

"Yes, really."

"Okay, okay," he held up his hands. "You can have the bedroom. But just until we get this straightened out."

"I've got a call in to Roberta."

"I left a message for Fred. Seems like they reconciled and went on a second honeymoon."

"They have to come back eventually."

"Ya think?"

Meg took a deep breath. Rusty's earlier snarky comments had gotten to her, but she held her tongue. She decided to keep her temper, since the boys were there. No use starting World War III in front of their sons. Boy, the minute she got Rusty alone, he'd hear about it.

"Come on. Let's go. There's a nature center in Oak Bend."

"I'll drive."

"Why?"

"Because my car's bigger. More room. Put the address in the GPS."

She shrugged. "Okay."

They piled into the car and Meg accessed the GPS on her phone.

"You can use mine. It's bigger," Rusty said.

"I'm sure everything of yours is bigger," she hissed. "But I'm happy with mine."

He shot her a salacious grin. "Yep. Just as long as you know."

"Shut it, will you?" She fiddled with her cell, then gave him the first instruction. She rolled down the window. "What a beautiful day."

"Perfect for golf. Tennis. Baseball. Hey! Maybe we can catch a game? I think there's a team up here. Look it up, will you?" Rusty kept his eyes on the road.

"A baseball game? In the country?"

"Baseball is the national pastime. It happens everywhere."

"Could we?" Charlie asked.

"What? Go to a baseball game?" Meg asked.

"Yeah."

"I'll see." She gave Rusty the next few turns to take then focused on her phone. "Found it. Hmm. Pine Grove is in Jefferson County. Let's see. There! There it is. Yep. The Jefferson Jaguars."

"Email me their schedule. I'll get tickets." Rusty put on his turn signal.

"We're here, guys!" As Rusty turned the car into the parking lot, Meg smiled. Her nerves settled. Soon she'd be in the woods and fields, on her home turf, and in control. The snarky, loud, jock would fade into the background. Maybe he'd even be happy to stay behind and play with his phone while she took the boys on an adventure. Her smile brightened.

The boys got out of the car.

"I'm thirsty," Tommy said.

"Here." Charlie offered his canteen to his new friend.

"What's that?"

"A canteen."

"What's a canteen?"

"It's kinda like a water bottle you refill."

"For hikers and campers," Meg put in, shooting a questioning glance at Rusty.

"Well, excuse me if I don't go camping. I like a comfortable bed and a bathroom."

"Figures," she muttered. "Come on boys."

There was a person there to collect a donation and give out maps of the center detailing trails and points of interest. Meg sat on a bench with a boy on either side.

"What do you want to see first?" She leafed through the small booklet. "Turtles, birds, or snakes?"

"Let's do the snakes last. Like in another lifetime, maybe?" Rusty piped up.

"Afraid?" Meg cocked an eyebrow.

"Just thinking of the boys."

"Birds, Mom."

"Okay." Meg pulled two pairs of binoculars from her backpack. She slipped one around her neck and handed the other one to her son.

"Can you share with Tommy?"

Charlie nodded.

"Good. Let's see. Hmm. There are water birds near the big pond. Probably see the turtles there, too. Take this path." She pointed to the right. Charlie ran ahead with Tommy right behind.

"How long is this nature crap gonna take?" Rusty followed Meg.

"However long it takes. Suck it up." She lifted her chin and moved faster, leaving him to catch up.

As they neared the pond, Meg pulled the boys aside to hide behind a small thicket.

"Look! See?" She pointed. "It's a redwing blackbird. Can you see the red on his wing?"

Charlie nodded.

"No. Where?" Tommy asked.

Charlie handed him the binocs. "Look through this at the tree."

Sure enough, another bird joined the first.

"I see him! I see him! Look, Dad!" Tommy pointed.

Rusty grabbed Meg's binocs, jerking her up against him.

"Where? Where?"

"Wait a minute. Geez. Can't you ask first?"

She slipped the wide loop over her head and handed the glasses to Rusty.

"Missed it." He thrust the spyglasses into her hand. "Let me guess. A blackbird with red on his wing. Right?"

"Brilliant deduction," Meg muttered under her breath.

"Mom! Look! A heron!" Charlie pointed.

Meg pulled up the binocs. "I think it's an egret, Charlie."

"Egret, heron. What's the difference?" Rusty asked.

"One is light brown and the other is white."

"Oh. Don't need those things to see. Where is it?"

"Maybe if you paid attention..." Meg barely held her temper.

"Yeah, Dad. Come on. Don't be a dick."

Meg's eyes widened. She turned to stare at Rusty.

"Okay, okay. Sometimes my language leaves...uh, well, you know."

"I don't know."

"Mom, what does being a dick mean?" Charlie raised innocent eyes to Meg.

She glared at Rusty. "Nothing good, Charlie."

"I'll tell you later," Tommy said.

"Thank you, Rusty Reisse, for my son's first lesson in bad language."

Meg pushed to her feet and headed for the pond. Rusty stayed behind. Charlie caught up to his mom. Meg looped an arm around his shoulders as she explained about the red-eared sliders they might see. She glanced over to see Rusty furiously typing on his cell.

Good. Let him lose himself in his stupid phone.

There was a small dock jutting out over the water. Meg and the boys went to the end. Turtles sun-bathed on exposed rocks and even on some of the grassy beach area.

"Turtles are reptiles. They're cold-blooded. They don't make their own body heat. They have to absorb heat from the sun."

As she continued, both boys asked questions. Then they had a contest—who could spot the biggest turtle and then the smallest one. When Tommy won for finding the smallest turtle, Charlie gave him a hug.

"In baseball, when one guy hits a home run, the other guys do high five. Or slap him on the butt. In football, they do a chest bump."

"Like this?" Charlie asked.

"No. Like this." Tommy demonstrated.

Watching her son learn the manly art of congratulations, sports-style, Meg swallowed a smile. Maybe having Tommy around would be a good thing for Charlie?

Rusty, running to join them, caught her eye.

"I did it! I got tickets for the Jefferson Jaguar's home game on Saturday afternoon. We got fifth row behind first base!"

"Really?" Tommy asked.

"Yep. Nothing but the best for you, slugger."

"Fine, fine. We'll go to a movie." Meg frowned.

Rusty grabbed her arm. "No siree. You're coming. I got four tickets."

Charlie and Tommy yelled and leaped, scaring the turtles. About half a dozen slid back into the lake.

"Whoopee. A baseball game." Meg sank down on a bench.

"You're gonna love it." Rusty's grin ran from ear-to-ear.

"Am I?"

"I've always wanted to go to a baseball game," Charlie said.

"You never told me."

"Aw. I knew you didn't want to."

"Okay. So I guess we're going. How much were the tickets?"

"They're on me. Since you're spending so much time schlepping us through nature. It's the least I can do."

"I don't want any gifts from you. We can pay our own way."

"How about you cook three dinners and two breakfasts and we'll call it even."

"Fine." She stood up and strode off. "This way to the bird feeders."

Rusty followed, shaking his head. "Gratitude."

"You might have asked me first."

"Oh? Really? And did your husband ask you every time he wanted to buy you something? Maybe you were never grateful. Maybe that's why he walked out?"

"What?" She froze.

"You're divorced, right?" Rusty and the boys stopped.

Meg took a minute to steady her voice. "He didn't walk out."

Charlie hugged his mother.

"My husband died in a car accident. Two years ago." Fast blinking almost controlled the tears. Two slipped down her cheek. She wiped them away quickly. "Let's go."

Rusty took her arm. He looked at Charlie, then at Meg. "I'm sorry. I didn't know."

Pulling away from him, she gave a curt nod. "This way to the feeders."

AT NOON, CHARLIE TUGGED on his mother's sleeve.

"I'm hungry."

"Me, too," Tommy added.

"Okay, get in the car and we'll find someplace to eat. I saw a restaurant in downtown Pine Grove," Rusty said.

"Downtown Pine Grove?" Meg laughed. "I'd hardly call it downtown."

"Whatever. I think it was called Homers. Let's go there."

"Do you know the way?"

"In this one-horse town? Damn right I do."

"Burgers and fries!" Tommy yelled in the backseat.

The boys hooted and hollered all the way, making Meg smile. It had been a very long time since she'd seen Charlie so joyful. As much as she despised Rusty, Tommy proved to be good for her son. Maybe they'd find a way to get along.

She could hear her therapist in her head. *You gotta let things go a little, Meg. Not everything's a big deal. Sure, losing John was. But give yourself a break. Learn to go with the flow.*

Go with the flow? Really? Her therapist didn't have her whole world turned on its ass in a heartbeat. She didn't lose everything. She didn't face the destruction of every dream she'd had. Nope, it didn't happen to Dr. Middleton. It had happened to her, Meg Gunderson, and no one else. Go with the flow? She might as well try to touch the moon.

Rusty requested a table outside.

"For little Miss Nature Girl here."

"I have the perfect table. Right by the water."

"Great. After you," Rusty said, stepping aside so she could go first. Suspicious, Meg shot a look at him before she followed the head waiter to a table. A colorful umbrella provided shade. The restaurant had a dock the length of the building jutting out slightly over Cedar Lake. Meg's heart squeezed. This was just the type of place John would have loved. Damn, she missed him.

The waiter pulled out her chair.

"This is so cool! Look. A boat!" Charlie pointed to a speedboat with a skier behind.

Meg tried to keep fried food away from her son, but she let it go today. He ordered the same as his new companion—a cheeseburger and fries. She and the boys ordered lemonade. Rusty had a beer.

Sitting back, she took in the sight of the beautiful lake, gleaming in the sun, its coastline hugged by small, neat houses. Each one had its own dock. Most had boats, too. While the lake wasn't big, it provided a quiet place to drop a fishing line and munch on a sandwich while you waited for a catch.

She and John had rented a quiet cabin in the woods upstate for their honeymoon. Her mind tripped back to the most glorious two weeks she'd ever spent with anyone. John had been protective, thoughtful, sweet, and the perfect lover. She sighed.

"Something wrong?" Rusty burst into her thoughts like Godzilla stomping into a village.

"Just remembering."

"Good memories?"

"The best."

"Wish I had some of those." He shrugged and turned away.

Meg raised her eyebrows.

"Ducks! Mom, ducks. Can we feed the ducks?" Charlie asked, taking a roll from the basket of bread on the table.

"Sure."

"Come on, Tommy."

"Careful! Don't fall in!" Meg called. "Don't you have any good memories of Tommy's mother?"

"Not really. She got knocked up. So we got married. We'd only been together about three months. The marriage? A disaster. Only good thing to come from it was Tommy."

"What a shame."

"What?"

"I don't mean about Tommy. But about your marriage. Your ex. No good memories? It's

sad."

"I've never had more than six months with any woman. By then, the warts come out. And I'm gone."

"Whose warts? Hers or yours?"

"Touché. Hers, actually."

"John and I were married for twelve years. Twelve of the happiest years of my life."

"Maybe I'll get there. Some day."

"Not if you don't hang around more than six months."

"I suppose. I'm busy. Broadcasting. Doing events. My son. I have a full life."

"I hope it works out for you."

"Do you?" He cocked an eyebrow at her.

"Maybe. Maybe I do."

He laughed. "Guess I'm growing on you."

"Uh, no. But Tommy is good for Charlie."

"And Charlie is good for Tommy."

"Might be better all-around if you found another house and sent Tommy over to play with Charlie."

"Funny. But I was thinking the same thing about you. Let's pick up a paper on the way home. Check out the rentals."

"I'm not moving," Meg said.

"Neither am I."

Meg's frown hardened. She narrowed her eyes and stared at Rusty. His face was a mask, leaving her unable to guess his thoughts. Surely, he'd cave at some point, right? All she had to do was outlast him. Damn, didn't her father use to call her pigheaded? Well, maybe now it wasn't such a bad thing.

When the waiter came with the food, Rusty called the boys back to the table.

"Dad, the ducks ate all the bread. We threw it in and they came over. Some of them fought with each other. Ducks are great. Can we get a duck?"

Rusty pointed at his son's plate. "Eat. No, we can't get a duck. There's no place to put a duck. Besides, we have Coco. She's enough to take care of. Eat."

Tommy quieted down and opened his burger. He spilled catsup on his plate but managed to get some on the burger.

"We can come back and feed the ducks again, Tommy."

"We can?" His face brightened. He looked up at Meg.

"Of course. This isn't far from the house."

The boy grinned and took a bite of his burger. Meg stole a side glance at Rusty. Frowning, he glared at her. She couldn't help but smile.

AFTER AN ACTIVE DAY, the boys fell asleep on the sofa. Rusty carried them to their beds.

"Two down," Rusty said, opening the fridge. He took out a beer. "Want one?"

She shook her head.

"Game's on." Before she could answer, he'd plopped down in front of the television. Coco joined Meg in the kitchen. The big dog stood by the back door.

"Coco needs to go out," she called into the living room.

"She can wait. Bases are loaded. Jake Lawrence is up. One out."

Meg had zero idea what he was talking about. She hunted around until she found the leash.

"Come on, girl." Meg fastened the lead on the dog and opened the door. At eight o'clock in late June, the sun was still out. The big dog pulled Meg toward the back of the expansive lawn, made up of crabgrass and weeds of an unknown variety. It stretched all the way to woods.

Meg let out the retractable leash, giving Coco room to roam. She followed the canine, who kept her nose to the ground, picking up every scent for miles. Crickets serenaded. An ancient, cracked bird feeder hung empty on a low-hanging branch.

"We'll fill it tomorrow," Meg said to the dog. But after examination, she realized she'd have to get a new one. "Small investment to have a summer filled with birds, don't you think?"

The dog looked back at her and gave a low woof in agreement. They stopped at the edge of the forest. Coco did her business then trotted over to a rock outcropping. Meg sat with the pooch at her feet. Absently, she draped a palm over the dog's rump and stroked her.

The clear night showcased a fabulous splash of stars. Meg searched the sky for her favorite constellations. She ticked them off, one after another.

"The Big Dipper. Little Dipper. Cassiopeia." Another plus to being in the country—sharing constellations with her son. Charlie hadn't seen them before because they weren't visible in New York City. She'd taken him to the Planetarium, and they saw the show, but it wasn't the same as seeing them for real.

Meg hugged her knees. Coco moved closer, placing her massive head on Meg's arm.

"Oh, Coco. I wish John was here. He'd love you. Always was a dog person." She sighed.

The ache in her heart had calmed some over two years. There wasn't a day went by when she didn't think of him and wonder what his opinion would have been on this issue or that. Though she'd stopped crying every night, Meg still felt his absence keenly.

Despite John's leaving her well-fixed financially, Meg continued to teach. She needed a reason to get out of bed every morning. Moody and silent some days, Charlie didn't open up about his feelings. She figured those were the times when he missed his father most.

She took a deep breath. No doubt about it, fresh country air had it all over what passed for air in New York City.

Coco rolled on her back. Meg took the hint and rubbed the dog's belly. After a day with the slobbery, affectionate animal, Meg stowed her fear of big dogs and became Coco's best friend.

When the chill of the night air penetrated her shirt, Meg returned to the house.

"Where have you been?" Rusty stood in the archway leading from the kitchen to the dining room.

"What?"

"I've been calling you. You missed a phenomenal play. Lawrence jumped on the first pitch, and—"

Meg held up her palm. "I don't care. I don't like baseball. I don't understand it. Stupid game. Grown men swinging a piece of wood at a little ball, then running around. Dumb."

If she had slugged Rusty with a two-ton bat she couldn't have knocked him as senseless as she did with her words.

"What? What did you say? Baseball is *dumb*? The national pas-time? The sport I spent seventeen years of my life playing. The sport I'm totally devoted to? Dumb? Woman, what's wrong with you?"

"Nothing. By the way. I walked the dog. I'm going to bed."

"At nine thirty?"

"I'd rather read than watch stupid sports."

"You wound me. And show your ignorance."

"Me, ignorant? You're the ignorant one. You don't know a black-bird from a robin, a turtle from a tortoise. You have zero knowledge of the world around you. I bet you haven't read a book in twenty years." She shot him a sideways glance.

"Stop insulting me. I know plenty. I'm not ignorant at all. You're the ignorant one," he said, poking her shoulder with his forefinger. "Do you even know who Babe Ruth is?"

"A baby? What do I need to know about a baby for?"

He clutched at his heart and feigned an attack. "Oh my God. You really don't know who he is, do you?"

"Should I?"

"Only the greatest baseball player who ever lived."

She glared at him.

"Of course, some might argue Willie Mays was better."

She cocked an eyebrow. "Stupid sports."

"At least I went along on your little nature jaunt."

"Yeah? Hating every minute."

"I learned a few things. I can now tell an egret from a, what's the brown one called?" He arched his eyebrows.

"A heron. You can't even retain information for twelve hours. Neanderthal." She pushed by him, heading for the bedroom.

"Neanderthal? Are you calling me a caveman?" Anger tinged his tone.

"If the loincloth fits, wear it." She entered the bedroom. The door closed with a loud click.

Meg undressed and got under the covers. Tears stung her eyes. Why did she have to be saddled with this arrogant man? At least she could talk to Charlie. No way could she ponder the questions of the universe with Mr. Sports Nut.

As she rested her head on her pillow, she remembered. Crap! She'd have to endure an entire baseball game with brainless on Saturday. What a waste of time! Frowning, she scrunched her face into the pillow and forced the unpleasant thought from her brain. Focusing on the sweet smells of fresh summer air and the companionship of the giant beast he called a dog, Meg shut her eyes, and sleep came quickly.

Chapter Four

Rusty's anger simmered under the surface, barely contained. He'd been called a lot of things in his day, most often by other ballplayers and women. But stupid and Neanderthal were not among them. *Why Miss Snotty Little Prissy know-it-all! Thinks she's better than me. Bullshit. She'd be lucky to lick my—well, she would. Be lucky. She can kiss my ass.*

After a sleepless night on the sofa bed, he regretted caving so fast and giving her the bedroom. At least he had the baseball game to look forward to. Oh, and the meals she'd promised to prepare. Would she try to poison him? He considered letting Coco be his food taster. The bitch would do or say anything to get control of the house.

He awoke grumpy, never a good sign. The smell of brewing coffee soothed his ruffled feathers. Of course, with his automatic coffeemaker at home and Mrs. MacDougal to set it up in the afternoon, he awoke every morning to the same delicious aroma—without the bitchy lip. He threw back the covers and grabbed his robe. Yeah, he slept nude. She'd just have to get over it. He padded into the kitchen.

"How do you take it?" she asked.

"I'll do it. Thank you." His tone could be as bitchy as hers.

"Oh, so it's like that, is it?" She rested a hand on her hip.

"Like what? I don't know what you mean."

"Don't pull the bitchy woman act with me. I've known more bitchy women than you, and I can spot that crap a mile away. Just get over yourself, Rusty. I'm being nice here."

"Nice? Let me get the dictionary. Obviously, you don't know the meaning of the word."

Before she answered, he spied two small faces peeking around the archway. Damn. The boys. He couldn't let her have it the way she deserved—not in front of them. They wouldn't understand. They'd think he was bullying her. And, of course, he would have been. But Meg Gunderson was one babe who could dish it out as good as a man.

"Hi, boys."

"Hi, Dad," Tommy said, sitting at the table. Charlie followed.

Meg kissed the top of her son's head. "Morning, guys. Scrambled eggs for breakfast."

Rusty added milk and sugar to his coffee and took a seat. He snarfed down half a mug before speaking.

"So what's on the schedule for today, little Miss Tour Guide?"

"Dad." Tommy kicked his father under the table.

Meg shot Rusty a hostile glance. "It's supposed to be hot today. I thought we might go swimming in the lake, then have a picnic down by town hall. There's a playground there and some picnic tables."

"You've sure done your homework, haven't you? You know this town forward and backward."

She ignored him and continued. "Since I'm not making lunch, I thought we could stop at The Cozy Café and pick up something. Their ad in the paper says they make sandwiches and are known for their scones." She faced Rusty. "Do you know what a scone is?"

Heat exploded in him. If she'd have been a man, he'd have decked her. He counted to ten, pushed to his feet and strode from the room. The last thing he heard was Charlie's voice.

"Mom!"

Rusty headed for the shower. In there, he could swear to his heart's content. He turned on the water, stepped in and let fly with every word he knew. Grabbing the soap, he cleaned his body, then washed his hair.

By the time he was done, he'd calmed down. A plan formed in his head. He got dressed, combed his hair, and then joined the others.

The boys jumped into bathing suits and were waiting at the door.

"Can we take Coco?" Tommy asked.

"Sure." Rusty picked up the leash. Coco barked once, then waited to be hooked up.

"You're welcome." Meg looked at him.

"Huh?" Rusty raised his brows.

"For walking the dog and making breakfast."

"Oh, yeah. Thanks. Come on, guys."

"Charlie, do you know how to swim?"

The boy nodded.

"He knows the four basic strokes," Meg put in.

"Good. Then no one needs life vests, right? Oh, can you swim?"

"I was on the swim team in college." Meg stuck out her chin.

"Well, bully for you. So you like some sports?"

"The ones requiring skill and not just brute strength."

Once again, anger bubbled in his veins. But Rusty controlled himself. Coco pushed out the door first. The boys followed, then Meg and Rusty. The kids ran ahead. Meg stuffed towels in a canvas bag. Rusty took her arm.

"Why don't you give it a rest?"

"What?"

"You've been riding me pretty hard. What have I done to you? Nothing."

"You're arrogant. You have a superior attitude, with nothing to be superior about."

"Sez you. You don't know who I am, do you?"

"Are you someone?"

"I was famous in my baseball days with the Nighthawks."

"Oh, really? Well rah, rah and bully for you."

"There you go. Nasty mouth."

"At least it isn't foul."

"There's more than one way to have a foul mouth. Can't you even try to be pleasant? For Charlie's sake?"

She glanced at the ground. "I suppose. He did say something to me."

"Oh, really? The boy has class. Must get it from his father."

"There you go! How do you expect me to stop, when you don't?"

"Okay, you have a point."

A triumphant look spread across her face.

"Truce? Just for today?" he asked.

"Truce. Yes. For today."

He stuck out his hand, and she shook it. They joined the boys in Rusty's SUV. He pulled out and headed for the lake.

Meg directed him to a small parking lot near the public access dock. Charlie and Tommy raced to the water while Rusty and Meg unloaded the food and towels.

They joined the boys and Rusty calmed. At least she'd stopped for now. But for two months? No way. This bitch couldn't be nice to him for five minutes, let alone two months.

When they got down to the lake, the unexpected happened. As she shimmied out of her shorts, his eye was drawn to her adorable little butt, wiggling right in front of him. Boom! Blood started pumping to his dick. Oh no, no, no. This could not be happening. Not her. Not the bitch. He turned away, hoping his dick would forget what it saw.

He threw off his shirt and ran to the dock. "Last one in is a rotten egg," he said, diving into the water. The cold lake water solved his problem. He surfaced and faced the dock. Shit. There she was, wearing a one-piece bathing suit. Did they still make those? Even a one-piece couldn't hide her luscious curves. Staring at her chest, he couldn't decide whether she was a "B" or "C" cup. Did it matter? Whatever their size, they called to him.

With her hands on her hips, her feet spread apart, the wind tossing her hair over her forehead, she was the cutest, sexiest woman he'd ever seen.

She executed a perfect dive, leaving hardly any splash. Damn. The woman had game.

THE COOL WATER REDUCED Meg's body temperature to normal. She didn't mean to stare at Rusty. It's not like she hadn't seen him half-naked before. But damn, the man had a body. Whoa. Trim, some ab definition. Not bad for a guy nearing forty.

He had perfect proportions, and everything was exactly the way she liked it, hair, skin, muscle. The man was sex on legs. At least that's what her old college roommate would have said. And she'd be right. Sure, he was obnoxious, full of himself, entitled, and arrogant, but he had something else, an easy sexuality—in the way he moved, or stood, or something. Keeping her gaze on him ratcheted her body up to high alert.

This was not good. She dove into the water to dial down her response to an almost naked Rusty Reisse. *Okay, so maybe athletes have fantastic bodies, but what about the mind?*

She had to control her tongue and stop insulting him. Especially in front of the kids. She had already embarrassed Charlie, and Tommy had looked hurt.

Time to put on her big girl panties and man up. Leave Rusty alone. If the fantasy of sleeping with him happened to breeze through her mind—so what? A woman could have sex with a man without any conversation at all, couldn't she?

When she pulled herself up on the ladder, Rusty was already on the dock. He handed her a towel. She felt his gaze smooth over her like a warm hand. Was it her imagination? After all, he hated her guts, she doubted he'd be lusting after her.

"Nice dive." He turned away.

"Thanks."

"Can you teach me?" Tommy asked.

"Sure."

"Me, too, Mom?"

"Okay boys, line up."

Thankful to be turning her attention to the children, Meg relaxed. Teaching kids was in her wheelhouse. Patient and encouraging, she had the boys diving within half an hour. Pumped with their new-found expertise, they kept diving in and climbing out again, and again, and again.

"Let's swim out to the float." Meg looked around. Where was Rusty? Damn, he was on his phone. "You, too, Bat Man." She grinned at her new nickname for the jerk with the attitude.

He nodded, obviously not listening. Meg dove in and was at the float in a heartbeat. She watched the two boys, making sure they were safe.

Meg sat back, watching the boys dive. From time to time, her gaze traveled to Rusty. With his pacing and hand waving, he seemed to be having an animated conversation—not in a good way. Could it be his ex-wife? Maybe a girlfriend? Wow, yeah. She'd totally ignored the idea Rusty was probably a player and had several girlfriends on the string at the same time. Her immediate reaction? Not envy, right? Pity instead.

Meg wasn't alone, she had Harold, didn't she? Yeah, dull-as-paint Harold. She sighed. Harold was better than no one. Did she love him? No way! She cared about him somewhat. He was an assistant principal at her school. He did smooth the way for her on a number of occasions. But in bed? Harold was about as exciting as a slug.

She didn't have many opportunities to sleep with him anyway. He lived with his aging mother and with Charlie in the house, he sure as hell wasn't staying overnight in her bed. At least he wasn't demanding. A quickie after Charlie was asleep sufficed. Harold liked the arrangement the way it was—except for this summer. She recalled their conversation.

"What do you have to go away for?"

"Fresh air. Charlie and I need a change."

"For the whole summer?"

"Yep."

"Why can't you go for a week? Like most people?"

"We're not most people."

"It's just like you to take off for months at a time, leaving me here alone."

"You're not alone. You have your mother." Meg had attempted to hide a smile.

"You know what I mean."

"Don't worry. I'll see you when we get back. Charlie and I need time alone together."

Harold had been grumpy about it, refusing to come over and say goodbye the night before she left. It was just as well, as she had so many things to think about and tasks to cross off her list. The last thing she needed was Harold bitching, moaning, and whining about her leaving. What did she see in him, anyway? He was someone to have dinner with, catch a movie with, and who understood her challenges as a teacher. She sighed. But nothing more. In the excitement department, Harold scored a zero.

As she watched, Rusty returned his cell to his pants on the dock and dove in. Coco did the same, swimming slower, following him. Meg watched him do the crawl, the muscles in his shoulders and back worked, rippling their energy through his arms. A tingle shot through her. Couldn't those arms hold a woman tight, shield her from the hurts of life? He had a strong stroke and was climbing up the ladder on the float within minutes. Coco attempted to follow but failed. Rusty boosted her up.

The pain of being alone seared through her. If only. When John held her, her world brightened, colors intensified, love flowed. Without him, fear, and the chill of loneliness penetrated her bones. About six months ago, she gave up hope of ever finding another man like John. She'd turned her full attention to her son. Charlie's life had been shaken to its roots. He needed her. Whenever she went out, if she returned later than expected, Charlie flew into hysterics.

His fear she'd die rocked her. Although she reassured him it wouldn't happen, life held no guarantees. She'd believed she and John would grow old together, but Fate had other ideas. She and Charlie had a therapist to help them cope and find a way to continue living. It helped, but only time would erase the bone-chilling fear of losing his mother, too.

Rusty and the Rottie shook off, pelting Meg with droplets of cold water, yanking her out of her reverie.

"Leave someone at home?" She tried to avoid staring at the water dripping down his magnificent chest but failed.

He narrowed his eyes. "Were you listening in?"

"From here? You're joking."

"Yeah. Sort of. An ex-girlfriend. You?"

His expression indicated he didn't think she had.

"A boyfriend." No way was she going to let on what a loser Harold was.

"You? A boyfriend? Really? Some professorial type, no doubt."

"Assistant Principal."

"Figures."

The boys cannonballed into the water, soaking Meg and Rusty, interrupting their conversation. Coco barked. Thank God. Harold was the last topic she wanted to discuss.

MEG FIXED A SIMPLE dinner of grilled chicken, baked potatoes, and salad. At six, Rusty rushed in. Picking up his plate, he headed for the living room.

"Sorry, but I have a game."

"A what?"

"Game. I'm still working. I promised to do color commentary on the radio. They'll patch me in through my phone."

"What's color commentary?"

His face scrunched up. "It's…it's…I talk about the game. Instead of television, they let me do it remote. I can't stop working. I have a contract. But in order to be with Tommy, I have to do this. I hope you understand. Can you get Tommy to bed for me?"

"Sure."

She sat with the boys at the dinner table. Swimming had sparked their appetites. They ate heartily, then went to their room to play while Meg cleaned up.

She stopped in her room and rummaged through the books she'd brought, selecting just the one she wanted before she headed to the boys' room.

The sound of the baseball game buzzed in the background. She heard Rusty talking as if there was someone else in the room. She barely recognized his animated, professional voice. She'd have to stop by and see what all the fuss was about.

She knocked on the boys' door.

"Come in," Charlie called.

"Ready guys? Pj's on. It's story time."

Tommy looked up from the Legos he'd been playing with. "What's story time?"

Meg's heart lurched.

"My mom reads to me every night. Doesn't yours?"

"I don't have a mom. I mean, I do. But she doesn't live with us. Can't you read?" Tommy turned to Charlie.

"Sure I can. But this is more fun than reading by myself."

"Oh. Okay." Tommy's face flushed.

"Come on, Tommy. This is for you, too."

Meg slipped off her sandals and got on the bed. A twin didn't leave much room for her plus two boys, but they managed. Charlie and Tommy climbed on, with one on either side of her. She looped her arms around their shoulders and opened the book.

"We're reading the Hardy Boys. Charlie and I have just started this one. We're on chapter three. Charlie, would you tell Tommy what's happened so far?"

While her son recounted the tale up to that point, Meg listened, grinning at his animated attitude.

"Got it?" Charlie asked.

Tommy nodded.

"Since you're on the right, Tommy, you'll be my page-turner. When I tell you, please turn the page."

As she read, the boys grew sleepy. They cuddled into her shoulders. Charlie fell asleep first, then Tommy. She laid Charlie down, closed the book, then wondered what to do with Tommy, fast asleep, resting against her.

"I'll get him," came a masculine voice from the doorway. She looked up to see Rusty lounging against the frame. "Commercial," he said in a stage whisper as he approached the bed. Effortlessly, he picked up his son and deposited him gently in his bed. He pulled up the covers and kissed his forehead.

Meg pushed to her feet, kissed Charlie, then tiptoed to the door.

"How long have you been standing there?" she asked.

"Long enough. Hardy Boys, eh? My favorites as a kid, too."

Meg doused the light and closed the door. Rusty headed back to the living room, chattering away on his phone. She followed. Leaning against the wall, she waited for another commercial break to speak.

"Don't you read to Tommy?"

"I'm not home often when he goes to bed."

"Didn't his mother?"

"She's an actress. Rarely home at night."

"What a shame. Do you mind if I include him with Charlie?"

"Not at all. Oops. Gotta go. Hey, Joe. Skip Quincy's at the plate. Yeah. After his bonehead play at short last inning, he has a lot to make up for..."

Meg wandered into the kitchen. The night was clear and the temperature perfect. Too restless to read, she donned a sweatshirt, poured a glass of wine, leashed Coco, and went outside.

She liked walking the Rottweiler. Rusty seemed relieved to be rid of the responsibility. Coco had grown fond of Meg, following her from room-to-room. The big animal, her newest best friend, created an aura of safety. The dog gave out a woof and strained at the leash.

"Okay, girl. I'll let you go." With some trepidation, Meg snapped off the lead and let Coco run free. After all, she wasn't Meg's dog. But she figured the canine wouldn't run off. She'd stick close, guarding Meg. Coco loped to the edge of the woods. Meg followed.

A howl broke the stillness of the night. Meg stopped dead. The bloodcurdling noise was loud, which meant it was close. The moonlight made two keen eyes glitter in the darkness. It was a coyote, not ten feet from Meg.

Coco stepped in front. A low growl emanated from deep in her chest. The wild animal froze, staring. Coco's loud, ferocious bark echoed in the stillness. Sweat trickled down between Meg's breasts and on her palms. Muscles in her shoulders tightened as her adrenaline pumped. The fur on the back of the coyote's neck stood up. The animal faced off with the dog. Tension thickened the air. Meg's breathing became shallow. As fear shot through her, she inched backward toward the house. Coco stepped out of the blackness of the night. Meg saw the hair on the back of her neck rise as another warning growl escaped Coco's throat.

The dog prepared to lunge.

"No, Coco!"

As quickly as the coyote appeared, it disappeared. In a flash, it turned and ran back into the woods. With the break in the tension, Meg's legs jumped into action. She raced back to the house, with Coco right behind her. No way would she hang around, waiting for the creature to return—maybe with friends. She flew into the house, struggling to catch her breath. Coco bounded in right behind. Meg shut the screen door, then the wooden door as well, and locked it.

Collapsing on the kitchen floor, she reached out for Coco. The dog licked her face and stood while Meg hugged her, crying. Rusty came in, still talking on the phone. He gestured, shrugging, his eyebrows rose.

Gulping air, Meg could hardly speak. Her hands trembled.

"Thanks, Joe. Another great game for the New York Nighthawks, winning five to three over the Boston Bluejays. Goodnight." He put the phone down and crouched.

"What the hell happened?"

Meg swept the tears away with her fingers. Rusty reached up on the table for a paper napkin and handed it to her.

"Coyote." Meg spit out.

"Oh my God! Really?"

Meg nodded. She took a deep breath and let it out.

"Are you okay?"

She nodded. "Coco saved me."

"She did?" His eyebrows shot up.

"She faced off against it."

"Coco?"

"Yep. She's bigger than it was, too. And she growled and barked. Scared it away. So we came back. Fast."

"And you're okay?"

"Thanks to Coco." Meg hugged the dog. The fear drained from her, leaving her limp.

Rusty took her upper arm and helped her stand. She wobbled for a moment. He snaked his arm around her waist, steadying her. Meg lost control. She fell into his chest, sobbing. He held her tight.

"It's okay. You're safe now," he said, his voice deep and soothing.

Coco barked once.

"Shh. She's okay." Rusty reached down with one hand and petted his dog. Then he stroked the back of Meg's hair. "Do you want a drink?"

She pushed away. "I'm sorry. I don't usually lose control." She reached for more napkins.

"Hey, I get it. I'd be shittin' in my pants, too."

She glared at him.

"Okay. Sorry. Come on. One shot. You'll feel better."

"Game over?" She took a seat, watching him get the bottle of whiskey from the cabinet.

"Yeah. Thanks for taking care of Tommy."

"He's a great kid."

"Yeah? Thanks. Wish the school agreed with you."

"Oh?"

"Here, drink this." He placed a shot in front of her. Meg studied his face, but his expression didn't give away why he changed the subject. Hmm, so Tommy had some trouble at school? Rusty had clammed up. Not one to pry, Meg resisted the urge to ask questions.

"Thanks." She belted the shot down in one gulp. The warmth the alcohol created soothed her. It would help her sleep.

"Do you want to talk about it?"

"Nothing more to tell." She checked her watch. "I'd better get to bed."

"Yeah. Thanks again for Tommy."

"I'll read to both boys every night. If that's okay with you?"

"That'd be great."

"Done." Already feeling the effects of the drink, she pushed up from the table. "Goodnight." Not completely steady on her feet, she managed to make it to the hallway.

"Goodnight," Rusty called.

In a daze, Meg undressed. After snuggling down under the covers and turning off the light, she remembered the glow of the coyote's eyes. Fear coursed through her again. Suddenly the bed dipped and a big body lay next to her. It was Coco. Meg rolled on her side and hugged the dog.

A moment before she fell asleep, she felt the bed dip as the animal left.

COCO LUMBERED INTO the kitchen. Rusty finished his nightcap. He opened the cabinet and pulled out half a dozen dog treats.

"You were brave, Coco. You protected Meg. Here you go." He offered the Rottie the freeze-dried chicken. She gobbled them up in a flash. "Good girl."

He washed his glass and put it in the drying rack, then stood by the back door, staring out at the lawn, dimly lit by a bright, full moon. A shudder raced through him. Wildlife right at his backdoor. Who would have thought danger could be so close? What if the coyote had attacked Meg? Sweat broke out on his forehead. What if he'd killed her? What would happen to Charlie?

A chill made him tremble. It would be a horrible disaster. Thank God for the dog. Of course, coyotes are kind of small, but still. If it had been rabid or hungry or something, Meg might have been a goner.

He turned out the light and headed for the living room. Coco followed. As he pulled out the sofa-bed, he thought about the scene in the boys' room. A lump formed in his throat. His mother had read to him every night. Yes, The Hardy Boys, too. How could he have forgotten?

He heard Tommy say he had no mother. The words pricked Rusty's heart. His mother had been so wonderful, so loving, giving him all her time and attention. Now his son had to grow up with no mother—a giant void—and a father who traveled too much, worked too hard, especially at night. Hell, the kid was practically an orphan.

His eyes wetted. How could he have let that happen? Too busy, too caught up trying to make a ton of money so he could pay for Tommy's college and leave him a legacy. But what kind of legacy is money alone? Rusty's mother and stepfather didn't have much. They didn't leave him a dime when they passed. But they left him a legacy of love.

His boyhood memories of his father and mother, who'd had three miscarriages before she carried him to term. How they had doted on him! He remembered Christmas mornings, filled with wonderful presents. Not expensive stuff but plenty of gifts.

Rusty stripped down to his boxers and eased into bed. Linking his fingers behind his head, he stared at the ceiling. How could he fix this? Maybe this summer, he could bond better with Tommy. They could do stuff, even if he had to work night games.

Envy rose in his chest. Meg had such an easy relationship with Charlie. He noticed how the boy clung to his mother as she read. How comfortable they were with each other. Not Rusty. He'd never been at ease around kids. Tommy was a great kid, Meg even said so. He'd have to pay more attention to the boy. Listen more. Maybe even cuddle with him. Emotion closed his throat. He loved his son, fiercely, since the moment the boy was born. Maybe now he'd have to find a different way to show it.

Coco jumped up on the bed, licked Rusty's face, then left, trotting toward the boy's room. At least there was one thing he'd done for his son. He'd gotten him a dog. A big, protective dog. Coco slept on Tommy's bed every night. The boy adored her, and she let him do anything he wanted to her.

Rusty smiled. At least he'd made one good decision regarding his son. He rolled over. He needed sleep and to get his act together regarding the boy. Maybe he could pick up some parenting tips from the bitch on wheels? If only she'd stop insulting him. He sighed and fell asleep.

Something landed on him, waking him in the morning. It was Tommy. Rusty wrestled with the boy, trapping him between his legs and rolling them over one way then back the other. Tommy laughed until he couldn't breathe. Rusty hugged his son to him and kissed his head.

The smell of bacon and coffee tantalized Rusty's tastebuds.

"Bacon!" Tommy said, when he caught his breath.

"And coffee." Rusty threw the covers off and stood up. He stretched his arms all the way up as high as they would go and yawned.

"Nice," she said, shaking her head.

Meg headed for the bathroom. Rusty grabbed the bedspread and wound it around his waist.

"This is how I sleep. You're the one who wanted to switch rooms," he called after her.

"Come on, Dad. Be nice. She's cooking."

"Okay, okay." Rusty took his clothes into the dining room. Once dressed, he joined the others in the kitchen. The boys were eating bacon, eggs, and toast. Meg stood at the stove.

"Ready?" she asked.

"Yes. Thank you. Looks great."

She spooned some eggs on each of two plates and handed him one. Then she sat with the others. Rusty helped himself to bacon and toast. The little domestic scene touched his heart. *Don't get comfortable. She hates you. Thinks you're dumb. This is temporary.*

"Do you have plans for today?"

"Nope."

"I thought I'd take Tommy to watch batting practice at the Jefferson Jaguar's stadium. Charlie, would you like to come along?"

"Sure. Yeah. Thanks. Can I, Mom?"

"And you're not inviting me?"

"You hate the game. Said so. Numerous times. I thought you might like to have some time to yourself."

"It's okay. If you don't want to invite me."

"I didn't say that." Rusty shoveled a forkful of eggs into his mouth.

"Can Mom come?" Charlie asked.

"Of course, she can. All she had to do was ask nicely." Rusty glared at Meg.

"Thank you. Of course, I'll come. Might as well try to learn something, since we're going to a game on Saturday."

Rusty didn't know how it would go with her there, but he had no choice. He expected his pleasant day with the boys to end up flying out the window as Ms. Wet Blanket tagged along. Ugh. He tried to smile but failed.

Chapter Five

Baseball practice? What was I thinking? Meg stepped into the shower. *No one takes my son anywhere without me.* She soaped up and washed her hair. After rinsing off, she turned off the spray and stepped out. Meg always toweled her hair dry first, then her body. Wrapping the towel around her, she tucked it into her breasts and combed her fingers through her hair.

"Tommy, just a sec..." came a masculine voice and blam! Rusty bumped into her, knocking her against the sink. She grabbed the towel, securing it. He stared, his gaze roaming from her head to her toes, for what seemed like forever.

"Sorry. So sorry. I didn't know you were in here." He backed out, palms raised.

"I'll only be a minute." Meg scooped up her clothes and, gripping her towel, dashed into the bedroom. She shut the door and leaned back against it, waiting as she steadied her breathing. She'd been almost naked in the bathroom with Rusty. Damn! Her pulse raced. If he had been one minute earlier, she would have stood in all her nude glory in front of him, open for his eyes.

She shivered. Why should she care? If Harold had walked in on her? She chuckled. She'd have ignored him and been annoyed he was in the way. She swallowed. The heat of Rusty's stare almost burned the towel off her body.

She dressed quickly and brushed her hair. After checking her purse, she made a beeline for the front door. Rusty and the boys were waiting.

Tommy sported an enormous baseball glove on his left hand. Rusty checked his watch.

"Ready?"

"Yes."

"Let's go."

She touched his arm. "One thing. New rule. No entering the bathroom without knocking first. Okay?"

Rusty's face colored. "Okay. Yeah. Good idea."

The boys nodded.

"Why are you bringing that?" she asked, pointing to the glove.

"In case a foul ball comes to me." Tommy smiled and punched the pocket of the glove.

"Oh, I see." She nodded. Nope, she had no clue what he was talking about.

They got in Rusty's car. He set the GPS and threw the vehicle in gear.

When they arrived at the stadium, Meg was surprised at how small it was.

"The major league stadiums are a lot bigger," Rusty offered, anticipating her question.

She nodded. Frankly, this was much less intimidating. Men in uniform littered the field. They seemed to be playing catch. One guy stood with the bat, threw the ball up and hit it to another player.

"I'm hungry," Tommy piped up.

"Me, too." Charlie looked up at his mom.

"How about a hot dog?" Rusty reached for his wallet.

Ugh. Junk food. But it's the ballpark. Guess you have to. Meg took Charlie's hand, but he pulled away.

"I'm too old, Mom."

She sighed and nodded. "Okay." His childhood was zooming by too fast.

Armed with hot dogs, soda, and fries, they took seats in the first row. The stands were mostly empty. Meg wore a turquoise tank top cut low enough to offer a little cleavage and white shorts. Rusty droned on about the game, practice, and what the men on the field were doing.

She tried to focus on his words, but one-by-one the players moseyed over to the stands.

"Howdy, little lady. Come to watch practice?" asked one tall, good-looking young man.

"Meg Gunderson. This is my son, Charlie, and his friend, Tommy."

"Nice to meet you, boys. I'm Frank Todd. I play second base." He tipped his cap.

"We're coming to the game on Saturday," Tommy added.

"Fantastic." Frank Todd autographed a ball and handed it to Meg. He couldn't take his eyes off her. "It is Miss Gunderson or Mrs. Gunderson?"

"Mrs."

"He your husband?"

"Him?" she laughed. "No. No. I'm a widow."

"Oh. I'm sorry for your loss." But Frank's grin appeared anything but sorry. "Can I call you for dinner sometime?"

Frank whipped his phone out of his back pocket. Meg dictated her number. She glanced over at Rusty and shrugged. His stormy expression pleased her. Guess he didn't think a ballplayer could be interested in her. Maybe he was jealous? Really? Couldn't be because he hated her.

Rex Charlton, center fielder, pushed Frank out of the way.

"Coach wants you," he said. Then he sidled up to the stands and shot Meg a five-hundred-watt smile.

"What's your name, little lady, and where have you been all my life?"

One by one, players took up a spot in front of Meg, each giving her a signed ball and asking for her number.

Rusty ignored the parade of horny men and stuck to explaining the game to Tommy and Charlie. Every time she glanced over she stifled a laugh. Rusty was jealous of the attention paid to Meg. Seemed as if none of the Jaguars recognized him, but they all wanted to talk to Meg.

A whistle blew and the men lined up. Coach mumbled something she couldn't hear. They broke into two teams. One took the field while the other sat on the bench, with one man at a time coming to the plate to bat.

Meg focused on Rusty's commentary—explaining how the game was played. The noonday sun heated the bleachers.

"Have you guys had enough? We're coming back Saturday anyway. Anyone want to go for a swim in the lake?"

The boys agreed. They packed up their trash. When the children ran ahead, Rusty sidled up to her.

"They're all a bunch of horndogs, you know. Lookin' to get into your pants."

Widening her eyes, she stared at him. "Oh? Were you like that?"

Red shot up from his neck to color his face. He fumbled for words. She laughed.

"I thought so. Takes one to know one, right?"

"I hope you're not going to go out with any of them."

"Why should you care?"

"I'd hate to see your heart broken."

"Really? Your concern for my heart is touching. Or would be. If I believed it. Is this another ploy to get me to go home?"

He shook his head. "Just the truth."

"Right. Like I believe you." She stalked off. He had some nerve.

She hadn't had much male attention since John had died. She'd be damned if she'd let snarly Rusty spoil the way it made her feel. Would she go out with any of them? Who knows? Probably not. Charlie hated it when she went out. He was anxious until she returned. Still, it flattered her to be asked.

She waited for Rusty to catch up. "I might just go out with all of them. See who's best in bed."

Rusty choked, coughing. Meg laughed all the way to the car.

STILL REELING FROM walking in on Meg in the bathroom, Rusty worked to focus on teaching professional baseball to the boys. Seeing her standing there, all flush from the heat of the water, flustered and vulnerable, he barely controlled himself. Blood started pumping to his dick. Recovery took several minutes. Then, the apology, of course. Was he sorry? Not one damn bit. He couldn't remember when he'd last seen a woman look so enticing. He wanted her, there, then, right in the bathroom.

Visions of hoisting her up on the vanity and sinking into her wet warmth ran through his brain. Shit! Of all the women he could fantasize about, why did it have to be the bitch on wheels? But she was different in the bathroom. Her lips parted slightly, her cheeks pink, her skin perfect—and her blond hair, flopped over her forehead, captivated him. It was an innocent Marilyn Monroe look. Sucked him in every time.

He'd wanted to kiss her. Take her in his arms, dispense with the towel and shed his clothes. To feel her bare skin up against his, her breasts pushing into his chest, her hips flush with his—heaven. Even remembering got his motor running.

When they reached the ballpark, he steeled himself for non-stop insults and snarky comments. He didn't see Frank Todd approach. Damn, the guy was practically a stalker—standing there, giving her the third degree, and picking up her number to boot. Shit. Rusty didn't even have her number. Not that he wanted it or anything. But it might come in handy since they were sharing the house.

She didn't drop one unpleasant word his way until he tried to give her a heads-up. Like a lamb among wolves, she had no idea about predatory ballplayers. He tried to warn her, but she snapped back with a comment he never expected. Would she sleep with them all? He doubted it. Little Miss Priss? "Please knock at the bathroom door." Yeah, right. She was a babe in the woods, and they knew it. They'd take her body and stomp on her heart without looking back.

But she didn't listen. So, fuck her. Too damn bad. He'd spoken up. Jealousy burned in his chest. He wanted her to want him. Why? So he could turn her down. He smiled. It would be a victory. Little Miss Superior and whammo! He'd shoot her down, show her who's smart. But now with the Jaguars leaving a trail of drool to her door, he had competition. Hah. Rivals had never scared him before. He'd been a star player for the New York Nighthawks—always victorious.

"Hey, you almost passed the driveway." Meg pointed.

"Yeah." Rusty turned the car.

"Where were you?"

"Right here."

"No, really. Your mind wasn't."

The boys chattered in the backseat about their favorite Jaguar players. Rusty had tuned them out. All he could think about was Meg. Worst idea he could have because she couldn't stand him, and he wanted to sleep with her like a bear wants honey. Oh the towel, barely big enough to cover her cute butt and blocking his path to heaven.

He grabbed his swimsuit and headed for the dining room. Within twenty minutes, they were ready to head to the lake. Rusty couldn't believe how sexy a woman could look in a one-piece. The blue of the material matched her eyes. And it hugged her tight, giving him a nice view of her form. His imagination could do the rest.

"Let's go." Rusty slung a towel over his shoulders and opened the door.

He allowed the boys to go first, then glanced at Meg. He caught her checking him out. Good. Let her see he's still in damn good shape. With a sweep of his arm, he stepped out of the way. Was he being chivalrous? No way. Rusty wanted another peek at the view from the rear. He chuckled to himself. Watching her walk in her suit was enough to give a man wood.

"You've been doing a lot of cooking. After the lake, let's have dinner at Homer's. My treat."

She faced him. "Nice."

The boys in the back cheered. "Burgers and fries!" Charlie shouted.

"Uh, no. No way are you eating fries twice in one day. Veggies tonight."

Charlie stuck his lip out and folded his skinny arms over his chest.

"You can have some of mine," Tommy said.

"Nope, Tom. No more fries for you, either. Meg's right. Veggies."

She stared with her mouth open. Hell, if the Jaguars could win her by being super nice and charming, so could Rusty, couldn't he?

SITTING ON THE DECK, in her bathing suit, at Homer's, Meg nursed a wine spritzer while the boys fed bread to the ducks. Facing Rusty, she narrowed her eyes.

"You've been nice all day. What's up?"

"Can't a guy be nice to the girl he's sharing a house with? His roommate?"

"Guess I am your roommate, aren't I?"

Rusty shrugged.

"This sudden turn-around come from somewhere."

"Maybe you're growing on me."

"Oh, I see. Like a fungus?"

"You said it. I didn't." Rusty grinned.

"Whatever the reason, thank you." She didn't believe him for a minute. He was up to something, and she needed to find out what. Rusty wanted this place to himself. He must be hatching some diabolical plot to get her to leave. She must figure it out before he pulled it off.

Rusty being charming could put any woman off her game. But Meg wasn't any woman. She didn't buy all the crap guys handed you to get you into bed. She smiled. Always trying to get a woman to spread her legs. She wondered why they didn't simply try honesty? How about, "Hey, I think you're hot, and I'd really like to have sex with you."

A giggle escaped her mouth.

"What's so funny?" Rusty put down his beer.

"Nothing."

"That's rude, you know. Thinking of something funny and not sharing it."

"Okay. You want it. Here it is. I was wondering why guys think they have to jump through a lot of hoops, turn on the charm, and shovel a load of BS at a woman in order to get her to sleep with them. Why don't they try the direct approach? Just say, I think you're hot and I want to have sex with you."

Rusty's gaze connected with hers. "Because it's the fastest way to get slapped, slugged, shot, or run over by a car."

Meg laughed.

"You think a woman would say yes? No way."

"Have you ever tried it?" She raised her eyebrows.

"Only when I was way too drunk to know what I was doing."

"And did it work?"

"I have the emergency room bills to prove it didn't."

Meg cracked up. "What's the best way to get a woman into bed?"

"Make her think you don't want to sleep with her. Be a gentleman, don't make a pass. She'll wonder why, think there's something wrong with her, and do her best to seduce you."

"And your idea works?"

"Every time." He grinned.

"What's funny?" Charlie asked.

Rusty changed the subject. "How are the ducks?"

While the boys chattered on about the mallards, the waiter brought their food. Rusty and Meg agreed on a compromise—the boys could have burgers if they agreed to eat salad instead of fries.

"I like salad," Charlie said, digging into his while his mom put catsup on his burger.

"I've never had salad," Tommy said.

Meg shot Rusty a dirty look. He shrugged.

"Do you like lettuce?" Charlie asked.

Tommy nodded.

"Then you'll like salad."

As they drove home, the sky clouded over. Thunder rolled through the town.

"The lady at The Cozy Café said sometimes a storm comes out of nowhere." Meg glanced up at the sky.

"Rain doesn't come from nowhere, Mom. It comes from clouds."

"Right, Charlie."

"Dad taught me that."

"What happened to your dad?" Tommy asked.

"He's died in a car crash. It wasn't his fault. A truck hit him."

Silence in the car gave way to another low rumble. They made it inside as huge raindrops pelted their heads. Rusty closed the door, then joined the rest at the picture window. Coco trotted into the room barking. Rusty pulled her close and petted her.

"She hates storms," Tommy said.

They watched as rain danced on the pavement. It fell in sheets, like angry waves.

"Can we watch a movie?" Charlie asked.

"Good idea. The video case is in my room. Take Tommy. Decide what you'd like to see." She turned to Rusty. "Okay with you?"

He nodded, and the boys raced into her room.

She stood by the window watching as the storm slowly moved away. The rain continued but the furious power had passed.

"Eight o'clock. I have a game to call tonight."

"Do you need the television?"

"I can watch on my computer," he said. "Okay if I set it up in the kitchen?"

"Sure."

"Why don't you watch with me? You might learn something so on Saturday you won't be such an ignorant doofus."

"I'm not a doofus."

"Okay, then ignorant."

She shook her head. "I'll read instead."

"What are you reading that's so much more interesting than live sports?"

"You wouldn't understand."

"Try me."

"I like reading. I read a lot of romance books. It's nice to remember what a loving relationship is like."

"I thought you had a boyfriend?"

"Yeah. Well. He's kind of a placeholder."

"A placeholder? Until Mr. Right comes along?"

"Mr. Right already came...and went. Just someone to go to the movies with."

"Oh. Yeah. Sorry." He paused. "Like a friend?"

"Sort of. It's complicated."

"So you read romance to live vicariously instead of having your own life?"

"That's pretty harsh."

"But true, no?"

She shrugged. "Maybe. I don't want to talk about it."

"I see."

"I read mysteries, too. I love seeing the bad guy get found out and punished."

"So you're into punishment?" He wiggled his eyebrows.

Meg laughed. "Like justice, you know? When you've been through what I've been through, you stop believing in justice, fairness. In good things happen to good people. You think life is just random. Mysteries, where they always get the bad guy, make me believe justice still exists."

She stared at her hands. Rusty pushed to his feet. He stopped to rub her back, then left the room, returning a few minutes later with his computer.

Meg stared out the window. The rain had petered off. Coco stood by the back door.

"Mind if I take the dog out?"

"Be my guest."

She fastened the leash and opened the door. The rain didn't bother her. She needed fresh air. And to get away from Rusty. Whatever made her open up to a man she didn't even know? If she'd met him in the City, she'd never have given him a second thought. Here she was, pouring out her deepest thoughts to someone who could care less. He just wanted company while he watched the damn game.

Meg had opened up to her therapist, but no one else. Why did she find it so easy to talk to Rusty? Such an ignorant, chauvinistic man, yet there she was, sharing her thoughts about justice with him. At least he didn't laugh or call her a name. Funny, he knew just what to do—nothing, say nothing. His pat on her back was almost as good as a hug. Okay, so maybe he did know something. Maybe he wasn't the dumbass she'd pegged him to be.

Coco trotted alongside Meg to the woods. They walked from one end of the property to the other. The canine did her business, then they headed back. Meg figured Coco had scared the coyote aware permanently and was grateful.

"Come on girl, race you home!" Meg took off, and Coco got the hint. She put on the speed, easily beating Meg back to the house. Rusty watched the game—cringing when Coco shook off rain. Meg dried her hair with a paper towel.

"I'm going to put the boys to bed," she whispered.

He nodded.

Cuddling with them, she read only half a chapter before they were both asleep. She managed to lift Tommy long enough to transfer him to his bed. She tucked them in, kissed them goodnight, doused the light, and tiptoed out of the room.

In the kitchen, Coco had curled up on the floor next to Rusty while he chatted away on his phone about the game. He looked up when she entered and then patted the chair next to him.

She smiled but shook her head. She'd had enough baseball for one day.

Once in her nightgown and snuggled into bed, she checked her phone. Sure enough, there were messages from three of the players she'd met. And, yes, Frank Todd, was first on the list.

Her door creaked open, alerting Meg. She sat up. Coco lumbered in, stopping next to the bed. She licked Meg's hand, then sat.

"Coco! Coco!" The deep voice penetrated the bedroom.

Rusty appeared in the doorway. "There she is. Sorry. She likes to make the rounds. You know. Check to make sure everyone's okay before she settles down with Tom."

Meg leaned over and kissed the top of the rottweiler's head.

"Did you like the baseball?" He lingered, lounging against the jamb.

"You mean the players."

"No. The game."

"Oh, that." She grinned at him. "It was okay."

"The real game'll be better. Trust me."

"We'll see."

"Come on, girl. I'm talking to the dog." His face flushed. "Goodnight."

"Goodnight, Coco. 'Night, Rusty."

He raised his palm, then closed the door.

Frowning, Meg settled down. Coco considered her one of the pack, the family. But Rusty was the last man on Earth right for her. She'd hate to break the dog's heart, but as soon as she could toss Rusty to the curb, the better.

Chapter Six

Rusty tried to focus on the game. Seeing Meg in her nightgown in bed destroyed his concentration. *Hmm, let's see, someone got a double and is now on second base. Or did he steal third? Pitcher is coming up to bat. I thought they were using a pinch hitter?* He took a swig of his beer, but he was way beyond alcohol.

Fighting to control his libido, he forced himself to watch the screen. Sure enough, the batter wasn't the pitcher, but the Nighthawks first baseman. Geez. If he wasn't careful his broadcasting career would disappear.

During the commercial, his mind wandered back to Meg's words. How hard it must be to feel like the victim of a great injustice? Hmm. Maybe his knocking up Angela had been an injustice, too. Not really. At least he had Tommy to show for it. Did he resent her for taking off and dumping their son on him? You're damn right he did. Every time he didn't know what to do, which seemed like every day of the boy's life, he cursed out Angela.

If she'd been around, she'd have helped, told him the right things to do. He was kidding himself. Angela didn't have a motherly bone in her body. She wouldn't have known any more than Rusty did, what a temper tantrum was, how to handle a fever, or how to make it go away? And a hundred other things making him feel helpless, like the world's biggest fool. Here was this tiny baby making an idiot out of his father. Parenting had been a rough road for the ballplayer.

He continued announcing the game until it finished at eleven with the Nighthawks winning with a two-run homer in the tenth. Exhausted, Rusty turned off the computer and stretched his arms up over his head. Yawning, he put the laptop back in the living room, turned out the lights, and locked the doors. Coco yawned and trotted off to Tommy's room.

Almost too tired to open the sofa bed, Rusty considered sleeping on it as is. He rejected the idea.

"I'll fall off in the middle of the night."

Marshaling his reserve strength, he opened it, stripped down to his boxers, and fell into bed. Images of Meg flitted through his brain. How beautiful she'd looked, blushing and smiling at the players as they peppered her with compliments. He guessed she didn't have a ton of hot guys fawning over her. And he couldn't imagine why not.

At the stadium, she'd asked some good questions and some totally idiotic ones. But she was new to baseball, so he excused her ignorance. She'd been subdued, letting him take the lead, leaving Charlie to ask questions and get excited about meeting the players and watching them practice. He didn't think she'd do it. He expected her to put it down, talk up stupid science shit, and not let Charlie join in with him and Tommy. But she didn't. Hmm.

Before he could figure it out, he fell asleep.

Coco's wet tongue woke him up shortly after sunrise. Feeling grumpy, he planned to yell at the dog until the warm, delicious scent of brewing coffee met his nose. He whipped down the covers and padded to the bathroom. After slipping jeans over his boxers, he headed for the kitchen.

His eyes almost popped out when he saw the clock.

"Six?" he choked the word out.

"Yeah. Summer sun wakes me up. Coffee?" Meg stood at the counter with a mug in her hand.

"Oh, yeah."

She poured the hot liquid. Rusty added milk and sugar. Before he could sit down, she spoke.

"Let's sit on the deck. Keep it quiet for the boys. And it's probably nice out there."

He nodded and opened the door. Coco bounded outside, almost knocking him down. The coffee sloshed out of the mug and onto his chest.

"Shit! Fuck!" He grimaced as the coffee burned his bare skin.

Meg wetted a dish towel with cold water. She slapped it on the burn and held it there.

"Better?"

"A little."

She replaced her hand with his. "Hold it for a sec." Within a minute, she returned with a hand full of ice. She pulled his hand away and held the cubes to the burn. He jumped.

"Jesus! That's cold."

"It's supposed to be. It'll stop the pain and the burning."

"Who are you, Nurse Nancy?"

"Ah. The snark is back. You must be feeling better."

He lifted her hand up and substituted his. Not that he didn't like her touching him, rather he liked it too much.

"Let's see." She bent down and pried up his hand.

"I'm fine."

"Come on. Let me look."

He frowned but stopped resisting. She leaned in close, then kissed the injured area.

"Oops. Sorry. A Charlie habit."

Rusty's pulse shot up. Heat traveled through him and his groin raced to high alert. He shoved her away.

"You don't have to be rude. Just trying to make you feel better." She huffed.

"Thanks. But I can hold the ice myself."

Grabbing the half-empty mug, she pushed to her feet. "I'll get a re-fill."

Rusty sat in the chair and glared at Coco. "Naughty girl."

The dog flopped down on the deck, rested her head on her paws, and appeared contrite.

Meg returned and placed the full mug on the table. "It's not her fault. You don't take her out enough. Here we are in the country and when we go someplace, you don't let her come. She's a big dog cooped up all the time. No wonder she made a run for it when she saw the open door."

He looked at the ground. "I suppose."

"You know I'm right. Just won't admit it." She raised her chin.

"Why do you have to be right all the time?"

"I'm right when I'm right, is all."

"It's a thing with you, isn't it?"

"Is it? Never thought about it. I'm pretty smart."

"But you have a way of putting things. Makes a person want to hit you in the face with a cream pie."

Her eyes widened and her cheeks flushed. Rusty couldn't help but laugh.

"You need to let things go, ya know?" he choked out.

"I let plenty of things go. Especially with you."

"Oh yeah?" He cocked an eyebrow.

"Never mind. Let me see." She bent down, eased his hand away and examined the burn. "It's still red. Looks like it'll heal okay. I don't think we need to go to the emergency room." She dabbed at it with a wet paper towel. Then smoothed her fingers over his skin, setting off shock waves.

"Thank you, Dr. Gunderson." He shoved her hand away. If she didn't stop, something embarrassing would happen.

"Snarky again. And rude! I was just trying to help."

"Help from over there." He pointed across the table.

Damn, her touch sent all the wrong signals. His body didn't know she was a stuck-up bitch. It recognized foreplay when it happened.

Blood started pumping to his dick. He could not, under any circumstances, get hard now.

Coco stood up and leaped off the deck, chasing some Canada Geese off the lawn. Rusty smiled. Damn, the dog always had his back.

"Good girl, Coco!" Meg called. "Those geese are annoying."

"Good coffee," he said.

"Thanks. Cereal for breakfast. Hot cereal. Oatmeal with brown sugar, strawberries, and cream."

"Wow!"

She smiled. "Oatmeal is good for you."

"I don't think Tommy's ever had oatmeal."

"Your Mrs. MacDougal takes care of all his meals?"

"I'm not home at dinner."

"What about breakfast?"

"We're always rushing. Frozen waffles. Cold cereal."

She frowned. "That's too bad. I make a real breakfast for Charlie every morning."

"Mrs. MacDougal doesn't come until noon."

"I see." Meg nodded.

"Look, I know I should do better with his food. He gets a good lunch and dinner. I'm doing the best I can."

"Where's your wife, if you don't mind me asking?"

"I do mind. But I'll tell you anyway. We're divorced and I don't know where the hell she is. Happy?" He frowned.

"You don't have to bite my head off."

"You asked."

"I'm sorry." She placed her hand on his forearm and stared into his eyes. "I think it's terrible for a mother to desert her husband and child. It must be difficult for you to earn a living and be mother and father to Tommy."

"It's not a walk in the park. You know all about it, don't you?"

She cast her gaze to the ground and nodded. "About the stuff I said last night. Can you please forget it? I shouldn't have opened my mouth."

Rusty squeezed her hand. "Why not? We both have hurdles in our lives. Although Angela's not dead, she might as well be. She hasn't seen Tommy since he was a month old."

"That's terrible."

Warmth coursed through Rusty's veins. Outside of the therapist he and Tommy saw, no one else understood. Meg did. Her soft acceptance drew him. Two boats adrift in the same sea, he figured. Maybe they could learn from each other?

WHEN HER FINGERS MADE contact with his bare skin, heat flared in her face. What was she thinking? Touching him? It was bad enough when he walked into the kitchen bare-chested. She almost dropped her coffee. Unable to tear her gaze from his pecs, she'd forced herself to face the other way.

Sitting on the deck, she grabbed glimpses of his torso when he wasn't looking. Damn it. Rusty was a fine-looking man. Heat grew in her veins, making her squirm. Embarrassment kept her gaze from his. What had she been thinking when she opened up to him last night?

"Listen, about what I said last night? I was just tired. Forget it."

"So you're taking it back?"

"It sounds pretty stupid now."

"I don't think it's stupid. Justice? I've cursed out Angela a thousand times since she left Tommy with me and filed for divorce. Hell, the hardest thing I've ever done is raising him on my own. It'd rather face a pitcher with a hundred-and-ten-mile-an-hour fastball every day of the week than raise my son by myself. But I have no choice. So, yeah. I get it. Anger. Betrayal. Desertion. And fear."

"It's not like I could get mad at John. I mean, he didn't choose to die. I'm sure he'd much rather be here, teaching Charlie to play ball or catch a frog."

"Just because you don't think you have the right to be angry doesn't mean you don't get pissed off."

She faced him. "Yeah. Sometimes I do."

"Welcome to the club. Not that it gets you anywhere. I've read every book from Dr. Spock to Mr. Rogers. And still, when I come home tired and Tommy's whiny or sick...I get mad. Mad I have to deal with it by myself. And mad at myself for being such an asshole."

"You do?"

"Yeah. So don't be embarrassed. You didn't say anything I haven't felt a million times. Believe me. Being a single parent—it's damn hard."

Emotions gathered in her chest rendering her speechless. Outside of her therapist, no one had ever spoken so honestly about her circumstances before. Rusty had hit at the heart. Tears stung her eyes. He took her hand in both of his.

"It's okay, Meg, to speak the truth."

She nodded and tried to blink back the wetness in her eyes, but two drops escaped. Rusty wiped them away with his thumbs. Lifting her mug to hide her face, she took a swallow. Maybe he wasn't such a Neanderthal after all?

"What do you want to do today?" He changed the subject

"There's a boy scout trail in the woods. It's not too far from here. Maybe a twenty-minute drive? We could take a picnic lunch?"

"Sounds good. Maybe The Cozy Café would make up a basket?"

"Wonderful."

"Do you want to call them?"

"Sure. Let's wait until the boys are up. See what they want."

"Okay."

She sat back, watching two red-winged blackbirds fly back and forth. An easy silence grew between the adults.

Coco returned. She took a big drink from her water bowl and went inside.

"She's going to get Tommy up." Rusty rose. "Time for me to shower and dress."

"Don't get dressed on my account," Meg said.

Rusty stopped and stared for a moment before laughing.

Stop flirting!

"I mean—"

"I know exactly what you mean. Thanks for the compliment."

She grinned as he exited. Boy, she was in trouble now. Looked like the truce had morphed into something else.

Could there possibly be a friendship between two such different people? Could she learn to like baseball? Could Rusty get over his fear of snakes?

Meg returned to the kitchen and put the water on to boil for oatmeal. Voices drifted in from the living room. Soon hurricanes Charlie and Tommy would burst on the scene. As she set the table, a sense of peace flowed through her. Maybe she could make this work—at least for the summer?

The boys flew into the room with Coco not far behind. Meg filled the dog's dish and put it on the floor.

"What's for breakfast?"

"Oatmeal with brown sugar, strawberries, and cream."

"Oh boy!" Charlie said, heading for the silverware drawer.

"I've never had oatmeal," Tommy said.

"You'll love it. Charlie, you two set the table. Here are the bowls, Tommy. Would you please put one at each place?"

The boys handled their tasks with ease, just like any family.

SATURDAY ARRIVED WAY before Meg was ready. Ugh, a baseball game. Hours and hours of something she was clueless about. She'd have to listen to Rusty. Pay attention. Learn. About something she had zero interest in. Less than zero—maybe minus one hundred.

Every day, Charlie had asked her how much longer until the game. She'd have to shove her impatience about baseball away and try to be enthusiastic. Who knew her little egghead son would be interested in sports?

Charlie ran into her room at seven and jumped on her.

"Get up, Mom!"

"Huh?"

"It's the game!"

"Oh, yes. Game day. But not 'til later."

"Rusty said two o'clock. Only seven hours."

"Good math. Okay. I'm up." Meg yawned and threw off the covers. "Why don't you get dressed?"

Charlie raced out of the room.

Meg brushed her hair and tied the sash on her robe. Like a robot, she hit the kitchen and started the coffeemaker. Tommy and Charlie, chattering away, entered fifteen minutes later.

"Eggs?"

"Can we have pancakes?" Tommy asked. "Please?" He grinned.

"Sure. But I'm out of blueberries."

"Your pancakes are good even without them."

Rusty could take lessons from his son in the charm department. Meg couldn't resist the boy. She gathered the necessary ingredients. "Why don't you boys make your beds while you wait?"

"Okay." Charlie tapped Tommy's shoulder. "Let's go."

Meg flipped on the radio. Unable to find her favorite classical music station, she stopped at a local country music one. The song, "Here You Come Again" by Dolly Parton came on Meg sang along and danced a few steps as she poured batter on the hot griddle pan.

While the food cooked, she checked her phone. Oh, God, text number bazillion from Harold. He'd sent texts and emails she'd neglected to answer. Settling for him in the City because there hadn't been anyone else had been the easy thing. But now, living with Rusty and the attention from the ballplayers, Harold didn't cut it.

John had been the love of her life. After he died, she'd accepted that their kind of relationship came along only once. Enter Harold, Mr. Mediocre-but-better-than-nothing. Or was he? At first, being alone tortured Meg. But after the first year, she found solitude soothing, peaceful.

In the country, she relished her time to read or walk with Coco. When Rusty had his game and the boys were in bed, Meg had time to think. Coco stayed by her side, as if the dog knew Meg needed a silent companion.

Slowly it dawned on her, Harold had become nothing more than an annoying thorn in her side. He had to go. She admitted to herself not responding to his texts and emails had been cowardly, but she'd had enough unpleasantness in her life. She needed to heal, without Harold. Snapping her phone shut, she flipped the hotcakes.

"Getting calls at this hour? Your boyfriend must miss you."

The masculine voice made her jump.

"You're up early."

"Dodging my question?"

"I don't owe you any explanations about my private life."

"I must be right or you'd have denied it."

She frowned. Rusty could be infuriating. "Anyone who annoys me gets no pancakes."

"Ouch. Okay. I'm sorry." He raised his palms, then poured himself a cup of coffee. "Need a refill?"

She nodded. He filled her mug.

"Today's the big day. Your first game. Are you excited?" He took a sip.

"Dread is the word coming to mind."

"Really?" His eyebrows shot up.

"Yep. How long does a game usually last?"

"Hard to say. Usually about three hours. If it's a pitcher's duel, it can be over in two. But if it's tied in the ninth, then it goes to extra innings. Which continues until the tie is broken."

"Oh my God? Isn't there a time limit of some sort?"

Rusty shook his head. "Nope. No ties in baseball. The Mets once had a game go twenty-six innings."

Her eyebrows shot up. "Twenty-six? How long did it take?"

"Dunno. Maybe eight, nine hours."

"Nine hours at the stadium?" She turned to face him.

"Calm down. It's rare. Probably about two, two and a half, tops."

She let out a breath. "Oh, thank God."

"Why? Are you really dreading it?"

"Maybe."

"Then don't go." He shrugged.

"What?"

"You heard me. Stay home. I'll take the boys. I don't want your sour comments or incessant asking when it'll be over to ruin it for the kids."

She put her hands on her hips. "Well, thanks a lot."

"You're welcome. Hey, don't burn those."

She lifted the pan off the flame. "Guess they're done. Please call the boys."

As she parceled out the hotcakes, she thought about his words. *He's right.* If she was going to go, it had to be with a reasonably cheery attitude. The idea of staying home appealed. But she'd never let Charlie have a new experience like this without her tagging along.

Besides, she wanted to see the players again. Especially Frank Todd. She hadn't answered their texts. Maybe because she hadn't considered their pleas to join them for dinner serious.

When the boys sat down, Charlie turned to his mother with a request.

"Mom, Tommy says I can't go to the game without a baseball glove."

"What?"

"Yeah. For catching fly balls."

"You're not going to be playing."

"In the stands, Meg," Tommy added.

"Oh?"

"Makes it more fun if you can go home with a fly ball you caught," Rusty said.

"So can I get a glove, Mom? Please?"

Meg shrugged. "Why not?"

"We can go shopping after breakfast," Rusty said, smiling at Meg. *Wonderful. A baseball glove. What's next? A football helmet?*

RUSTY SMILED TO HIMSELF. Telling Meg she didn't have to go to the game had been brilliant. Her reaction had been textbook. He played her like a fine violin. He wanted her along, wanted her to see, hear, and feel baseball—to understand the thrill of the game. Maybe then she'd stop putting it down and calling it Neanderthal and stupid.

He dressed in his best jeans and pulled his old Nighthawks jersey over his head. He'd have to get a jersey for Charlie. He poked his head into the boy's room.

"Tommy, wear your Nighthawks jersey."

"Okay, Dad."

"Charlie, we'll get you one in time for the next Jaguar game."

"Thanks."

Pride pumped Rusty's chest. Little Miss Mensa Chick would be spending the day in his arena, his wheelhouse, his comfort zone. His biggest struggle would be not lording it over her that she didn't know jack-shit and he knew everything.

"Boys! Time to hit the road." Rusty shoved his well-worn wallet in his back pocket.

"Boys? Where are you going? Wherever Charlie goes, I go, too." Meg crossed her arms over her chest.

Don't hide the goods, honey.

"I'm taking them to get a baseball glove for Charlie. You can come, too."

"Damn right I can come."

Rusty grabbed her arm. "I'm not trying to take Charlie away from you. I just figured the last thing you'd want to do is spend time looking over mitts. Figured you'd rather read a book."

"Maybe. But where Charlie goes, I go. And what's a mitt, anyway? I thought you were going to buy a glove?"

Rusty smiled. *Like taking candy from a baby.* "A mitt is another word for a baseball glove."

"Oh."

Barely able to contain a laugh, Rusty turned away. The boys raced to the front door.

"There they are! Future infielders of America! Let's go." He opened the door, stood to the side, and did a half bow. "Ladies first."

Meg raised her chin slightly and headed for the car. Rusty chuckled to himself. Watching her squirm would make his day. He rolled his eyes. *Who doesn't know what a mitt is?*

They went to several stores, finally ending up at a local sporting goods shop. The prices there were easily fifty percent more than a chain store. But they had Wilson and Rawlings top-of-the-line kids' gloves. Rusty picked out several for Charlie to try on.

"This Wilson is the best," Rusty said to the salesman. "We'll take it." He reached for his wallet until a hand on his arm stopped him.

"The glove is a hundred dollars."

"Yeah? So? Tommy's glove cost more."

"I don't want to spend so much on something Charlie may use once."

"Trust me. Once he gets baseball fever, he'll have the glove on every weekend. It's my treat. He's a good kid."

Meg blanched. "Every weekend?"

"You'll see. Baseball and boys go together."

"Like?"

"Ham-and-swiss, peanut-butter-and-jelly, and love-and-marriage."

Meg cocked an eyebrow at him.

"Don't be a doofus. Let the kid have the glove. He'll use it this summer. Trust me."

"Okay. But I'll pay for it."

"Why do you have to be like that? Can't Charlie get a present from a friend?"

"Yeah, Mom. Can't I?"

With three sets of eyes pleading with her, she gave in. "All right."

"Good. As I said, we'll take it. Can you take the tags off? We're going to the game today. He needs it."

"Sure. Who's playing?" the salesman asked, pulling small scissors from his pocket.

"The Jaguars," Tommy piped up.

"They're having a great season. Keep your eye on Frank Todd. He's their slugger, their biggest star."

"Really? Good to know. I got a text from him a couple of days ago. Guess I'll answer him now," Meg said, whipping out her phone.

"You actually got a text from Frank Todd?" Rusty's mouth hung open.

"He said he would get in touch."

"What did he say?"

"He invited me to dinner."

"He asked you out on a date?"

She nodded while a smug smile played on her lips.

Holy shit! He thought the guys were just flirting, fooling around, having some fun. He had no idea Todd had been serious.

"Guess you don't know everything, Mr. Reisse," she said.

He frowned. She won that round. Damn. He'd underestimated her charm or how horny Frank Todd was.

"Are you Rusty Reisse?" the salesman asked.

Rusty nodded.

"Can I have your autograph?"

"Sure, sure."

Rusty signed, charged the glove to his American Express card and they left. All his cockiness drained away. When it came to the Jaguars, maybe Meg held the trump card after all.

Chapter Seven

Meg could not believe she'd texted Frank Todd she'd have dinner with him after the game. It's not like she wanted to have dinner with the ballplayer, but it would piss Rusty off if she did. So, whammo, behaving like a child, she sent him a flirtatious text about how much she looked forward to getting to know him. Ugh. Big lie.

It was bad enough she had to listen to Rusty rattle on incessantly about baseball. Now she'd add Frank Todd to the list of men who couldn't talk about anything else. Then she'd have to fend off his advances after dinner. She gasped. And leave Charlie!

She'd made a rule. Until they'd fully recovered—if possible—she'd never go anywhere without Charlie. This eliminated the possibility of something tragic happening to one of them. Her son had seemed relieved when she came up with the idea.

The parents of Charlie's friends understood and always invited Meg along on playdates. Sometimes she went, other times she didn't—but only if Charlie felt comfortable. The suddenness of John's death had shaken Meg and Charlie to their roots. No longer believing everyone returns safely, the mother and son clung to each other.

Rusty didn't get it. Meg didn't blame him, but she wished he'd back off when she insisted upon going along. How would Charlie feel if Meg went on a dinner date with Frank Todd? She had no clue. Pushing the dilemma out of her mind, she returned to the house to change. Since a date might happen after the game, she dressed in a low-cut tank top, cotton skirt, and sandals.

"You're going to a ball game. Beer. Hot Dogs. Foul balls. Not to a dance."

"And out to dinner with Frank Todd afterward," she dropped in.

"Really?" Rusty's eyebrows shot up.

"Yep." She grinned.

It was almost worth setting a date with Frank, to see Rusty jealous. Keeping him off balance had become her favorite pastime. But why should she care if he got jealous? After all, he was nothing but a nuisance, right? An enforced roommate she'd been trying to shake since the get-go. Yeah, right.

Was Rusty Reisse getting under her skin? Meg frowned. Caring for him would be totally unacceptable. So the man was sexy? So what? And what about the hot Jaguars? It didn't mean she'd be developing feelings for Rusty. Her friends, mothers of Charlie's friends, assured her she could sleep with someone without falling in love, without being engaged, or without even liking the guy much. Sex was sex and could have nothing to do with love. Like scratching an itch, they'd said. Who was she to disagree?

Whew. Yes, she could find Rusty attractive in an animalistic kind of way but not have feelings for him. Relieved she'd sorted it out, she took a deep, calming breath.

"Watch out for Todd. I hear he's a player."

"Takes one to know one?" She arched an eyebrow at him, enjoying the blush spreading over his face.

"Guys. Got your gloves?" He called to the boys.

They raised their hands, then ran to the car.

"Let's go." Rusty grabbed Meg's arm. "You're getting in over your head. Nice little schoolteachers don't date big, bad ballplayers."

Meg ripped her arm out of his grasp. "I can take care of myself."

"Really? I doubt it."

"I've managed to go toe-to-toe with you and come out ahead."

His mouth opened, but no words came out.

"I rest my case. Don't worry about me. I'm a lot stronger than you think."

"I don't doubt it." He held the door for her, then followed. "But I also doubt Frank Todd is asking you out because he's looking for a ready-made family."

Meg whirled around. "Stop it! No, Frank Todd isn't looking to marry me and adopt Charlie. And I'm not looking for a husband and father for my son. Maybe we're looking for a pleasant evening spent in the company of an attractive member of the opposite sex."

Rusty burst out laughing. "Lady, you've got a lot to learn about ballplayers."

"Oh, shut up." She flounced down the stairs and into the vehicle.

Although his arrogance infuriated her, what he said made sense. No, Frank Todd wasn't looking for a family. Most likely, he was looking to get laid. Well, if sex was on his mind, he'd called the wrong woman. Meg compressed her lips into a firm frown. She'd be damned if she'd be anyone's one-night stand.

RUSTY STILL COULDN'T believe sweet little Meg was going out with that animal, Frank Todd. Oh, sure, she could handle anyone verbally, but Frank wouldn't be using words. And he'd be persuasive. Hard to resist for a lonely lady who needed a roll in the hay.

Whoa! Rusty's eyes widened as he steered the car toward the stadium. Did he just say to himself Meg needed to get laid? Wow. Maybe he needed to slow down. If it's what she needed, Frank Todd could provide the answer. But not nearly as well as Rusty Reisse. He smiled to himself for a moment. *Wait a minute. Do I want to sleep with this chick? Can't be. Her nasty mouth is a total turn-off. Right?*

A quick surge of blood to his groin argued with his head. Damn, he did. *Shit. Crap.* No way, no way, no he had to stop thinking about her. Meg was the enemy, and he needed to keep her in that camp. He already had trouble with his ex-girlfriend, Maria, who had no idea why he left town and could care less about Tommy. No way should he take on this chick. Besides, she'd never give him the time of day, right? Wrong. He'd spied her looking him over a couple of times. And it made his pulse jump.

Physical attraction. Being a healthy male, he'd reacted to her, like he did to any pretty female. It's simple chemistry, hormones, whatever—certainly nothing beyond. Then why did he care if Frank Todd seduced Meg? The answer? He didn't. Let him fuck her brains out. It wouldn't matter one bit to Rusty.

He pulled into the lot and picked a space close to the entrance. The lot was barely half-full. But they were early.

"These little regional teams have a hard time filling the stands," Rusty said as he put the car in park.

"So it's a good thing we're going to the game?" Meg asked.

"Yeah. Maybe we should plan to go again."

"Yes!" The boys hollered at the same time.

Putting their gloves on, the boys piled out of the vehicle and headed for the gate.

"This better be good," Meg said, almost under her breath.

"Give it a chance, will you?" Rusty replied.

"Okay." She smiled.

"That's better." Rusty started singing "Take Me Out to the Ball Game."

Meg laughed and shook her head. Tommy joined in. Charlie watched.

"You never taught him the song?" Rusty asked.

"No need."

"Your husband never wanted to go to a ballgame?"

She shook her head. "Not that he ever said to me. A tennis match, yes. Baseball? No."

"Too bad. It's America's Pastime. And the kid doesn't even know the song."

"Rub it in a little, why don't you?"

"If you weren't so high-and-mighty about Charlie maybe being the next Albert Einstein, I might let it go. Might offer to teach him the song myself."

"I'm glad to see you know who Albert Einstein is."

"You know, if you were a man, I'd slug you." Rusty growled, walking faster. He whipped the tickets out of his pocket and ushered the boys in. He flipped her ticket to her but didn't wait. Charlie stopped.

"Mom?" As he looked around, his voice quavered, his body stiffened.

"She's right behind us," Rusty said.

Much smaller in comparison with a major league stadium, it still loomed large to a little boy. Rusty took Charlie's hand. "See? Here she comes."

He noticed the boy relax as soon as he spotted Meg. A lightbulb went off in Rusty's head. *Oh my God! The boy is afraid to be without his mother. Must be afraid she'll die like his dad?*

Emotion swept through him. He'd never considered the residual fallout from the sudden death of the boy's father. What a heavy load. His eyes wetted for a second.

MEG'S EYES TOOK IN the entire arena. Now it wasn't simply practice, the stands were filling up. Hot dog, ice cream, popcorn, and soda vendors spread out along an alley. In the back were a half-dozen picnic tables.

Dawdling to take in everything, she realized Charlie wasn't with her. Hearing a familiar voice call out, she sped up. She thought he'd be okay with Rusty but guessed he still needed to keep her in sight, especially in a new place.

"I'm here, Charlie." Meg waved. "Thanks for not waiting for me." She directed her comment to Rusty.

"I'm so sorry. I never. Well. I'm sorry." He gripped her forearm for a moment before turning his gaze away.

"Guess you didn't get it before, but you do now."

She shot the snarky comment to Rusty and immediately regretted it. When her gaze connected with his, she saw something unexpected. She thought he'd send her a frown at her irresponsibility in letting Charlie get ahead. Instead, she saw sadness and understanding. And was there wetness there? Did Rusty mist up? Impossible.

The adults flanked the children. With tickets in the first row, they'd be practically on the field. Meg caught the excitement in the air. The allure of baseball included the delicious aroma of cheap-ass hot dogs and popcorn, the buzz of the crowd, and the thwack of hard balls hitting gloves as players warmed up. The experience bombarded her senses. Her mouth salivated.

"Where are we sitting?" Tommy asked.

Rusty glanced at the tickets and led the way. "Over here."

They filed down the aisle to the front row, then made their way across to almost first base.

"Best seats in the house," Rusty said.

Tommy nodded.

"Who's hungry?" Rusty asked.

"Me," piped up a deep voice.

Rusty raised his gaze to connect with Frank Todd's. The ballplayer leaned up against the stands in front of Meg.

He doffed his cap. "Hi, Meg. Are you with this old guy?"

A deep voice saying her name drew her attention. She looked up and there was Frank Todd, his dark eyes a few feet from hers. A shiver shot down her spine.

"Yes, she's with me, Frank. Keep your mitts to yourself."

Surprised to be claimed by Rusty, she raised her eyebrows and faced him.

"Are you dating him?" Frank asked.

"Actually, she's living with me," Rusty piped up.

"What? I am not."

"Are you not living in the same house?" Rusty's tone was all innocence.

"Are you?" Frank asked.

"We're roommates. We are absolutely, positively *not* living together—in the biblical sense."

A lazy, sexy smile spread across Frank's face. "That's all I needed to know."

She smiled back.

"I'll pick you up in the parking lot, after the game. Give me time to shower and dress."

She nodded.

Charlie tugged on her blouse. "Mom. Are you going somewhere with him?"

"Mr. Todd is taking me to dinner after the game."

Charlie's eyes widened. "Mom. Remember our rule."

"I know, sweetheart. But Mr. Todd will be very careful driving. Won't you?" She glanced at the ballplayer, who nodded in response.

Tears filled her son's eyes. "You always said Dad was a good driver, too."

"Oh, Charlie." Emotion choked Meg. Tears clouded her blues.

"What happened?" Frank Todd asked.

Meg gave a brief explanation.

"Say, Charlie, boy. Why don't you come with us?"

"Really?" Charlie sniffled.

"Sure. We'll go out the three of us."

Meg had never wanted to kiss a man more than right then and there.

"Can I, Mom?"

"If Mr. Todd says so."

"Frank. It's Frank."

"Okay, Charlie. What do you say?"

"Thank you...Frank. Oh boy!"

Frank Todd reached over and cupped Meg's chin. He wiped away a small tear on her cheek.

"See you after the game. Wish me luck."

She sighed. Charlie jumped up and down in his seat. Meg faced Rusty.

"And you said he's a player. I guess not."

Rusty shrugged, but his frown hinted at his true feelings. His expression tugged at Meg's heart. She didn't care for Frank Todd and regretted her effort to make Rusty jealous. Her mother had always said jealousy was a dangerous emotion. Meg agreed.

He raised his gaze to hers. She smiled and squeezed his hand. He shot her a questioning glance. How could she explain to him what she didn't understand herself?

"Food?" she asked.

"Oh, yeah. Who wants a hot dog?"

Rusty took the orders. The boys went with him to help carry everything. While they were gone, she watched Frank field the ball. Every few minutes, he looked over at her. A sense of panic grabbed her. What the hell was she doing? What did she want? Her throat tightened. She wanted John back, that's what she wanted. But he'd never return, and she had to get on with her life. She checked her watch. The game was about to begin. The loudspeaker came on.

"Ladies and Gentlemen. Please stand for our national anthem."

Before she could turn around, Charlie, Tommy, and Rusty had returned to their seats. They passed the food around and stood up. Meg sang along. She noted Frank held his cap over his heart. In a sidelong glance, she saw Rusty put his hand over his heart and sing. She did the same.

When the song finished, the audience applauded and cheered. "Play ball!" came from the loudspeaker. A sense of tension grabbed Meg.

"The Jaguars are playing the Minisink Marshalls, their biggest rival. This should be a good game," Rusty said.

Meg smiled and took a bite of her hot dog. Charlie sat up straight in his seat, cheering for the Jaguars between eating and slugs of soda. The boy appeared more animated than she'd seen since John passed. Tommy cheered right along with him. And so did Rusty. She figured she might as well get with the program.

"Go, Jaguars!" she hollered.

Rusty shot her a big grin.

Frank Todd got up to bat and hit a home run! The crowd went wild. Meg rose from her seat, cheering, screaming, and hollering. Rusty gave her a high-five. All was right with the world.

RUSTY HAD NEVER BELIEVED in miracles before, but watching Meg Gunderson get into the Jaguars game, cheering, downing two hot dogs and a shit-ton of soda blew his mind. Totally convinced she was a prissy bitch, he tossed his assessment out the window. Anyone watching would swear the woman sitting two seats away was a lifelong Jaguars fan who never missed a game.

Meg and Charlie high-fived, hooted, hollered, and yelled together. Rusty scratched his head. Where had she been hiding this persona? The rapport and love between mother and son smacked him in the face. He wished he had such an easy relationship with Tommy.

Tommy and Charlie had raised their gloves half a dozen times to catch foul balls but caught none. Then it happened. One of the Marshalls took a swing and fouled one off right to the stands near first base.

The ball sailed directly at Meg. She screamed and, bending over, covered her head with her arms. Charlie and Tommy froze.

Rusty grabbed the glove from his son and raised it. He dove across the seats to Meg, extending his arm. The stadium grew quiet. The only sound was the thwack of the ball hitting the glove. Rusty ended up in Meg's lap, arm outstretched, ball in glove.

He vaulted to a standing position, waving to show the fans. Meg came out of her crouch. The crowd cheered. Many stood and applauded. The announcer came on the loudspeaker.

"Well, will you look at that? Looks like the New York Nighthawks' very own Rusty Reisse! And he made the catch. Say, Rusty is she your girlfriend?"

The crowd chanted "Rus-tee, Rus-tee," over and over again. He took a bow, then grabbed Meg's hand and made her stand, too. Then the chant changed to "kiss him, kiss him."

Meg's face turned several shades of pink. She sank down on her chair, shaking her head. But the crowd wouldn't stop. Laughing, she pulled him over and kissed his cheek! Rusty cheered and raised his gloved hand with the ball again. Then the umpire blew the whistle and play resumed.

Meg collapsed, fanning herself. Charlie and Tommy argued over the ball.

"My dad caught it. So, it's mine."

"But it was coming at my mother. So, it's mine."

Rusty returned the glove to his son and faced Meg.

"You okay?"

She nodded. "Fine, now. Damn. My heart's racing."

"It was headed straight for you."

"Thank you. You saved me."

"And I'd do it again."

"I owe you one."

"No, you don't. You'd have done the same for me." His gaze met hers.

Rusty spoke to his son. "Tommy, how many foul balls do you have at home? From professional games?"

"I don't remember."

"Yes, you do. Come on. How many?"

"Five."

"Five!" Charlie said.

"Yeah. Right, Charlie. Five is a lot, isn't it? So how about we give this one to Charlie, because he doesn't have any."

"But you caught it," Tommy argued.

"Then I should keep it? But I don't want it. Besides, it was headed right for Charlie's mother. If she knew how, she might have caught it. So maybe the ball belongs to Charlie?"

"Okay." Tommy handed the ball to his new friend.

"Thanks." Charlie took possession of his new prize.

"Way to go, Tom," Rusty said, giving his son a high-five and a hug.

Charlie rubbed his hands over the leather covering.

"Want me to keep it for you?" Meg asked her son.

He nodded and handed it over. She tucked it into her purse.

"Maybe we should have bought you a glove today," Rusty said.

Rusty turned his attention back to the game. The Jaguars got their second homerun from Frank Todd. He doffed his cap at Meg as he headed for first base. *Fucking showoff.*

"Frank Todd's having a great game. Looks like you bring him luck."

"Maybe. But that's all I'm bringing him," Meg replied, shooting a sharp glance at Rusty.

He sighed. When these players turned on the heat, a woman would have a hard time resisting. He could only hope Charlie being there would keep the second baseman in line. Why did he care? So what if Meg dumped Charlie at home and screwed Frank Todd's brains out? What would it mean to him?

He didn't have the answer for the question that kept running through his mind. While he had no insight as to why, it did matter. It mattered a whole lot. Todd better watch his step. Naïve Meg would be easy pickins for a player like Todd, with his smooth lines and good looks.

No one would be taking advantage of Meg Gunderson, least of all a ballplayer, while there was breath in Rusty's body. Now he'd decided on the issue, he turned his attention back to baseball.

"Hey, Earth-to-Rusty. What's that?" Meg tugged on his shirt.

"What?"

"She wants to know what the infield fly rule is, Dad," Tommy said.

"The infield fly rule? The most complicated in baseball…" he began.

Chapter Eight

The Jaguars won the game six to five, with Frank Todd batting in the winning run in the bottom of the ninth. Meg stretched. Time to face her date with Frank. She turned on her phone. There were eleven texts from Harold. She replied.

It's over, Harold. Please stop texting me. We're done.

"I guess you have your big date with Todd." Rusty pushed to his feet.

Dread filled her. Charlie and Harold did not get along, so she saw Harold mostly at school functions. When he'd stop by for dinner from time to time, Charlie would play in his room. Once in a while, he'd stay until Charlie was safely in bed. Then they'd have sex. It hadn't been very satisfying. But she reminded herself John had been the gold standard as a lover, and she shouldn't expect anyone else to measure up.

When she told Harold their relationship was over, relief washed through her. She preferred being alone to being with him, which probably went for any other man, too. If she couldn't have John, why settle for a second-rate stand-in?

"To make sure you're not stranded here, Tommy and I will wait until Todd shows up."

"You don't have to."

"Oh, yes I do."

"Don't you trust him?"

"Not for a second."

"You think he'd stand me up?"

"I have no idea."

"Oh. So, you're waiting to make sure he shows up?"

"Exactly."

"Hmm." She glanced at Rusty. He shifted his weight, hands in the pockets of his shorts, his brow furrowed. Something about him reminded her of her father when she had her first date. Straining not to laugh, she turned away. Rusty was as obvious as the smell of a freshly peeled onion. When being protective, he could be kinda cute, almost likable.

"Hey, there!" A handsome, dark-haired man strode toward them. "Meg?"

"Hi. You met Charlie."

Frank Todd bent down to shake the boy's hand.

"How'd you like the game?"

"It was awesome." Charlie beamed.

"Congratulations," Meg said. "On your home run."

"And two RBI's, too."

"What's an RBI?" Meg tilted her head slightly.

Frank laughed. "We have a lot to talk about. My car's over there." As he made tracks to his vehicle, Rusty grabbed his arm.

"You're Rusty Reisse, right? Old-timer?"

"Not exactly old timer yet."

"Oh, okay. Sorry."

"Have her back at a reasonable hour."

"Are you her father?"

"Just a friend."

"I see."

"And no funny business."

"Her son is the best chaperone going."

"Good. Just remember that."

"I see. So it's like that? Does she know?"

"Know what?"

"Old and dense, too." Frank shook his head.

"I don't know what you're talking about. We're friends. I'm just keeping an eye on her."

"So that's what you call it?"

"What else?"

Frank laughed. "If you don't know, I'm not going to tell you."

"Fine. Be respectful."

"Don't worry, old man. I'll have her home at a reasonable hour."

Frank opened the car door for Meg. She opened the back door for Charlie. The three buckled in and Frank turned over the motor.

"Where are we going?" Charlie asked.

"There's a place with great burgers called Mickey's. Do you like burgers, Charlie?"

"Yeah. But Mom doesn't let me have 'em much."

Frank cocked an eyebrow at Meg.

"Tonight's okay. It's a victory celebration." She picked at the hem of her top.

"Right! A victory celebration. Which do you like better, Charlie? A regular burger or a cheeseburger?"

Within fifteen minutes they were seated at a table by a picture window in a rustic restaurant with a bar. Several bar patrons stopped by the table to congratulate Frank and ask for his autograph. Charlie had stars in his eyes. Frank appeared to be a huge star with tons of attention from fans.

Meg chewed her lip. John's success in finance had been quiet success. He'd never been asked for his autograph. Would Charlie forget his father in favor of a baseball star? No way. No one could forget John, the funniest, smartest, kindest man she'd ever known. Her brow furrowed. Frank won Charlie over in two seconds. She sighed.

"You're much nicer than my mother's boyfriend."

"You have a boyfriend?" Frank raised his eyebrows.

"Had. Had a boyfriend. We broke up."

"You did? Yay!" Charlie said.

"Not the old guy, Reisse?"

She shook her head. "A colleague at school."

"Glad he's out of the picture."

"Me, too," Charlie piped up.

"You like baseball?"

"This was my first game," Charlie replied.

"Well, let me tell you about the time I got my first grand slam."

"What's a grand slam?"

With Charlie hanging on his every word, Frank spent the meal recounting his best moments in baseball for Meg and her son. He carried on, bragging shamelessly. Meg, bored, tried to show interest, but it appeared Frank didn't even care. Charlie's attention was enough. Mesmerized by Frank's stories, the boy asked a ton of questions.

When dinner was over, Meg couldn't wait to get home.

"It's past Charlie's bedtime. We'd better go."

"Aw, Mom."

"Sorry. It's time"

Her watch read eight o'clock, not quite her son's bedtime, but close enough. She couldn't wait to escape the bone-crushing boredom of endless baseball stories. Frank paid the check and they shuffled out to the parking lot.

On the drive home, Charlie fell asleep in the backseat.

"Why don't we drop him, and you come back to my place for a nightcap?"

"I don't think so. It's been a long day." She pretended to yawn.

"It's not even eight thirty yet."

"We started early."

"I bet I can find a way to wake you up." He threw her a salacious glance.

Meg sat in silence. Fortunately, they pulled up in front of the house before he uttered another come-on. Guilt at turning him down nagged at her. Frank had been such a good sport about Charlie, but sex wasn't a thank you, or a tip. It had to be heartfelt for Meg.

Frank picked up Charlie and carried him into the house.

"Where should I put him?"

"In here." She led the way. Rusty jumped up from the living room sofa and the pro ballgame on television to follow them. Frank laid Charlie on his bed. Meg undressed him and tucked him in. Frank took her hand and led her to the door. Rusty lounged against the door jam.

"Back early?"

"Yep. Just to drop her son off."

"Oh?" Rusty faced Meg. "Are you going out again?"

She shook her head. "It's late. I'll walk you to your car."

Frank frowned but followed her outside. Rusty adjusted his position. *So he's going to eavesdrop? Fine. I'll give him something to remember.*

When they reached the vehicle, Frank stopped. He snaked his arms around her waist.

"Are you sure you don't want to come to my place?" He nuzzled her neck.

"I'm sure."

"Can I at least have a goodnight kiss?"

When she stepped closer, Frank lowered his mouth to hers. He swept her tight against his chest while his mouth ravished hers. Meg closed her eyes and reveled in his delicious taste and the feel of him against her. Damn, the man knew how to kiss!

His hands held her, then slid down to cup her rear end. He held her so close, she could feel his erection growing. As if a fire alarm went off, the first touch of hardness alerted her to stop. She gently pushed away from him, moving back, breaking his hold.

"Wow." She looked up at him.

His dark eyes, smoky with desire, glittered in the moonlight. His lust evident, she put on the brakes. Maybe a roll in the hay with Frank

Todd wouldn't be so bad, but she didn't feel it. All during dinner, he monologued. Never once asked her about her job or how she liked living in the City, or anything.

Meg figured men who are selfish outside of bed are often selfish in bed, too. She'd not be sampling the sexual techniques of Frank Todd, thank you very much.

"Thank you for a wonderful evening and for treating us to a great dinner."

"My pleasure."

"And Charlie. Well, you simply made his whole day. I'm sure I'm going to be hearing about it and about you for weeks to come."

He stepped closer. "Would you have dinner with me again? Just you?"

"I don't know if Charlie's ready to let go of me. But thank you."

"You have my number. Any time you want to pick up where we're leaving off, just text."

"I will. Thank you again, Frank."

Meg stood in the driveway, watching him start his car and drive away. She sighed. A first real date, sort of. Harold, who had known her for years, didn't count.

"Well, well, well. Turned him down?" Rusty leaned against the door jamb.

"None of your business."

"Must have. Or you wouldn't be here. What happened? Charm wear off by dessert?"

"Oh, shut up." She pushed by him and headed for the kitchen. She poured a glass of cabernet and slipped out on the back deck. Emotion overwhelmed her. Harold had never shown any interest in Charlie. The man had been a last resort—on a good day. When she simply couldn't stand to be without another adult around, she'd call Harold. He'd never threatened her world, or Charlie's. Her son had asked her if she'd marry Harold. When she got through laughing, she reassured him it would never happen.

But tonight, Charlie had opened up to Frank. He'd admired him, questioned him and hung on every word the ballplayer uttered. He seemed to worship the man. In the past, Charlie's hero worship had been saved for his father. Would he discard John in favor of Frank Todd?

The thought broke her heart. Talk about a full-time job—keeping love alive for a dead husband and father took the cake. He deserved that, didn't he? Didn't John have a right to her heart—and Charlie's—forever?

Yet she sensed the boy slipping away from the image of his father, to replace it with someone else, even someone he barely knew. And it hurt Meg's heart—killed her to watch him devote all his attention to Frank.

The idea that Charlie was ready to move on stunned her. She took a good swallow of the red liquid and put her glass on the railing. Burying her face in her hands, she let loose.

"What? What's the matter? What did the asshole do? I'll kill him." Rusty's words pierced the haze of sadness surrounding her.

"Nothing. He didn't do anything."

"Did you turn him down?"

"And he took it like a gentleman."

"I'll bet."

"He did. Honest."

"Then what's wrong?"

"Charlie," she choked out.

"He did something to Charlie? I'll kill him."

"No, no." She waved her hands, sighed and took a deep breath. Somehow, putting words to her feelings made it real.

"Then what?"

"Charlie was mesmerized by Frank. It's like he was in love, like Frank was his new idol. John has always been Charlie's idol." She burst into tears. "What if Charlie forgets John?" Control gone, she sobbed. Before she could stop, Rusty had folded her into his embrace. Weak, shaken, and confused, she melted into him. He tucked her head into his shoulder and let her cry.

Energy gone after a few minutes, she wound down to sniffling. She rested propped against the strength of his body. Even though her legs got wobbly, she didn't slip as his arms, like two iron bands, held her.

"I'm sorry," she whispered until he cut her off.

"Shhh."

Time stopped for Meg as she clung to Rusty. He stroked the back of her head, then her back.

"No worries," he whispered.

"But what if?"

"Shh. Sit." He eased her down on a comfortable chair, grabbed his glass and pulled up a seat. "Let me explain."

"You have the answer?"

"Listen."

She nodded and picked up her drink with a trembling hand.

"My father was amazing. He could fix anything, answer any question. He danced like a pro, hit a ball farther than anyone I knew. He was incredible, the best at everything—except maybe being a father. He left when I was twelve. I've never seen or heard from him since."

Meg gasped. Rusty raised his hand.

"Wait! Before you go feeling sorry for me. My mother was great. About two years later, she married a nice guy. Harry Reisse. Harry couldn't do any of the things my dad could. But he made a decent living, came home every night, and didn't fall in a liquor bottle. He adopted me."

Rusty broke to take another swig of beer. Meg squeezed his hand.

"Harry loved me, and I grew fond of him. But all these years? I never forgot my father. Never stopped loving him, admiring him, and wanting to be like him—in most ways."

"I didn't know."

"Don't worry about Charlie. You've both done a good job with him. He'll never forget his father. Christ, he talks about him all the time."

"I love that about Charlie."

"He's a good kid. But boys need someone to look up to. They need heroes. Makes growing up easier. Heroes provide a guide. Like a path, you know? So if he looks up to the asshole, Frank Todd, don't worry about it. He's not trading his father for Frank."

Meg took a deep, shuddering breath. "Thank you."

"You're welcome. Charlie's a great kid. Your husband would be proud."

Meg pushed to her feet, kissed the top of Rusty's head, and headed for the bedroom. "I'm tired."

"How did you like the game?"

"Oh, gee. Thank you for the tickets. It was amazing."

"Would you go again?"

"Of course. But not tomorrow, okay?"

"Oh, okay. But you will go again?"

"Yes. And I stand corrected. Baseball is not stupid. It's a complex and challenging sport."

Rusty gave a small bow. "Thank you. It is."

"Goodnight."

"Goodnight. Oh, one thing."

She faced him. "Hmm?"

"Are you going out with Frank again?"

She shook her head. "Nope. Too much focus on himself. He didn't even ask me what I do for a living."

"Selfish bastard."

"Don't look so happy about it."

Rusty's grin turned sheepish.

"'Night."

Undressing quickly, she didn't bother with her nightgown. She simply fell into bed and was asleep within a minute, ignoring the eleven new texts from Harold.

Chapter Nine

Even Meg slept in the next morning. She awoke at seven, not six, padded into the kitchen and started coffee. One peek out the window at the rising sun gave her an idea.

"A science day." While she mixed batter for pancakes and sipped her coffee, ideas whirled in her brain. She dressed, then hunted throughout the house for supplies—a cardboard box, rubber gloves, and sunscreen.

Sleepy boys wandered into the kitchen.

"Pancakes," she said.

They took their seats.

"Something smells great." Rusty entered, scratching his chest. Damn, in sweats alone the man looked enticing. Although she couldn't take her eyes off his chest, she tried to cover up her response.

"Please. No half-naked men at the table."

"Oh, sorry. Be right back." He scooted out of the room. Tommy and Charlie giggled.

Rusty returned sporting a snug T-shirt which emphasized his muscles. Meg tore her gaze away and flipped the hotcakes. After doling out three plates worth, she sat down to finish her coffee.

"What are we doing today?" Charlie asked, his mouth half-full of food.

"Well, I thought we might do something different."

Rusty cocked an eyebrow at her.

"What?" Tommy asked.

"Explore the woods. It rained last night. I thought we might hunt for salamanders. We can get a fish tank and make an environment for them. Keep them as pets until we leave."

"Oh boy! I love salamanders!" Charlie bounced in his chair.

"What's a salamander?"

Meg sat next to Tommy and explained about the small, boneless, red newts. Rusty focused on his food but moved closer. She had a hunch he didn't know what a salamander was either.

"Can I go, Dad?"

"If Meg says it's okay."

"Of course, he can come."

The boys high-fived each other.

"When you're finished, go get dressed. Long pants and long-sleeved shirts." Meg faced Rusty. "And you, too."

"Oh me? I'm not going."

"Why not?"

"It's kid's stuff."

Meg cocked an eyebrow. "Really? Didn't you say something about the social worker demanding you spend time with your son?"

"And I am. But creepy crawly things? You probably like snakes, too."

"Actually, I do."

"Ugh. No thanks."

"Come on. Show Tommy how macho you are. Face down a two-inch salamander."

"Very funny." He scowled.

"Okay. I promise to handle all the creepy crawly things. You don't have to touch anything."

"Really? You'd do that for me?"

"I intended to all along. Unless the boys want to touch them."

"Good."

"Then you're coming?" She raised her eyebrows.

The boys ran around the corner.

"Dad! Why aren't you dressed?" Tommy asked.

Rusty shrugged. "Guess he answered for me." He rose from his seat and brought his dish to the sink. "I'm getting dressed right now."

Meg hid a smile behind her hand. "Boys, can you load the dishwasher while I take Coco out?"

They set right to the task. Meg leashed the dog and headed for the backyard. Coco walked beside her, matching her stride. Meg gave her a pat on the head. "You're a good dog, Coco. Not a beast, like I thought."

The dog smiled at her and drooled. Rusty explained he hired a dog walker to handle the Rottie. Meg liked taking the animal for a stroll. A few moments of peace and quiet suited her. She let her mind wander.

Did she really open up to Rusty last night? Yeah. He'd surprised her with his depth of understanding. His words had comforted her. She didn't expect anything so profound and personal. Knowing more about him piqued her interest. Underneath his stupid macho bravado crap, who was this man? Little by little, he'd revealed a softer side. Maybe they could actually become friends? She frowned. *When day becomes night, maybe.*

Before they left, Tommy had a request.

"Can we take Coco with us?"

"Coco? In the woods? Do you have tick stuff for her?" Meg turned to Rusty.

He shrugged.

"It's not fair. We leave her home all the time because dogs aren't allowed anyplace. But the woods is outside. Can we?" Tommy's brown eyes pleaded.

"Why not? Let's go to the store and get her a flea and tick collar. Then she can come along."

"She can protect us against bears," Charlie piped up.

Rusty, in a long-sleeved T-shirt and snug jeans, opened the door. "After you."

They leashed Coco and took her to the car. She jumped in the backseat first. The boys arranged themselves around the dog. She settled down with her head on Tommy's lap.

THEY TRAMPED OVER THE lawn and halted at the edge of the forest.

"I'll take the leash," Tommy said.

Meg nodded. She slipped off her backpack. Before they entered, she laid out the rules and passed a handful of pink cloth strips to Charlie.

"What are those for?" Rusty asked.

"Charlie's going to tie those around tree trunks to mark our path. We don't know our way around these woods. It'll keep us from getting lost."

"Pink?"

"Okay. I ripped apart an old T-shirt. We have ties in the city we use when we go camping. I forgot to bring them."

"Camping? You?"

"Uh huh. You don't take Tommy camping, do you?"

"Honey, the Plaza hotel is as close to camping as I get."

"That's too bad."

"Lead on. Let's go."

Meg pushed aside the brush and led the way. Charlie followed, then Tommy with Coco and Rusty, bringing up the rear.

"Look on the ground. Rain brings salamanders out. They are mostly bright red and should be easy to spot. When you find one, give a shout," Meg said, box in hand.

"I see one!" Charlie hollered, bending down.

They crowded around, staring at the tiny creature.

"Pick him up by the tail, Charlie. Be very gentle. They don't have bones, only cartilage. They're delicate."

The boy did as his mother instructed. She slipped the box under his hand and he dropped the little newt in.

"I found one! I found one!" Tommy dropped the leash and bent down to examine the critter. Coco woofed.

"Rusty! Grab the dog before she steps on it," Meg said. She joined Tommy. "You sure did. Do you want to pick it up? You have to be very, very gentle. It's easy to crush them."

"No. I don't think so. I don't know how."

"Why don't you try? Just close your fingers around his tail enough so you can pick him up. I'll put the box under you, then you let go. Give it a try. They don't bite."

"They don't?"

"Nope. Nothing to be afraid of."

Tommy brought his shaking hand close to the salamander. It started to move.

"Sneak up behind him," Meg said.

Rusty leaned over behind his son, watching. Meg raised her gaze and made eye contact with him. He smiled and gave a slight nod. Tommy tried again. This time the tiny newt stayed still. Tommy picked him up by the tail, and Meg positioned the box underneath him. Tommy let go.

"Great! Now we have two. Can you boys tell them apart?"

A lengthy discussion ensued about which salamander was which and belonged to who. Next came name selection.

"I'm going to call mine Frank, after Frank Todd." Charlie smiled.

"I'm going to call mine Hardy, after the Hardy Boys," Tommy said.

Meg stood up and shoved the box in Rusty's face. "Aren't they cute?"

He jumped back, making everyone laugh. "Go on, touch it, Dad. It's not slimy or anything."

"Come on, Rusty," Meg said.

He wore a weak smile as he reached one tentative finger into the box. A quick touch and he pulled back. "There. Happy? Right, Tommy, they're not slimy. They're kind of cute, too."

"Told ya," Meg said, under her breath.

"I heard that," Rusty sniffed.

They tramped on for another hour but didn't find more salamanders. Something on the ground zipped by Rusty. He jumped.

"What the hell was that?"

"Snake." Meg reached into her backpack. She pulled out an old towel.

"Snake?" Rusty moved back quickly.

"Stand still everyone. You, too, Coco."

Meg searched the ground until she spotted where the snake had stopped. With a stealthy step or two, she threw the towel over the reptile. Then she crept up and felt through the towel until her hands came in contact with it. She'd slipped on thin rubber gloves.

"Found it. Just a minute." Working quickly but carefully, she grabbed the snake and pulled it out from under the towel. It was about a foot long.

"Garter snake."

"A snake is a snake. Get it away from me," Rusty said, turning pale.

"Don't be a baby. They don't bite. This thing is more afraid of you than you are of it."

"I wouldn't bet on that," Rusty mumbled.

Meg shot him a hostile glare. "Way to go, scaring your son."

Charlie rushed over. "Mom caught a garter snake, Tommy. Come look!"

"A snake?" The boy shook his head. Charlie grabbed a handful of his friend's shirt and pulled him along. "Come on. Don't be a wuss. They don't bite. They're really cool."

Dragging his feet, Tommy joined Charlie and Meg. She held the snake just behind the head and at the tail. While she talked, explaining what it was and how it lived, and why it was good, Rusty inched closer.

"Want to touch it?"

Rusty shook his head. Tommy put out a tentative finger.

"Snakes aren't slimy either," Charlie said. "See?" He took Tommy's hand and pulled it until his finger touched the snake.

"Now you." Meg turned her gaze on Rusty.

He shook his head.

"Come on, Dad. I did it." Tommy took his father by the hand and held a finger to the snake.

"Damn. You're right. He's not slimy."

Meg put the terrified snake back on the ground. It slithered away so fast, they couldn't see where it went.

"See? It's moving at, like, a hundred miles an hour. The damn things sneak up on you and then, wham! They're around your neck before you can blink."

Meg laughed. "Not a garter snake. They eat bugs, little things and aren't constrictors."

"Constrictors?"

"Like the boa constrictor. Those are the snakes that squeeze you to death. They don't live here in this climate. You've nothing to worry about." She patted his arm.

They continued wending their way through the woods with Charlie marking trees. Meg pointed out birds they hadn't seen before. When she turned to face the children to explain which bird perched above, Rusty stood listening as well.

"I'm hungry," Charlie said.

"Me, too." Tommy joined in.

"Okay. Lunch break."

"Lunch?" Rusty looked at Meg.

"Yep. Packed PB&J sandwiches, water, chips, and cupcakes."

"In your backpack?"

She nodded.

"It must weigh a ton."

"It will be lighter after we eat. Look for a flat rock, boys. We need a place to sit."

Tommy found the perfect spot. Rusty held the box with the salamanders. Meg passed out sandwiches. Everyone ate quietly. The boys watched the salamanders. When they finished eating and gathering up their trash, it was time to head home.

"Tommy, I'm putting you in charge of finding the pink ties and removing them, okay."

He nodded.

"Don't run ahead. Don't take down the tie until we reach you. Okay?"

"Okay." Tommy located the next pink tie, then called to the others. They joined him. Charlie ran ahead, while Rusty fell in step with Meg.

"Why didn't you let me carry the heavy stuff?"

"I wasn't sure you wouldn't bolt. Besides, in a backpack, it's easy."

"Tommy's having a great time. You've got his attention and he's not afraid. Amazing."

"He's a great kid."

"Thanks."

When they returned home, Rusty took them to the pet store to get food and a tank for Hardy and Frank, the salamanders. Once they got home, Meg took the boys out back to gather grass, leaves and other shrubbery to create a woodsy environment for the newts. Meg found a small yogurt container she cut down and filled with water. The boys dropped some dried bugs in, which is what salamanders eat.

The sky clouded up and rain threatened. Rusty set the boys up with a movie in the living room. Meg put up a pot of coffee and then moved outside, waiting for the storm to hit.

"Shit!" Rusty entered the kitchen, cursing.

Meg turned. "What the?"

"There was a yellow jacket in the stuff in the salamander tank. I looked in and the bastard stung me."

"Where?"

"Here." Rusty pointed to his earlobe, which had already begun to swell. "I'm allergic to bees, I think."

"Oh my God. You are?" Meg rose from her chair. She examined the sting. The area had begun to swell.

She yelled into the living room. "Boys! Come here. Quick!"

MEG TOOK A DEEP BREATH. The earlobe didn't look good, it had doubled in size in a matter of minutes. She took a deep breath then grabbed her phone.

"Charlie, get the GPS and punch in the nearest hospital. Tommy get in the car. Rusty, give me the car keys."

"What happened?" Tommy asked, his voice laced with fear.

"I'll explain when we get on the road."

Within a minute, Tommy and Rusty were fastened in the back. Charlie sat in the front and manned the GPS.

"It says we're only eight miles away, Mom."

"Good. Thanks." Meg pushed down hard on the accelerator. "How's it feel, Rusty?"

"Hurts like hell," he said.

One glance in the rearview mirror and she saw the swelling had grown. Color drained from Rusty's face.

"Are you gonna be okay, Dad?"

"Sure, sure. Once they get me to the hospital, they'll give me a shot and I'll be fine."

Rusty's voice lacked confidence. Tommy began to cry. Rusty gripped his boy's shoulders.

Meg increased the speed. She concentrated on negotiating the backroad curves while staying on the road. She had to get him there safely. Adrenaline pumped through her veins as she forced herself to focus.

"Next right, Mom," Charlie said.

Another quick glance in the rearview mirror showed a line of red creeping down his neck. Panic seized her for a moment.

"Stop it!" she said to herself. "Focus."

"You're doin' great, Meg," Rusty said, his voice weak.

She tried to smile, while she kept the pressure on the gas pedal.

"One more mile," Charlie said. "There it is. On the left." Charlie pointed.

Meg narrowed her eyes, searching for the entrance. She hit the brake, slowing the car to make the turn without a mishap. Zooming to the front of the building, she threw the car in park and turned off the motor.

"Miss. You can't park here," said an attendant.

"This is an emergency!" Meg hollered out the window.

She jumped out of the car. "Charlie, you stay here."

Yanking open the back door, she helped Rusty get out of the car. A nurse ran out to greet them. Meg quickly explained the problem. The woman took Rusty inside. Meg took Tommy by the hand. "Come on, Charlie."

As they went in, there was a loud crack of thunder and rain poured from the sky. The woman at the desk asked questions and Meg answered as best she could.

"He might have insurance information in his wallet. Where is he? I'll get it. Tommy, you and Charlie stay here."

"I want my dad," Tommy bawled, bursting into tears.

Meg looked around helplessly. "Let me go check on him. I don't think kids are allowed in."

"Come on boys. Have a seat. I can't let you back there. They're taking good care of your father." The nurse showed the boys to a seat. Charlie hugged Tommy.

"I bet he's going to be okay," he said to his friend.

Meg rushed into the back. "Where is he?"

"Third door on your left."

Rusty lay sprawled across a bed with a doctor and nurse at his side. Meg stepped to the left, out of the way of the medical team on the right. Rusty's whole face had ballooned. His eyes were puffy slits, his breathing shallow.

"Don't leave," he huffed out.

Meg glanced at the doctor, who nodded. "We're going to give you a shot of epinephrine, and oxygen. You need to stay until the swelling goes down and you are breathing normally again."

Meg nodded. She took Rusty's hand in both of hers. "I'll be here as long as you need me."

"Tommy?"

"He's okay. He's in the waiting room with Charlie."

Rusty's hand gripped hers.

"I hate shots."

"Who doesn't? Squeeze my hand if it hurts."

"Hold on," the doctor said.

Rusty tightened his grip. He turned his head toward Meg so he wouldn't have to watch the needle go in. A nurse came around next to Meg with an oxygen mask. She fit it over his nose and mouth.

"Your children are in the waiting room?" she asked.

"Yes," Meg replied.

"I'll check in on them in a minute."

Rusty gave a small smile.

"Don't try to talk. Just breathe." The nurse smiled at Rusty and left the room.

"I'll check back in a few minutes." The doctor left the room.

Rusty's head lay back on the pillow. His body had gone limp, but his grip remained strong. Meg's heartbeat still raced. She watched him with intense eyes. The swelling started to recede.

"Can you breathe?"

He nodded. She raised his hand to her lips. They sat in silence for fifteen minutes. When color returned to his skin and the swelling went down, Meg let out a breath.

"You scared the shit out of me," she said.

He laughed and wagged a finger at her. "Bad language," he managed to say through the oxygen equipment.

"This calls for it. Bet it scared you, too."

He nodded.

The nurse popped her head in. "The boys are asking for you, Miss."

"I'll be right back." Meg pushed to her feet and hit the waiting room. Tommy flew at her, tears streaming down his face. She held him tight. "Your dad's gonna be okay. They gave him some medicine to make the swelling go down."

"Can I see him?"

"Not yet. I'll come and get you when they say it's okay."

She returned to Rusty. His eyes were closed. Terrified he had died, she poked him. Startled, he jerked.

"Just making sure you're still alive."

"Thanks." He shot her a frown but laced his fingers with hers.

After an hour, the doctor returned.

"I think you can go home now. We're going to give you an EpiPen, in case you have any further symptoms. If they are severe, please return."

"How long do we have to watch him?" Meg asked.

"Symptoms can return up to about seventy-two hours. So, keep an eye on him."

"Thank you, I will."

"Very good. Mr. Reisse. Here you go." The doctor gave Rusty a prescription and shook his hand, then Meg's, too. "Mrs. Reisse."

Wide-eyed, she tried to hide her shock at being mistaken for his wife. When they stopped in the waiting room, Tommy flew at his father. Rusty plopped into a chair, pulling his son onto his lap. Tommy fastened a death grip around his father, burying his face in his dad's shirt. Meg couldn't hear the soft words Rusty spoke. He held the boy and stroked his back.

Tears threatened. This was a side of Rusty she had not seen. He kissed his son's head, then pushed to his feet.

"Come on, Slugger. Let's clear up the paperwork and go home."

When they went outside, the pavement was wet, but the storm had passed. The sun tried to make an appearance, dancing around puffy clouds.

Rusty moved into the backseat with Tommy. "Who's up for pizza and a movie?"

The boys cheered.

"Who wants meatball and who wants pepperoni," Meg asked, as she put the car in gear.

Chapter Ten

They enjoyed a quiet evening and retired early. The next day was spent watching Frank and Hardy, the salamanders, and tracking down the yellow jacket. Charlie found him first and Meg killed him with her shoe.

Another storm rolled in, so movies became the day's entertainment. Deciding comfort food was called for, Meg prepared mac and cheese. Once the boys were safely tucked into bed, she put the kettle on for tea. The air, cooled by the storm, sent a chill through her.

"Tea on the deck?"

"Thanks." Rusty threw a blanket over his shoulder and padded outside.

Meg prepared mugs the way they liked them before joining him.

"Thanks for everything. You were amazing. Got me to the hospital so fast."

"You're welcome."

"The doctor said if we'd been half an hour later, it would have been touch-and-go. Maybe you saved my life."

"Maybe. And maybe not. Anyone would have done the same."

"Tommy's in love with Hardy."

"The salamander?" Meg took a sip of her tea.

"Yeah. I have to admit the thing is pretty cute. He loved the whole woods thing."

"Oh? Yeah? Good. I'm glad."

"So did I."

"You did? Even the snake."

"Well, I admit the snake wasn't exactly my favorite part, but it was okay. The rest was interesting. I never realized how many things—critters—live in the woods."

"Species? There are many animals, insects, and birds living there."

"Except for the bee thing, it was a good day. You're pretty smart."

"Thanks. I love the woods."

"I can see why."

"Are you okay? Feeling all right?"

"I am. Except it's cold out here. Come here. This blanket is big enough for two."

She joined him on the loveseat and tucked the blanket around her legs.

"Better?"

She nodded.

"I admit I didn't think we could ever work this out, but sharing the house is okay. Tommy adores you, and Charlie is his new best friend."

"After plotting ways to get you out of here, I admit you've broadened Charlie's perspective."

"Me and Frank Todd," Rusty snickered.

"Don't remind me."

"I can't believe he named his salamander after that sleazeball."

"He's not a sleazeball. Just not right for me."

"Correction noted."

They sat in comfortable silence, gazing at the moon and sipping tea. The truce between them continued and peace reigned. Meg sighed.

"Something wrong?"

"It's so peaceful here."

"Do you still miss your husband?"

"Every day."

"Guess that'll never change."

"I hope not."

"Maybe someday you'll have a life again."

She faced him. "A life? I have a life."

"You have a son. You're a parent."

"And a teacher."

"It's not a complete life."

"You should talk! Are you even seeing anyone?"

"I have been, yes."

"So your life is complete and mine isn't?"

"I didn't say that."

"Yes, you did."

"Come on, Meg. Things have been going so great, let's not fight."

"Then stop saying crappy things to me."

"I'm sorry, okay?"

"Fine." She compressed her lips into a fine line.

"No more fighting."

"Tommy looks like he suffers from the same fear Charlie does. He's worried something is going to happen to you and then he'll have no one."

"Technically, he'll have his mother. But it's the same as no one. I don't even know where to reach her. If something happened to me, Tommy would have to go to my sister."

"I bet it scares him."

Rusty nodded slowly. "It does. We don't talk about it. With me traveling, airplanes, cars whatever. It worries him sometimes. But this bee thing really shook him."

"I understand how he feels. Charlie would have reacted the same way if it had been me."

"He'll get used to it. In time."

"I suppose."

Rusty stood up and yawned. "Bedtime."

"Are you okay? I mean, do you feel normal again?"

"Almost. One more day ought to do it."

"Good."

"Thanks again." He leaned over and kissed her on the cheek. "You were a lifesaver."

When the door closed behind him, Meg touched her face. She hadn't expected either the verbal gratitude or the kiss. Maybe it was time to re-evaluate her opinion of Rusty Reisse.

She pulled the blanket higher and stared at the tree branches turned silvery in the moonlight. Peace washed over her. A new feeling of contentment warmed her. Would it last? Only time could tell.

"FRONT ROW SEATS FOR today's game! How about it?" Rusty waved tickets under Meg's nose.

"Can we go, Mom? Please? I wanna see Frank Todd hit a home run."

Even the idea of seeing Frank Todd didn't dampen Rusty's spirits. Since the hospital incident, he wanted to do something for Meg and the boys. She seemed to enjoy the first game.

"Come on, Meg. Ignore ole Frank."

"Where did you get such great seats last minute like this?" She crossed her arms over her chest.

"I have a friend in the box office."

"Really?" She arched an eyebrow.

"All right, all right, Miss Detective. I traded some of my memorabilia with him for the seats."

"What did you give away, Dad?"

"Nothing really. One of my caps."

"From your Nighthawks collection?" Tommy clutched his throat in a theatrical move.

"It's okay, Tom. I have a few more."

"Oh, good."

"Get your caps and gloves."

"I'll get the sunscreen," Meg added.

"So you're coming?"

"Wouldn't miss it. Maybe Frank will strike out for me." She grinned.

"I thought he already did."

Meg threw a dish towel at Rusty.

The boys fastened themselves in the backseat. They spent the entire trip punching the pockets in their gloves.

"We need to be ready for a foul ball," Charlie explained.

"Maybe I should wear a hardhat?" Meg laughed.

They arrived fifteen minutes before game time, allowing them to load up on hot dogs, soda, and popcorn. Frank Todd spotted Meg and waved. But he didn't have time before the game to come over and chat. Rusty secretly patted himself on the back for his timing.

After the national anthem, Frank doffed his cap to Meg, who waved back. Charlie could barely sit still.

"I think we have a future major leaguer there." Rusty hadn't stopped needling Meg. It had become his favorite pastime.

"Not unless baseball is played in a chemistry lab," she quipped.

Had to admire the lady. She gave back as good as she got.

The Jaguar's pitcher aimed and fired. The batter swung and missed.

"It's a good omen. Making the batter swing on the first pitch." Rusty took a swig of his beer.

"Did you ever notice how many superstitions there are in baseball? You'd think the game was invented in the Dark Ages." Meg sipped her soda.

Rusty raised his chin a tad. "Not superstitions. Just things. Good luck things."

"Superstition."

"One woman's superstition is another man's luck."

Meg snorted. "Good luck with that."

"See?" Rusty pointed at her. "You mentioned luck."

Meg laughed.

The game was tied until the seventh inning. Frank Todd hit a game-winning two-run homer. Charlie jumped up and yelled until he was hoarse. When Todd put his foot on home plate, the crowd came to their feet. Frank walked over to the stands and raised his cap. Then he bowed to Meg and returned to the dugout.

"Your mom's going to marry Frank Todd," Tommy said, nodding.

"Wow. Are you, Mom?"

"What? No way. No. No. I'm not going to marry anyone." Meg's face flushed.

Rusty's shoulders drooped. Why would her statement affect him at all? A brainiac like Meg Gunderson would be the last person on Rusty's marriage list, right? Besides, he didn't have a list, because he'd vowed never to take the plunge again—ever. Yet her pronouncement saddened him. She'd make a good wife for the right guy. Maybe the sadness had to do with Charlie never having a flesh-and-blood father. Rusty had no clue and dismissed the thought.

A secret smile played on his lips. Guess Frank Todd was out of luck. Rusty had a chuckle he thought was private, but Meg caught him.

"What's funny?"

"Poor ole Frank. He'll be disappointed when he finds out you plan to spend the rest of your life as a spinster."

"Spinster? What cave did you dig that word out of?"

"Don't they use it anymore?" Rusty looked away to hide a smile he couldn't stop.

"Antiquated. Do you know what it means?"

"Yeah. It means as old as your ideas about marriage."

"You've got a lotta nerve."

"I do, don't I?"

So busy needling her, he didn't see a foul ball coming their way.

"Dad!" Tommy yelled, firing his glove at Rusty.

He picked up the glove and lunged in front of Meg for the second time. The ball bounced out of Rusty's glove and right into Charlie's. Rusty picked the boy up.

"Hold it up high, Charlie so everyone can see."

The crowd gave the boy a standing ovation. The ball hadn't been hit by Frank Todd, but it didn't matter. Charlie had caught it on his own.

"Charlie! Way to go!" His mother gave him a brief hug, then a high-five.

"I caught it by myself."

"Yes, you did!" Meg grinned. "Thank you." She turned to Rusty.

"I didn't do anything."

"You saved me—again."

"Guess you're in the lucky seat. No, wait. Superstition."

"Stop." She gave him a playful slap on the shoulder. "Okay. I give. Luck isn't a superstition."

"Glad you finally saw it my way." He grinned.

"Don't I always?"

A DAY IN THE SUN, WATCHING the game and finally understanding it, calmed Meg. Being outside with the boys, eating hot dogs, watching an exciting sport added up to another great day brought to her by Rusty Reisse.

Okay, so she had jumped to wrong conclusions about baseball. It was a complex sport requiring skill, judgment, athletic ability, and tremendous concentration. Her assessment of Rusty had begun to rise. While he appeared to be an arrogant jerk on first meeting, he had improved greatly. It had been so long since she'd had a good time, without feeling guilty. She'd credited Rusty with making it happen, and she'd always be grateful.

As the car rounded the bend, close to the house, Meg spied a vehicle in their driveway.

"Oh no. Fred didn't rent the house to someone else for August, did he?" She chewed her lip.

"Not that I know of." Rusty's brow furrowed.

As he made the turn, Meg saw a man, sitting on the front step. Well, son-of-a-bitch! It was Harold Morrissey.

"What the Hell is he doing here?" Meg muttered to herself.

"You know this dude?"

"It's Harold."

"Mom, what's Harold doing on our steps?" Charlie asked.

Rusty parked the car. "Come on, boys. Let Meg talk to this guy alone." He shot her a concerned glance.

"So you're the one?" Stepping back out of the way, Harold gave Rusty a nasty scowl as he passed.

Rusty merely glared at the man and shepherded the boys inside.

Annoyed Harold had wrecked her perfect day, she put her hands on her hips and approached him.

"What are you doing here, Harold?"

"I came to save our relationship. But I see you are living with another man."

"I'm not living with him. We're roommates."

"I've heard it called lots of things, but roommates isn't one of them."

"I don't care what you've heard. It's none of your business." She glanced at the front door. It was open about an inch. So Rusty was listening.

"You are my business. Definitely my business. And this shacking up has got to stop. Right now!"

"Who do you think you are?"

"Your boyfriend. Your lover."

Meg laughed. "Don't go there."

"We've been together for a year."

"So what? I told you we're finished. And I meant it."

"A text. You broke it off in a text. Really, Meg? I thought you had more class."

"Look, Harold. You'd better leave. Insulting me won't get you anywhere."

"I'm not leaving without you."

"What?"

"Leave you here with that, that, hustler? Never. You need to be rescued, and I'm here to do the job."

"Get over yourself, Harold. I don't need rescuing. Rusty isn't a hustler. And I'm not leaving with you."

"I love you, Meg. I'm not leaving you." He grabbed her arm and held tight.

"Ouch! Let go!"

"No!" He yanked her across the path. She stumbled and fell up against him. He tried to kiss her, but she struggled and pushed away.

"Leave my mother alone!" Charlie bounded out of the house with Rusty right behind.

"Butt out, kid. This is between her and me."

"Take your hands off her," Rusty said.

"Fuck off, asshole." Harold dragged Meg toward his car. She kicked him in the shin. He dropped his hands. As she started to move away, he grabbed for her, but she eluded him. Then he strode toward her.

"Get away from me."

"I'm calling the cops," Tommy said, dialing.

"You're mine. Stop fighting it." Harold stepped closer.

"Bullshit!" Meg stood her ground.

When the word came out of her mouth, Harold slapped her hard, across the face. She flew sideways, down on the lawn and lay dazed.

At the sound of palm hitting cheek, Rusty charged.

"What the fuck did you do?" Rusty yelled, then drew his arm back, and punched Harold right in the jaw. He fell against the house and slid down on his butt. Charlie rushed over to his mother. He helped her up.

"You can't hit her." Rusty rubbed his fist.

The sound of a siren interrupted the melee. The patrol car pulled into the driveway. Two officers got out. One looked over Rusty and Meg.

"You two? Again?"

Then everyone talked at once. The other officer raised his hands. "Quiet down. Quiet! One at a time."

"He hit my mother," Charlie said, practically in tears.

The officers questioned everyone.

"Mister, I don't know where you live, but this lady has every right to share a house with whoever she wishes. She doesn't want to go with you. So I suggest you move along."

"But, Officer."

"Move along, buddy. Don't make me have to drag you down to the station house for assault."

"What about the fact that he punched me?" Harold pointed to Rusty.

"I'd punch someone who hit my woman, too. He was defending her. Don't push me. 'Cause I'm ready to write you up right now." The officer pulled a notebook out of his back pocket.

Harold blanched. "Okay. I'm going. But Meg. You haven't heard the last of me."

The second officer blocked Harold's path. "Yes, she has. Buddy. We have laws about stalking. And if I hear anything from this lady about you contacting her again, I'm gonna haul your ass in and you're going to jail."

Meg rubbed her cheek.

"Are you okay?" Rusty stood by her side, his arm around her shoulders.

"I think it's swelling."

"Get a picture, ma'am. Evidence." The officer took everyone's names. "We'll have a police report for you in a couple of days."

"What about my injury?" Harold stood up straight, his hand cupping his jaw.

"Don't go there, mister. You started this."

"I did not! She moved here. Moved in with this, this…"

"I told you. Move along now. Don't be calling names. You're tempting me to pull you in." The officer stood between Harold and Rusty. "And don't you get any ideas. One punch. Okay. But two? Nope. I'll haul you in for assault, too."

Still holding onto Meg, Rusty stepped back. She moved closer. His protection soothed her. The officer stayed until Harold backed his car out of the driveway.

"Fucking slut!" he screamed out the window.

His words were so harsh, it was as if he'd punched her. She burst into tears.

"Get outta here!" the cop yelled.

Harold stepped on the gas and the car lurched forward, speeding until he was out of site. Rusty folded Meg into his embrace, rubbing her back.

"Thank you, Officers," Rusty said.

"Yeah. Thanks. I hate him." Charlie shook hands with both policemen before they climbed back in their patrol car and drove off.

"We'd better get some ice on your face." Rusty opened the screen door. Meg went inside first.

"I'm going to lie down."

In a few minutes, Charlie knocked. "It's me, Mom."

"Come in."

"Here." He handed her a Ziplock bag containing ice cubes. "Rusty said to put this on your face."

"Thanks." She smiled at her son and put the bag against the swelling. "I'm sorry you had to see that."

"I hate Harold. I'm glad he's not coming around anymore."

"Me, too."

"I like Rusty."

"You do?"

"Yeah. He doesn't have a wife and you don't have a husband. Why don't you marry him?"

It hurt her to smile. "Thanks, Charlie. But I'm not ready to marry anyone, right now."

"Okay. But I'm putting him at the top of the list."

She kissed her son's head and closed her eyes. "I think I need to rest."

"Rusty's taking us out for ice cream."

"Great idea."

"See you later." Charlie hugged his mother and kissed her cheek.

Hovering between asleep and awake, she felt something. A soft, lightweight blanket had been spread over her and tucked in at the bottom. She detected lips on her forehead and a tender, gentle touch on her injured cheek. Was it Rusty? Conscious thought faded like mist in the hot sun and she was asleep before the door clicked closed.

Chapter Eleven

Meg woke up groggy. She sashed her robe and dragged herself into the kitchen. The aroma of coffee, probably leftover from yesterday, greeted her. No, wait, it smelled like fresh. Rusty wouldn't lower himself to make coffee, would he?

"Just the way you like it." Rusty thrust a mug of steaming brew in her hand.

"Thanks." She blinked, trying to wake up.

"It's a special blend, Kona and Dark Roast."

"Thanks. It's great. Where are the boys?"

"They're taking Coco on her morning walk. They're okay. I've been watching."

"Oh. Good. Coco knows where to go and what to do."

"Right. Sit. Sit. How are you feeling?"

"I look like a chipmunk."

He stifled a laugh. "You can hardly tell."

"Don't lie. It's obvious. One half of my face is bigger than the other."

She plunked down at the table and slumped over her mug. He joined her.

"Let me see." With one finger, Rusty tilted her chin up. His gaze perused her face, first one side, then the other. He ran his palm lightly over her smooth skin. She ignored the shiver shooting up her spine when he touched her. Then he used his thumb, ever so gently. It almost tickled. "Looks a little tender, but almost as good as new."

"It's okay. I'll live."

"I can't see you dating such a violent guy." He shook his head.

"He was never violent before."

"Guess you struck a chord."

"I did? It was me? Go ahead, blame the victim. It's just like you when a woman is involved."

"Hey! I didn't mean it. I meant he had some weak spot for you or something. Of course, it wasn't your fault. And no, you didn't deserve to be slapped. Geez. What do you think I am, a monster? A woman beater? Never. Not in a million years. I'm a lover, not a fighter."

"I'm sorry. Guess I'm grouchy this morning."

"With good reason. Let's go out to breakfast. My treat. How about cinnamon buns, bacon, and eggs at The Cozy Café?"

"Sounds good to me."

"How fast can you dress?"

"Fifteen minutes."

"I'll get the boys." Rusty headed out the back door.

Meg returned to her room and threw on shorts, a tank top, and sandals. She washed up and applied some light makeup. The idea of a delicious breakfast at The Cozy Café lifted her spirits. Hunger gripped her belly, but the last thing she wanted to do was cook. The image of Rusty trying to figure out how to use a frying pan brought a smile to her lips.

When she joined the guys at the front door, Charlie threw his arms around her.

"Are you okay, Mom?"

"I'm fine. Thanks, Charlie." She hugged him and kissed the top of his head.

"I'd like to beat up Harold."

"He's not coming back. You don't have to worry."

She felt him relax in her embrace. Her little man sticking up for her made her heart squeeze.

Rusty opened the car door for her. She opened the window and took a deep breath of fresh country air. The soft breeze caressed her bruised skin. The sun warmed her and brightened her spirits. Yes, there had been an ugly scene, but now Harold had to accept the break-up. Relief washed through her. Free to find someone else or enjoy being alone.

Rusty chatted with the boys about the game while Meg sat silently contemplating her life. While rooming with Rusty had been difficult at first, they'd fallen into a routine. He played catch with the boys in the afternoon, giving her time alone. She read to them at night, allowing him the chance to catch up on pro baseball games on television.

In a quiet way, Rusty had stepped into John's shoes, sort of, a little bit. He'd become her partner with the boys, teaching them about sports and joining in on their science adventures. As much as she'd never admit it, having a man around to help lift the burden a little had improved her mood. She didn't say no all the time to Charlie. She laughed more and so did he. They had a calm existence in this house in Pine Grove—even with Rusty's snarky comments and digs.

Although in the past, she'd fended off Charlie's requests for a dog, she liked Coco and enjoyed their morning walks and the sense of safety the mammoth canine created. Maybe a dog wasn't such a bad idea? She'd spring the idea on Charlie when they got back to the City.

Meg watched the swan couples on the lake. They say swans mate for life. What would John say? Hard to admit, but she knew he'd want her to find someone. Not a replacement, because no one could replace John, but maybe someone for a second chapter in her life and Charlie's.

It had been two years—two-and-a-half, actually. Had the time come for her to bring another man into their lives?

Rusty pulled into the small parking lot and the crew piled out of the car.

"Can I have a cinnamon bun, too?" Charlie asked.

"Sure." Meg walked slowly to the entrance. Rusty joined her.

"You were quiet on the ride out. Everything okay?"

She nodded. "Yeah. Just thinking."

"About what?"

"Stuff. Private stuff."

How could she tell him she might be ready to move into a new relationship? Surely he'd think she meant him, right? Rusty? He'd be the last person she'd hook up with. Even the idea made her laugh. Rusty? The arrogant, conceited, chauvinistic, ignorant jock? Never. But then an image of Rusty in a bathing suit flashed through her mind. She swallowed.

He held the door for her. The boys had already plopped down at a table by the window.

"Swans! Look, Mom. Swans!" Charlie ran to the door to the deck. Tommy followed. Meg and Rusty sat at the table.

"Was it you, last night?" Meg stared at him from under her lashes.

"Me?"

"Who covered me and kissed my forehead?"

Rusty turned several shades of red. "It might have been. Don't remember."

"Liar."

"Okay, okay. Yeah. It was me. If you're mad, I'm sorry."

"I'm not mad."

"Then I'm not sorry."

"It was a nice thing to do."

"Don't tell anyone. I have a reputation to maintain."

SHE LAUGHED. THE BOYS returned, buzzing with questions about swans. Meg explained they mate for life.

"Really? Nice to know some species make it work," Rusty said, under his breath.

Meg glanced up at him.

"What if one dies? Do they find someone else?" Charlie looked at her.

Meg hesitated. Before she could answer, the food arrived. Rusty shoveled in eggs while he buried his nose in his cellphone.

She focused on her meal, hoping Charlie would move on and she'd not have to answer his question. Since John died, the death of a spouse or partner had been one of Charlie's main topics. He'd fired all sorts of questions at her from the legality of marrying someone else to why did they give all his dad's stuff away? Meg answered each question honestly and to the best of her ability. But his never-ending curiosity stressed her.

When they finished their eggs, hot, grilled cinnamon buns arrived.

"I have the answer for you, Charlie." Rusty addressed the table.

"What?"

"When one mate of a pair of swans dies. What happens?"

Meg looked away.

"When one of a pair dies, the other one finds another mate. If they can't find another mate, they die of a broken heart," Rusty continued.

Silence. Charlie put his food down. His eyes filled.

"Those are swans, Charlie. Swans. Birds. Not humans." Meg shot Rusty a nasty look.

"It says so in Wikipedia."

"No one's going to die of a broken heart." Although after John died, there were days when she wondered if she would.

"Then you have to find a new partner, right?" Charlie took a bite of the confection.

Rusty faced her. "Well, Meg?"

She shoved a piece of cinnamon bun in her mouth and shrugged. No way would she be lured into answering. When the boys finished, they got up and wandered over to the bulletin board.

"Hey, Dad! What's a corn barbecue?" Tommy called over.

Rusty shrugged. "Don't know."

"Really?" Laura Dailey, the manager of The Cozy Café, piped up. "It's just one of the best events in Pine Grove all year."

The boys drew closer to the older woman.

"Hundreds of ears of corn, picked fresh from the field the same morning, are roasted on a grill. Nothing tastes more delicious."

Charlie licked his lips.

"And there's music and dancing. Our Mayor Mike and his band play. We have a raffle for gift baskets, and a few vendors, like Ike's Ice Cream. It's homemade."

"When is it?" Rusty asked.

"This Saturday. It's only ten dollars a person. All the money goes to our volunteer firehouse."

"Sounds like a good cause. You guys want to go? Meg?"

"Yes!" the boys said in unison.

"Sure." Meg smiled.

"Thanks for the info, Ms. Dailey." Rusty reached for his wallet.

"Please call me Laura. You're the folks renting Fred and Roberta's place?"

"We are," Meg said.

"Lots of rumors going around about y'all. I straightened everyone out. Said there's nothing improper going on in their house. There isn't, is there?"

"Nope. And nothing that's anyone else's business." Rusty shot a cool look at Laura.

"Okay. I'll pass it along."

"You do that. Ready to go, kids? Can I have the check, please?"

"Sure thing. I'll be right back." Laura hustled back behind the counter.

Rusty paid. The boys ran ahead. Rusty fell into step with Meg.

"So, Meg. You never answered the question."

"What question?"

"Are you going to die of a broken heart or find another mate?"

She stopped to face him. "I don't know. Have someone in mind?"

"Not Frank Todd."

She laughed. "No, not Frank Todd. Though Charlie might disagree."

The week passed quickly. Rusty and Meg took the boys swimming in the lake, to an amusement park, and a movie playing at the local theater. Every day they fed Hardy and Frank, the salamanders, and changed their water.

Surprised there was so much to do in the country, Meg was often too busy to read. Things with Rusty had calmed down. She still couldn't believe he'd tucked her in after Harold's assault. When Rusty busted Harold in the chops, Meg cheered silently. He'd taken care of her, even though Meg wasn't Rusty's responsibility. Hell, he didn't even like her. Yet he came to her rescue. Why?

His actions had given her pause. She'd been re-evaluating him, accepting him more and judging him less. Her guard dropped a little more each day. The corn barbecue was on August first. August already? Half the summer had flown by. Meg vowed to enjoy every minute.

RUSTY COULDN'T BELIEVE he was headed to a corn barbecue. He'd called Fred and had a laugh over it. Fred had called him Gomer Pyle. Sure, he joked about the hick town, but the longer he stayed in Pine Grove, the more it grew on him. Did he miss the Big City—the great food, the night clubs crawling with willing females, the noise, the congestion, the traffic, the sirens, the masses of tourists crowding the streets—hey, wait a minute! Maybe he didn't miss it so much.

He'd settled into a routine with Tommy and Charlie—and Meg, too. Things had calmed down. He'd credited himself with enormous patience. His learning to shut up had helped smooth things over with the schoolteacher. Was she still a stiff, arrogant, snobby, smart chick? Probably. But he'd gotten used to her and it didn't bother him anymore.

In fact, he'd found some positives with her, too. She could cook—which went a long way with Rusty. Most of the women he'd dated expected him to take them to fancy, expensive restaurants on every date. Not Meg. To be fair, there weren't a lot of fancy restaurants near Pine Grove. But she didn't complain, either. He admired her ability to cope with what was, and not bitch about how things should be. Whining, complaining women drove him nuts. Gold diggers, too. He'd been sucked in by them at the beginning of his career. When he first hit a major salary bump, money-hungry women came out of the woodwork like roaches.

Some of the old-timers warned him. But, of course, Rusty Reisse knew better. Maybe those women could take advantage of those guys, but not him—Rusty was on to them. Uh, no, he got taken for some major money by the most innocent looking chick ever. Fifty grand later, he'd learned his lesson.

His ex-girlfriend, Maria, wasn't cheap, but he'd made it clear he wasn't a money-machine. She'd pouted a little but accepted his limits. She gave the world's best blowjobs, so he'd loosened the reins on his bank account a little. Loud and temperamental, she made their relationship a struggle. When he said he was going away for the summer with Tommy, she'd blown like a firecracker, yelling and carrying on.

"What am I supposed to do while you're gone? Knit a sweater?" Their separation created the perfect opportunity to end things.

Bad experiences with women had made him wary. But Meg'd been different, she'd thrown him off-kilter. He didn't know what to expect. After a month together, they'd fallen into an easy companionship. How could he get along with a brainy chick, especially without sex? Was she like his little sister? Hell, no. No one with a body and face like hers could ever be his sister.

As soon as he got over hating her, he wanted to sleep with her. He had to laugh at himself. Sleep with her? She barely spoke to him. Sex with Meg would happen when fish flew. But he could dream, couldn't he? Aspire to a different class of woman, couldn't he? Strive to win over one who was so far out of his league, he could barely see her, couldn't he?

Fred had laughed at him on the phone.

"You'll never get into Meg's pants. She's sworn off normal men and only dates some weirdo from her school. I don't think she's even sleeping with him. Give it up, Rusty. Stay in your own backyard."

Fred's attitude had pissed him off. Meg didn't walk around like she was light-years above him, even if she was. Of course, he was famous, and she was nobody, but it didn't faze her. His fame rolled off her back like water from a duck.

He'd grown fond of Meg. Damn, she was smart, and he'd learned a shit-ton from her. And Tommy? The boy was smitten, for sure. He never got along with Maria. She'd been upfront about not wanting kids and had little patience for Rusty's son. Tommy did things to piss her off on purpose—driving his father crazy.

But not with Meg. Tommy liked her and did what she said. Sometimes, when she read to the boys at night, Rusty would lean against the door jamb and listen. He'd watch Tommy snuggle up to her, hanging on every word. The scene had made his heart swell. Meg had qualities he'd never looked for in a woman. She'd taken him by surprise, and he'd loved it.

When Harold, the asshole, had smacked her, Rusty flew into a rage. Barely able to control himself, he'd attacked, and been ready to beat the guy to a pulp. He couldn't stand men who were violent toward women. And toward Meg, so sweet and gentle. What a crime! Rusty found the punishment.

Contemplating the corn barbecue, he pulled out a button-down teal blue shirt, to match his eyes, and snug designer jeans. He needed to look his best because he'd had a hunch about tonight. Something between them had shifted after the shit with dickwad Harold. They hadn't spoken about it, but he sensed it. He needed to look good, in case their spark fanned to flame.

Meg wasn't into clothes. She didn't dress up around him, another quality he wasn't used to. She wore jeans or shorts and T-shirts or tank tops, no makeup, except a little lipstick. He couldn't get over how great she looked natural. Tonight, he hoped she'd be dressed for a party and not wearing old sweats.

"Ready guys?" Meg stood at the door.

Rusty's mouth hung open. Damn! She wore some kind of fancy fabric white dress. The revealing neckline, which tantalized him, had black trim, as did the hem. The thin straps were black, too. The dress fit snug through the body, outlined every curve, and flared out at the hips.

"You look amazing."

"You clean up pretty good yourself." She smiled.

Upon closer inspection, he detected makeup. Around the eyes, and maybe her cheeks and lipstick, of course.

"You'll be the prettiest girl there," slipped right out of Rusty's mouth, without stopping to be censored by his brain first.

Meg blushed. "I bet you say that to all the girls."

He took her arm and stopped her cold. "Never said it to a girl before in my life." Once again, his mouth forgot to consult his brain.

Her color deepened, and her gaze connected with his. "Great."

"Let's go, guys," Tommy said, breaking the spell.

"Yeah." Rusty held the door. *I'd better shut up before I get myself in trouble.* Still, he couldn't stop staring at her. Sexy, beautiful, and his date for this shindig—did a guy get any luckier?

WHEN SHE SAW RUSTY, Meg's eyes widened. Damn, the man looked good. The color of his shirt brought out the turquoise in his eyes. Rusty Reisse knew how to dress to make the most of his good looks. Still slim and athletic, his body taught jeans a few things. A flush of warmth swept through Meg. Attraction? No way. She couldn't possibly be sexually attracted to this Neanderthal baseball champ, could she?

A few unsatisfying romps in the hay with ole Harold had done nothing to quell her growing sexual appetite. She'd thought desire had gone to the grave with John—and it had for a year. But like a phoenix, it had risen and gripped her, filling her mind with sexy thoughts about Rusty.

Naughty, delicious fantasies about what he might do to her haunted her dreams. How many times had she imagined touching him? Any time he appeared bare-chested her body reacted. Heat flew through her veins and a certain private place throbbed. She almost had to sit on her hands to keep them from sliding them up his chest.

What was wrong with her? Rusty Reisse could never be the love of her life. She'd had it and it had disappeared, abruptly, never to be seen or felt again. Right? No one gets a love so strong twice in their life, do they? The last thing she wanted was Rusty Reisse in her bed, but her body disagreed.

Every time he touched her, be it to place his palm on the small of her back, grab her arm, or help her up or down something, a shock zinged up her spine and private places tingled. If he brushed by too close, her nipples hardened. Then she'd have to turn away so he didn't see. Damn her body! She couldn't trust herself around him.

Being in charge of her thoughts and feelings came naturally to Meg, except when Rusty entered the room. Like a stupid, fan-girl, her body cried out for him. Her self-control wore thin. How much longer she could hold out before she did something so embarrassing she'd have to leave the house? Hell, Rusty didn't want her. He didn't even like her. Making a pass at him would be a foolish mistake, but how much longer could she refrain from giving in to her desires?

Rusty opened the car door for her. When she got in, her dress rode up to mid-thigh before she pulled her leg in and smoothed it down. She watched Rusty's gaze follow the hem. A bead of sweat formed on his upper lip.

Really? Truth be told, she'd caught him, eyes glued to her chest, a number of times. When he realized she'd seen him, he'd turn three shades of red and faced the other way. She'd laughed behind her hand.

So, he was like every other male on Earth, curious. So what? It didn't mean a thing, especially not that he liked her. Why did she care if he liked her or not? She didn't respect him, so what if he did or didn't lust after her?

Wait a minute. She did respect him. Rusty had shown uncommon kindness to Charlie, including him with Tommy, teaching him all about baseball. Charlie adored him. Quoted the former star often, liked him more even than Frank Todd.

And Rusty had protected her—several times—from foul balls and Harold, the jerk. He'd been incredibly generous, though she didn't need it. John had left her well-fixed, financially. As Rusty drove them to the Pine Grove Community Field for the corn barbecue, Meg stared out the window and thought about him.

"We're here!" He put the car in park and shut off the engine.

The boys ran up to the entrance. The parking lot was graveled. Rusty offered his arm to help Meg across the stones. She took it to steady herself. High heels and gravel don't mix.

"You really do look beautiful tonight."

"Don't sound so shocked."

"I can't even give you a compliment, can I?"

"I'm sorry. Yes, you can. Thank you."

She didn't want compliments from him. Or his attention. Or his love. She'd learned to deal with widowhood, without love or affection, and survive. She didn't need this sexy baseball player rocking the boat.

She gripped his forearm. His muscle felt like he'd slipped a rock under his skin. A star baseball player had to have muscles, didn't he? The damned tingling started again, but she couldn't let go. Heat warmed her cheeks.

"You okay? You look flushed."

"I'm fine."

His pointing it out only made it worse. Once she stepped on the grass, she let go, smoothed down her skirt, and headed for the entrance.

"This is amazing," Rusty said.

She scanned the field, impressed by what she saw. There were three manned grills handling a mountain of unshucked corn. A table held plates, napkins, and tubs of ice holding water and soda. Across the way, Mayor Mike Foster and his band played. An ice cream truck and a bake-sale table were off to the left, a children's bouncy world was to the right. Three kegs of beer stood near the grills and someone, next to the beer, poured wine. Half-a-dozen tables with vendors rimmed the out-skirts of the field.

"I've never seen anything like this before. Have you?" he asked.

She shook her head. "They have everything."

"Where should we go first?"

"Corn?" She shrugged.

"Corn and beer." Rusty took her hand and headed for the food.

As they waited in line, Tommy and Charlie ran over.

"Can I get ice cream?" Charlie asked.

"After you have corn," Meg said.

"Me, too." Tommy chimed in.

"You heard the lady. Corn first."

Tommy made a face but went along. They grabbed the corn by the stem and peeled off the hot, charred outside layers. Inside, the kernels were golden yellow, bursting with fresh-from-the-stalk goodness. Meg showed the boys how to brush on butter.

"Take this. I'll get us beer."

"Wine for me."

"Red or white?"

"Rose?"

"I knew it." Rusty made a mock-angry face and went to get the drinks.

"Boys, put your corn on these plates and get water bottles." Meg spread out the plates, one in front of each chair. In a minute, they returned.

"Can we have soda instead?" Charlie.

"Okay. Special occasion." Meg sat back, watching the people.

The music started again. Tunes from the '60s and '70s, she guessed. Her foot started tapping. When they were all seated, Rusty raised his glass in a toast.

"To Meg. Most beautiful woman at the Corn Barbecue."

Tommy and Charlie followed. Meg laughed. Then the eating began. The boys finished their corn quickly. Meg slipped them ten-dollar bills. They came back with ice cream, then brownies from the bake-sale table.

Rusty refreshed their drinks, then ate two more ears of corn. Meg had a second ear and sipped her wine. The boys ran off to the bouncy room. The band came back from a break and struck up the David Cassidy song, "I Think I Love You."

Rusty offered his hand. "Dance?"

Chapter Twelve

Sure she'd reject him, he held his hand out anyway. To his surprise, she smiled and pushed to her feet.

"I love this song," she said, taking his hand.

Once they were in the circle of colored lights defining the dance floor, Rusty pulled her into his embrace. He slipped his arm around her waist and eased her closer until her breasts were flush against his pecs. Her sweet scent wafted to his nose. She rested her head on his shoulder. He took her hand and folded it against his chest. Her warm body melted into his. Emotion replaced words. He wanted to close his eyes, but narrowed them, instead, focusing on the feel and scent of Meg.

The song finished long before he was ready to let her go. She stepped back, her eyes hooded and dreamy. He moved to kiss her.

"Dad, Dad!" Tommy yanked on his sleeve. *Damn it to Hell.*

"What?" His voice sounded harsh, even to his own ears. Tommy stepped back. "I'm sorry. What is it, Tom?" He gentled his tone.

"Can I do the horseback ride?"

"Sure."

"It's five dollars."

Rusty peeled off a twenty. "Here. Two rides for you and two for Charlie."

"Thanks, Rusty." Charlie stood behind his friend.

Rusty looked at Meg. "Now, where were we?"

Mike's band broke into a fast dance with the song, "Mama Mia."

Meg moved to the music. Rusty joined her. As an athlete, he found dancing easy. Girls didn't like the guys who couldn't dance. In high school, he practiced with his sister for hours until he could master any beat, any step, fast or slow. He'd even won a dance contest junior year with his girlfriend—who went on to become a professional dancer.

Right at home on the dance floor, he moved to the rhythm with ease. Meg kept up, step for step, thrust for thrust. Dancing turned him on, too. Or was it watching her dance? Or was it dancing with her? Hell, what difference did it make? He kept moving. He danced closer, moving behind her. He fastened his hands on her waist and did a bump and grind against her luscious butt. She backed up into him and returned as good as she got.

She folded her fingers over his hands, holding them in place. Holy shit. As she pressed against him, blood pumped into his dick. Another minute or two and she'd feel it. He released her and put space between them. She shot him a quizzical, almost hurt, look. He smiled and shrugged. No way could he go so far.

Terrified of scaring her, Rusty slowed down. Sweat gathered on his forehead. At the next pause between songs, he headed for their table and mopped his face with a napkin. She joined him.

"Out of shape?" She quirked an eyebrow at him.

No. So turned on I can't keep my hands off you.

"Not exactly."

"You worked up a sweat. Not me."

"Oh?" He cocked an eyebrow. "You want to work up a sweat? Let's step behind that shed."

She laughed, but a rosy color pinked her cheeks.

"Are you saying you know how to make me sweat?" With flirty eyes and a sexy smile, she sashayed up closer.

"Oh, I think so."

"Do you?"

"You know I do." His last words were almost a whisper.

Barely hanging on to his control, Rusty grabbed his beer glass. "More wine?"

"Okay," she said, leaning against the table.

Shit, she's drunk, maybe? Tipsy? Fuck. A girl had to be sober for him to make the first pass. The last thing he needed was Meg waking up with regrets the next day. He simply could not take advantage of the situation. He needed her to come to him of her own accord, stone sober.

"I think you've had enough." Rusty put her glass down.

"I'll decide that."

"Charlie's here. Don't let him see you drunk," he whispered.

"I'm not drunk. A little high, maybe."

"A little high? You practically screwed me on the dance floor."

"I did? You were the one behind it." As soon as she recognized the pun, she burst out laughing. "Behind. Get it? Behind!"

"I get it, I get it. Come on, Meg. Sit. How about a Coke?"

"Wine."

"No."

He left and returned with another beer and a can of Coke. Meg sat at the table, her face propped up on her hands. He handed her the drink. She took a long slug.

"Oh, that's good. You were right. I've had enough."

He took her hand and brought it to his lips. She cupped his cheek, her eyes staring into his.

"When the hell are you two gonna get a room?" A man stopped at their table. "I could run a community pool on when you two are going to get it on."

"Barney!" His wife, Laura Dailey from The Cozy Café, took Barney's arm and pulled him away. "I'm so sorry. He's had too much beer. Please. Don't mind him. Go right ahead with whatever you were doing."

Meg's hand flew to her mouth. "Are we the town gossip?"

Rusty took her hand away from her face. "What do we care? So what? They're people with nothing better to do than poke their noses into our business."

"Is the whole town waiting for us to sleep together?"

Rusty shrugged.

"I've never been, never had people, never—gossip!" Meg fumbled for words.

"Hey, forget it. He's a drunk old man. Who cares what he thinks? Come on, it's eleven. Time to go home."

They found the boys asleep on the grass. Rusty carried each one to the car.

"My purse!" Meg tugged on his arm. "I left it."

"I'll get it." He headed for their table; Meg followed.

"Kiss her for Crissakes! Will you just kiss her?" Barney bellowed from the dance floor.

Embarrassment heated Rusty's cheeks. Sure, kiss her. Just one kiss, right? Just one kiss and he'd be sunk. He'd be a goner, putty in her hands. No way could there be just one kiss. One kiss would lead to much more. Something he wasn't ready or willing to do.

The boys saved him from that kiss on the dance floor. And now? He'd ignore Barney. Ah, there it was. He plucked it from the seat and turned, bumping into Meg. Dropping her bag, he grabbed her waist to keep her from falling.

She clasped his shoulders, pulling herself closer.

"Kiss her! Kiss her!" Barney hooted.

"Shut up, Barney!" Laura pushed him off the dance floor.

The music started up again. It was an ABBA song. Her dreamy eyes connected with his. Her breasts mashed against his chest, her lips, those beautiful lips, pink and inviting, were a breath away. Hell, Rusty was only human. He leaned forward, slightly, and met her lips with his. Her hands let go as her arms closed around his neck. He drew her so close a piece of paper couldn't slip between them. As hunger grew in him, he ravaged her mouth.

At the first pressure, her lips opened. He plunged in, tongue meeting tongue. He explored her mouth. His breathing ragged, he couldn't let go. He felt her panting, her softness tempting him. Her hips, flush, thrust into his.

Before his control slipped completely, Rusty took a breath and eased her away. Her eyes shone, her chest heaved, and her lips were slightly reddened from the kiss. Blood rushed to his dick, making it ready for action. Heat spread throughout his body. He was primed for more.

The sound of applause from Barney startled Rusty. He nabbed her bag, tucking it under his arm and took her hand.

"Come on."

Speechless, she looked at him with lust in her eyes. He dragged her to the car. "Time to go home," he muttered.

He opened the door. Meg slid in and fastened her seatbelt. He got behind the wheel and turned on the car. She faced him.

"Did you? Did we?"

"Shh. We'll talk about it at home. Let's get the boys in bed."

She grinned. "Yeah. Then we can get in bed."

He stared at her, wide-eyed, then threw the vehicle in gear and roared out of the parking lot.

ONE-BY-ONE, RUSTY CARRIED the boys inside. Meg undressed them and tucked them in, leaving a kiss on the forehead of each lad. Rusty watched. *Even three sheets to the wind, she's still a responsible mom.*

Before she finished, he left to put on a pot of coffee. Meg joined him in the kitchen.

"Look, before you say anything—" he began.

"Just one kiss? I don't think so." She stared at him with hot eyes, then pushed him against the wall. She yanked his head down and captured his mouth.

Rusty's willpower vanished. Pent up desire unleashed rushed through him like a tornado, swirling emotion and lust together, creating a powerful force. He wrapped his arms around her, holding her tight. Their mouths fused. When she ground her hips against his, a groan rumbled up from his chest. It was the final straw.

He raised his hand to cover her breast and squeezed. A low moan emanated from her throat, but she didn't push him away.

"Do you want to…"

"Yes," she breathed in his ear, cutting him off.

"Sure?"

"Yes! I know what I'm doing. I'm not drunk."

Were those words the green light he'd been hoping for? He unzipped the back of her dress.

"Last one naked is a rotten egg," she said, pulling the garment down.

"No fair. I've got buttons."

"Too bad." She smirked.

He attacked the buttons feverishly, keeping his eyes on her as she shed her clothes. Damn, no bra. She was half naked already. He swallowed and fumbled with his shirt. She slipped her dress to the floor, revealing white lace bikini panties.

"Let me help you." She grabbed his shirt and pulled him closer.

All he could do was stare as she ripped through his buttons and unzipped his fly. He undid the button on his jeans. She pushed them to the floor.

"Boxers. Off."

"Wait."

"No!"

He bent down to reach into his back pocket, which now lay on the floor, and pulled out his wallet. With a shaking hand, he extracted a condom.

"Oh. Yeah." She nodded.

He pushed his boxers to the floor, revealing his erection. Then he hitched thumbs into her panties and yanked them down with one motion. As he stood, he stopped to kiss her mound, then straightened up. Skin brushing skin ignited electricity between them. He had to have her. He couldn't wait. And from the blush creeping up her chest and neck, he figured she felt the same.

His gaze roamed her body, followed by his hands. Although his dick grew increasingly engorged, he needed to look and touch before he took her. He cupped a breast in each hand and kissed the peak. After giving them a squeeze, Rusty slid his palm down her belly to her core. Slipping a finger between her folds, he pressed against her, gently.

"Oh, God." She closed her eyes. "Hurry."

Looking around, he settled on the lowest counter. He lifted her up and parted her knees. She reached down to curl her fingers around his erection.

"Hot damn!" She looked at his pecs, then into his eyes. Raising her hand, she flattened her palm on his chest and slid it up and down while he rolled the condom over his dick.

He stepped closer and ran a finger up and down her slit, then stuck it inside her. "You're ready, baby." He raised her legs, hiking them over his shoulders and guided himself into her. Barely able to contain himself, he plunged in as far as he could.

"Oh, fuck," he muttered, closing his eyes as he pulled her hips closer.

Meg spread her hands behind her and arched her back. Rusty lowered his head to her breast. God, he'd wanted to suck those nipples a thousand times in the last month. Closing his lips around the hardened point, he almost grinned as she gasped when he pulled. He laved it with the flat of his tongue while he moved in and out of her.

"Damn, you're tight." Fire licked at his loins.

She dug her fingers in his hair and combed it back. Raising his head, she attacked his mouth. Rusty placed his palm on the small of her back to secure her and pounded into her. She let go as her head fell back, her eyes closed. She moaned with every thrust.

"Yes, yes, yes!" She swirled her tongue over her lips, inviting his to take them again. He did. Then he moved his mouth to the crook of her neck, breathing in her scent mixed with sexual arousal as he listened to her breathing.

"Damn!" She hollered as she climaxed, her internal muscles clenching around him, holding his dick tight before releasing and fluttering. Rusty's control, held by a thread, disappeared when she came. His balls tightened as heat rocketed through him and he found his release. Pleasure poured through him, reaching every fingertip and toe. He'd never come so hard and for so long before. He lowered his sweaty forehead to her damp chest.

"Amazing. That was amazing," he muttered, kissing her bare skin.

She hugged him, burying his mouth between her breasts. When he came up for air—with no apology, no explanation, no words at all—his gaze met hers.

There was understanding, not recrimination, in her gaze. Satisfaction and happiness shone through. He grinned.

"You're...wonderful," he said.

"So are you." Meg's steady gaze spread warmth between them.

Rusty backed away and headed for the bathroom. What just happened here? Damn, this would change everything.

WHEN HE RETURNED, RUSTY wrapped his fingers around her waist and lifted her off the counter.

"Sorry. It wasn't very romantic."

"You mean screwing me on the kitchen counter?"

"Yeah. I mean. I felt romantic."

She laughed.

"It's just been so long. I mean I've wanted to do that for so long—"

"You mean screw me on the kitchen counter?'

"Stop saying that. No. I mean make love to you. And it just. I couldn't. I mean waiting. Wasn't possible. I couldn't wait. You're so, so, wow, you know."

"Tongue-tied?"

He nodded.

She kissed him, then wound her arms around his middle. With her head on his chest, she muttered, "I needed that."

He took her shoulders and held her away, making eye contact. "What? That? I'm a *that*? *That* you can get from a sex toy, or your hand or even the God damn washing machine."

Her eyes filled. Her voice soft, she continued. "No. With you. I've wanted *that* with you—for a long time."

"With me?"

"Didn't you hear me?"

"I can't believe it."

"You're my best friend, but I wanted more. Tonight, I got it."

His voice softened. "Me, too. You said it for both of us. I've wanted you forever."

"Spend the night with me?"

"What about the boys?"

"I'm up before them. I'll make up the sofa before they get up."

"My pleasure, honey. My pleasure." When he picked her up and carried her to the bedroom, she giggled like a teenager. Dropping her on the bed, he followed.

Looming over Meg, his fingers brushed her hair back from her forehead. His eyes stared into hers, warmth and peace flowed through her. After John, she never expected to feel this way about another man, especially Rusty. But his sweetness crept into her heart. Still, she never dreamed he'd reciprocate her feelings. His desire for her surprised her.

"You're an amazing lover," she said, rubbing her knuckles against his scruff.

"You're inspirational."

"Really?"

"Don't you know how beautiful and sexy you are?"

"Me? An ole sweatpants, science nerd, mom like me?"

He laughed. "Take another look in the mirror. Maybe you'll see what I see."

"What?"

"A smart woman with a heart of gold."

Her eyes filled. A tear slipped down her temple, unchecked. He swiped at it with his thumb.

"What did I say?" His brow furrowed.

"The most beautiful thing in the world."

He kissed her. "You're the most beautiful thing in the world."

Stretching to her full length, Meg flattened her body against his. "Round two?"

"Make love? Maybe a little slower this time?"

"Slow works. I've got all night."

She hooked her leg over his hip, bringing his dick in close contact with her sex.

"Ah, the magic words."

"And those are?"

"All night," he chuckled, closing his fingers around her breast.

Chapter Thirteen

After making love to Meg a second time, Rusty snapped off the light.

"Hold me? Please?" Her voice was almost a whisper.

"Com'ere. Scoot over."

She eased closer. Rusty grabbed her waist, pulling her halfway onto his chest. He tucked her head into his shoulder, then shifted a few times.

"How's this?"

"Perfect." Meg sighed.

She'd given up dreaming of another man like John. Then Rusty blustered into her life and the light in her, dimmed for two years, sprang to life. Even though she had no idea where things with him would go, happiness in the moment satisfied her. She stroked his chest, combing her fingers through the smattering of hair there.

In the last few weeks, she'd grappled with the growing urge to touch him. Whenever he walked around shirtless, she obsessed about it. Now he was open to her fingers, her lips, her tongue, and she could hardly wait to explore.

Of course, the physical side of things would have to be put on the shelf during the day, when the boys were around. But she'd make the most of the nights. For once, Meg decided to satisfy her own cravings and not worry.

With each breath, she drank in his masculine scent. He'd impressed her by shaving and using aftershave before the dance—like he was getting ready for a date. She caught a whiff and it brought back being in his arms, swaying to music.

Closing her eyes, she snuggled into his embrace. A sense of safety surrounded her, bringing a restful sleep.

At six, her eyes popped open. She bounded out of bed and made her way on tiptoe to the sofa. She opened it and mussed the sheets a bit, then returned to the bedroom. Rusty looked so peaceful, snoozing away. She leaned over and kissed his bare shoulder. Groggy, he opened his eyes and reached for her, pulling her back on the bed.

"Hey, babe."

"Time for you to get up and switch to the sofa."

"The sofa?"

"Before the boys get up. We talked about it last night. Remember?"

"The only things I remember about last night involve your body parts."

She grinned. "Great. But we don't want the boys to know, right?"

"Oh. Yeah. Okay."

Slowly he eased his legs over the side of the bed and padded toward the living room.

"Boxers!" She grabbed him. "You don't sleep naked, right? Boxers."

"Oh. Right." He stopped and headed for the dining room. He rummaged around for a pair of clean ones, found one and slipped it on. Almost sleepwalking, he kissed her and got in the sofa-bed.

"Goodnight, sweetheart."

She laughed. "Goodnight." And returned to her bed. The side Rusty slept on was still warm. She slid there, scrunched his pillow under her head and fell back to sleep.

At seven thirty, a boy jumped on the bed. Startled, Meg sat up.

"Mom! Pancakes?"

"Oh, Charlie. You scared me. Sure sweetheart. Give me a minute."

"Where's your nightgown?"

His question wiped away the cobwebs from too little sleep. She clutched at the covers.

"I got warm. It's okay. You go ahead into the kitchen. I'll be there in a minute."

Charlie shrugged and went on his way.

Damn. She'd remembered to tell Rusty but forgot to tell herself. She threw off the covers, slipped her nightgown over her head and sashed her robe. When she entered the kitchen, the boys were arguing over chocolate chips versus blueberries for pancakes.

Meg pulled down the ingredients for pancakes. "No need to fight. Charlie, you can have blueberries and Tommy can have chocolate chips."

The sound of a yawn from a man drew her attention. She sported a small smile as she cracked the eggs. Suddenly, a masculine arm wound itself around her waist from behind.

"Good morning, Meg," rumbled a deep voice.

Someone lowered his head and kissed her neck before letting her go. "Morning."

There was silence for a moment. Meg held her breath, waiting for a comment or question from one of the boys, but none came. She released the air she'd been holding.

"Dad, Charlie says blueberries are better in pancakes. I say chocolate chips. Which one do you like better?"

"Oh, no. You're not sucking me into a debate. Both are good. Uh, Meg? I'll take mine plain." He padded over to the coffeemaker. First, he refilled her mug, then poured one of his own. He added just the right amount of milk and sugar and handed it to her.

"Who's going to take Coco out while I finish making pancakes?"

Both boys responded at the same time. Meg leashed the dog, gave instructions and let Charlie and Tommy outside.

"Not that I didn't love your good morning, but do you think it's wise to do it in front of the boys?" Meg stirred the batter.

"I've kissed Maria in front of Tommy. I don't want him to think I don't like the women I date. I want him to know kissing is normal, a good thing."

Meg sensed a blush heat her cheeks. "It is, but do we have to flaunt it?"

"Didn't you let the douchebag Harold kiss you in front of Charlie?" She shook her head.

"Really?" Rusty raised his eyebrows.

"I don't want Charlie to worry."

"Worry about what? Don't you think he should see a healthy male/female relationship?"

"I suppose."

"I'm not going to pretend we're not lovers."

"What do you mean?"

"If I want to kiss you, I will. If I want to hold your hand, I will. I think the boys should know we've gone beyond roommates."

"Waaay beyond." Meg grinned.

"No reason to keep secrets."

"But they don't have to catch us in bed, right?"

"Maybe not now. But if they did, would it be so bad?"

She shivered. "I'm not ready to deal with making explanations."

MEG PUT TWO PANCAKES on a plate and handed it to Rusty.

"Look, Meg, I may not be the best parent in the world. But I'm honest with Tommy. He knows who I'm sleeping with. When they spend the night, we're open about it. Tommy's used to seeing a man and woman in bed in the morning." Rusty reached for the syrup.

"Not Charlie. Harold never stayed over."

"I think it's a mistake."

"He's fragile. Still recovering."

"Don't you think he'd like to have a man around? Like to know you're not lonely?"

"I'm not sure he's ready to share me." She took a sip of her coffee.

"Share you? I know Charlie. Why can't it be all of us being together?"

Meg poured batter in the pan and added blueberries to one and chips to another.

"Maybe you're the one who needs to get used to making room in your life for another man." Rusty took a forkful of pancakes.

Before Meg could answer, the boys burst into the room. Coco panted.

"We almost caught a fox!" Charlie said.

"Yeah. Coco chased him away. She was awesome." Tommy petted his dog.

"Give her a couple of treats," Rusty said, chewing a pancake.

Meg served the boys their meal and put one on for herself. Rusty's words echoed in her mind. Was he right? Was she protecting Charlie or herself?

The boys chattered on about Coco's bravery, wolfed down their food and asked to be excused. John had insisted Charlie not simply get up and leave when he was through eating but ask first. Meg had continued the practice. Tommy had fallen in with it, too.

Rusty refilled his mug. "More?"

She raised her hand.

"So? What do you want to do?"

Meg sucked her lower lip over her teeth and shifted her weight.

"Unless you want to consider last night a one-night stand?" He raised his eyebrows.

Her eyes widened. She approached him. "Oh, no. No. Not at all."

He rested his hands on her waist. "Good. Then we're open?"

She nodded.

"And you'll deal with any fallout?"

She nodded again.

"Good." He lowered his mouth to hers for a brief kiss. Then he turned her around, gave her a gentle smack on her behind. "Let's get dressed and do something. I think the county fair is still going."

She shot him a smile and headed for her room. While she dressed, she noticed her body seemed lighter, as if Rusty had lifted a two-thousand-pound weight from her shoulders. She couldn't be more relieved. She and John had promised each other if anything ever happened to them, they wanted their partner to find someone else and have a life. When he'd asked Meg if she'd agreed, she'd lied and said she did. Her stomach had churned at the thought of John with someone else, even if she wasn't alive.

He'd been sincere. Maybe he was right. Things with Rusty had evolved, slowly, naturally. Although she didn't have as much in common with him as she had with John, something bound them together. Was it their sons? Their stubborn insistence on always being right? She laughed. Maybe it was their love for this house and the tiny town of Pine Grove?

She gave her head a shake and finished dressing. She'd seen the beautiful day unfolding outside and wanted to get underway. After all, she had a life to live, and maybe a new family to enjoy, didn't she?

She joined the guys at the front door. Rusty took her hand.

"Mom, is Rusty your new boyfriend?" Charlie looked up at his mom.

Rusty paused.

"I guess you could say so."

"Oh. Good. Good choice." Her son nodded, then opened the front door.

The smells of the fair greeted them in the parking lot. Funnel cakes, cotton candy, sausages and peppers, and hot dogs made her stomach rumble.

"Junk food heaven," Meg said.

"Mom, can I have—"

"Okay, yes, you can have some of this food. But no cotton candy, which is pure sugar and makes a disgusting mess. Let's see if they have ice cream."

Meg read from the program. "Sign says 4-H exhibits and animal contests."

"Ah. Here we go. Pig races! Potbelly pigs." Rusty laughed. "We can't miss those."

"What's a potbelly pig?" Tommy asked.

"Let's go find out." Rusty led the way.

Tommy won the pig race trifecta. Meg tucked his tiny trophy in her purse. Charlie begged to go on the rides. They all went on the Ferris Wheel together. Meg clutched Rusty when the wheel stopped at the top. He stole a kiss. Then another and another. The jolt from the machine when it started to turn startled her.

"Every boy's dream. Kissing his girl at the top of the Ferris Wheel."

She laughed. "Am I your girl?"

"Damn right you are." He slid his arm around her shoulders, and she snuggled into him. The day passed quickly. They had dinner at the sausage and pepper stand then, at eight o'clock, headed home. The boys fell asleep in the backseat. Rusty carried Charlie inside first.

"DAD?" A SLEEPY VOICE drew Rusty's attention. Tommy had awakened when his dad picked him up.

"You still awake?"

"Can I ask you a question?"

"Sure."

"If Meg's your girlfriend, then Maria isn't anymore? Or do you have two girlfriends?"

Rusty smiled. No fooling Tommy. The kid was sharp, he didn't miss anything.

"When I decided we should spend the summer here, Maria didn't like it."

"You had a fight?"

Rusty chuckled. "She said if I came up here, then we were finished."

"So she broke up with you?"

"Yep. I agreed we wouldn't see each other anymore."

"Good."

"I know you never liked her."

"She didn't like me."

"She wasn't into kids."

"I like Meg."

"I know you do. She likes you, too."

"She's fair. She doesn't give Charlie everything."

"Right. She's fair."

"If she's your girlfriend, why do you still sleep on the sofa?"

Rusty had no answer.

"I thought boyfriends and girlfriends slept in the same bed."

"Would it be okay with you if I slept in Meg's bed?"

He nodded. "I'm tired. I don't want to talk anymore."

Rusty carried Tommy into his room. Then he doused the light and tiptoed out.

Meg sat on the deck, a cup of tea in her hand. He joined her.

"What a great day." She grinned.

"Sure was." Rusty recounted his conversation with Tommy.

"Tommy's okay with us sharing a bed. Can you talk to Charlie?"

She shrugged. "I might be pushing it."

"Didn't you share a bed with John?"

"We were married."

"Doesn't mean much to a kid." Rusty sat in a chair next to Meg.

"I don't know."

"Try it. What's the worst that can happen?" Rusty rested his elbows on his knees.

Meg sat quietly, staring at the sky.

"Don't you want to spend the night with me?"

"More than anything." She touched his cheek.

"Okay. So, we spend the night tonight? And if the boys discover us, so what?"

"I have to wear a nightgown."

"Fine. I'm going to take the dog." Rusty leashed Coco and headed down the steps. Not exactly dying to take the beast for her nightly stroll, he needed time to think. What had he done? He'd convinced his son Meg was his girlfriend. Did she agree?

When he left Maria, he'd vowed this summer would be all about Tommy with no women. What did he do? He found a new woman. Meg was nothing like Maria or Angela, either. Ready to hate her at the outset, he'd found he respected her. She'd been cocky, arrogant, and downright pushy at first.

With Tommy, she exposed a softer side. He'd never been with a maternal woman, one who wanted kids or even liked kids. He figured he didn't need children, so dating women who weren't interested worked. Until he knocked up Angela. Tommy's birth hit Rusty like a ton of bricks. He'd done an about-face in thirty seconds.

The boy had changed his life. But Rusty didn't vary his dating habits and kept going out with non-child-friendly women. Conflicts between his son and whatever woman he'd been dating flared up time and time again. Seemed he couldn't get it right. Couldn't find a woman who'd like Tommy and Rusty, too.

Until he moved into this house. And now what? The minute he saw her with his son, he'd fallen. Meg was the perfect mother for Tommy. And her sweet smart side was the right woman for him. She challenged him to think, to be smarter and better than he'd ever been before. With her pushing him, he'd grown. Now he needed Meg like human beings need air and water.

Their relationship had to morph into long-term. Where could he ever find another woman as fantastic as Meg Gunderson? Nowhere. And he didn't need to, because he had her, right? Didn't he have her? He needed to sew this up, commit himself and her, as well. Only then could he breathe free and keep this happiness he'd never known before.

When he returned, he unleased the dog, gave her a treat and a few pets before joining Meg.

She pushed to her feet, yawned, and stretched.

"Are you trying to tell me something?"

"Maybe."

He looked at his watch. "Wow, ten o'clock already? Time for bed."

She laughed and followed him into the house. He stopped in the doorway.

"All night?"

"We'll see."

Chapter Fourteen

The next morning Meg and Rusty awoke before the boys. Snuggling closer to him, Meg whispered. "Just ten more minutes?"

"Yeah."

He circled his arm around her, then rested his hand on her breast. "Ahhh, yes." He closed his eyes and his fingers.

"If you're going to do that, ten minutes is going to become an hour."

"The boys'll be up soon." Rusty groaned. "We need a lock on the door."

Meg rolled the covers down and swung her legs over the side. "Nightgown," she muttered, shuffling along to the dresser. She whipped out sleepwear and shrugged on her robe. Yawning, she headed for the kitchen while Rusty went back to sleep.

Humming *I Think I Love You*, Meg put up coffee and took eggs from the fridge. Coco greeted her. Meg fed the dog, then opened the back door and took her mug to the deck. Early morning crows cawed their greeting.

Before she finished, Charlie and Tommy came in, arguing.

"Do."

"Do not."

"Do."

"Do not."

Meg sighed and returned to the stove. "Eggs today. Do and do not what?"

"Tommy said boyfriends and girlfriends sleep in the same bed. I said they don't."

Meg sensed her cheeks heat up. "Well, it depends..." she hemmed.

"My father said they do. Are you calling him a liar?"

"No."

"Why don't you ask him?"

"Where is he? He's not on the sofa." Charlie asked.

Oh, shit. Cat's out of the bag now.

"I know! I bet he's in the bedroom!" Tommy raced to the back of the house with Charlie in pursuit.

"He is not!"

Voices young and old carried through the house. Meg melted butter and counted out the eggs. *Let Rusty handle this.* A few moments later, the three guys entered the room.

"Tommy was right. Rusty was in your bed." Charlie cast her a look of betrayal.

"You never asked me. Yes, Rusty is sharing my bed. Yes, we are boyfriend and girlfriend. And yes, it's okay." She hugged her son.

"Harold never slept in your bed." Charlie raised a defiant chin.

"He wasn't a real boyfriend. Just sort of a friend."

Rusty and Tommy joined them for a four-way hug. Meg broke first.

"Let's eat and get going. I thought we had a trip planned for today?"

"Fishing in the Delaware!" Rusty raised his arm and fisted his hand.

"Fishing in the Delaware," the boys chanted.

"Okay then. Two eggs each. Tommy, you get the bread in the toaster. Charlie, you get the butter and Jam. Rusty, you pour the orange juice. Let's get this family movin'."

Her hand flew to her mouth. What had she said? Ignoring her slip, the boys went about their tasks. Rusty stopped on his way to the fridge to hug her and plant a kiss on her lips.

"I like the sound of that," he whispered.

They took their seats in the car, including Coco and headed to Log Hill. While Rusty drove, Meg led the boys in a million choruses of

"Row, Row, Row Your Boat." After fifteen minutes the dog barked, and they switched tunes.

Memories of rare weekend trips with John and Charlie flitted through her mind. Time to make new ones. Meg had resisted letting go for so long, yet today, she did. She took a moment to remember the early days with John and Charlie, then packed those into her heart and moved on.

They stopped at *Java the Hut* for large traveling mugs of coffee and Danish, then *The Cozy Café* for a picnic lunch. When they got on the scenic byway, Rusty spoke. "Do you like to fish?"

"I do. Never been fly fishing before."

"Wait until you see the flies I have."

"Dad, let's let Charlie use our lucky fly first."

"Okay, Tom."

Meg sat back and stared out the window. Sunshine coated everything with golden promise. The perfect weather buoyed her spirits with the expectation of laughter and fun. She resisted the urge to look into the future, deciding, instead, to simply enjoy the present for all it was worth.

They pulled into the parking lot of the public river access area. Rusty pulled out a tackle box and four fishing rods.

"You have four rods?"

"Don't think you're the first girl I tried to interest in fly fishing." He handed each one a rod.

"Come on. We need to get this gear on."

He had waders for himself, Meg, Tommy, and a spare kid's pair for Charlie.

"I researched this on the Internet. The fish are biting right down there." He pointed.

The group followed him down the bank of the river. Last in line, Meg delighted in watching the guys falling in together. Could this be her dream come true? Would she get a second chance?

RUSTY CLEANED THE FOUR fish they caught. He wrapped them in tin foil with lemon and butter and threw them on the grill. Meg prepared a salad. On the lawn, the boys played fetch with Coco. The song *I Think I Love You* kept playing in Meg's head. She hummed the tune, then sang the words, softly. Rusty turned to glance at her.

"Really?"

"What?" She raised her eyebrows.

He took three steps to the table, took her chin in his hand, and raised her mouth for a brief kiss. "Yes."

"What?"

"For your song."

"Oh?"

"Yes. I do."

Heat rose to her cheeks. "Really?"

He shrugged. "Yeah." And went back to tending the fish.

Meg swallowed and reached for the dressing. Did he mean it? Could he possibly love her, the condescending bitch who called him a Neanderthal?

"Fish's done." Rusty took the packets and put them on a platter.

"Boys! Dinner!"

Charlie and Tommy raced up the steps, followed by Coco.

"Go wash up. I'll feed the dog." Meg bent down to pet the pooch. Within ten minutes, they were seated at a table on the deck. Rusty poured wine for Meg and himself. Meg filled glasses with milk for the boys.

"It's amazing to eat the fish we just caught," Charlie said.

"I don't think I'll like fish." Tommy's mouth turned down in a frown as he stared at the food on his plate.

"Try it. It's great. Really." Rusty took a forkful. "With butter and lemon. You'll love it."

Tommy lifted the fork slowly. "Do you like it, Charlie?"

The other boy nodded and continued chewing.

Tommy picked up his fork and tasted the fish. "Not bad."

Rusty laughed.

After such a vigorous day, the boys tired early and couldn't stay awake for more than a few pages of the Hardy Boys. Rusty carried a sleeping Tommy to his own bed and kissed him goodnight. He signaled for Meg to meet him on the deck.

When she got there, five candles burned. A small glass of fine brandy sat by her chair.

"A nightcap." He took a sip.

"This is so romantic." She toed off her sandals and rested her feet on a chair next to Rusty. He curled his long fingers around her arch and squeezed.

"I'm famous for my foot rubs," he said.

"Oh? Let's see."

"Doubting me?" He raised his eyebrows. "Or just challenging me so you get one."

"Guilty as charged."

"All you had to do was ask." He dug his thumb into her flesh.

Meg sat back and closed her eyes. "It feels sooo good." A soft chuckle met her words.

He moved his chair and repositioned her foot in his lap. Every muscle in Meg's body calmed as peace grew. She relaxed so much she didn't notice his hands creeping up her leg. Within a few minutes, a foot rub had become a calf massage. She murmured little moans of pleasure as he made his way north.

When he got to her thighs, she opened her legs and her eyes. Pushing up the skirt of her little sundress, he bent to kiss the inside of her thigh. He pushed the skirt all the way to her waist.

"Ohh. Pink Panties. My favorite. They've gotta go." He palmed her butt with his left hand and lifted her up slightly, to slide the garment off with his right. "Much better."

She watched him spread her legs and dive in. When his tongue touched her core, she bucked.

"Hold still, lady," he muttered.

She combed her fingers through his hair. Her eyes drifted shut. "God damn, Rusty." The only response was a deep chuckle that tickled her private parts. He swirled his tongue around her center, then slipped a finger inside her.

"Wow," he muttered.

"Damn, Rusty. You, you, you..." words failed her as smoldering embers burst into flame inside her.

"Me, what? You like?" He raised his head.

"Hell, yes. Don't stop."

A quick laugh and he returned to stroking her with his tongue while he plunged two fingers in and out.

"I'm gonna come."

"Go ahead. Do it."

Although the night air had cooled, Meg's body was hot. She tugged on the waistband of his shorts.

"Drop 'em, mister."

"Ready?"

"Hell, yes. Take 'em off." She pulled harder.

"Whatever the lady wants." Rusty pushed to his feet and made quick work of his clothes, flinging them on a nearby chair. Meg giggled.

"You're in a hurry, too?"

"If this gets any bigger, it'll explode," he said, looking down at his dick. He retrieved his wallet and nabbed a condom. "Let's do it here." He sat in a chair and rolled the latex on. "Jump up," he said, patting his thighs.

"Never done it in a chair," she muttered, yanking her dress over her head and tossing it to keep Rusty's clothes company.

"No? Chair sex is fun." He wore a lustful grin. "Ride 'em, cowgirl."

She tried to mount him but slipped and slid and couldn't get her balance. He leaned over and wrapped his big hands around her waist and hoisted her in the air. Damn! She bent her knees as he lowered her onto his cock.

"Direct me." He nodded toward their coupling. Meg closed her fingers around him and placed him at her entrance. He eased her down and slipped right in.

"Oh, hot damn," he said, shutting his eyes. "So good. Amazing."

She flattened her palms on his chest to steady herself, then slowly pumped her hips until she hit a rhythm. Rusty opened his eyes and stared at her breasts.

"Gotta have those," he said, directing one toward his mouth. When he fastened on to her nipple, Meg moaned and increased her speed.

"You're, you're, hot damn. Rusty," she muttered, her eyes hooded, her mouth open and her tongue rolling over her bottom lip.

"I can't take it." He grabbed her hips and sped her up.

Intense need spiraled up in Meg. Then she went over the top. Her nipples hardened. All her muscles clenched tight, then released. Pure pleasure streamed through her.

"Holy shit," Rusty said, as he opened his eyes. With one hard pull, he held her down on him and groaned. Then he embraced her, crushing her breasts against his bare chest.

"God damn!" He kissed her neck and rubbed his palms up and down her back. She rested her face against his shoulder and licked his salty skin. "You taste good," she said.

"Me? Sweaty."

"Good." She snaked her arms under his and gripped his back. Happiness flowed in her veins. "Can we stay like this forever?"

"I wish."

He let go with one hand and brought it around to rest on her breast. He couldn't seem to get enough of touching those. It warmed her heart.

The night air chilled her.

"It's cold. Isn't this supposed to be summer?"

"Let's go to bed."

"I thought we already did?" She shot him a sly smile.

He laughed. "Come on." He lifted her off and padded to the bathroom. Meg brought their glasses inside, then scampered into the bedroom for her robe. After she washed up, she added an extra blanket and eased between the sheets. Rusty joined her.

"Thanks for preheating the bed." He moved to her side.

"My side, at least."

"We'll warm up faster if we're closer."

She snuggled into his embrace, breathing in his sexy scent. "I like your new aftershave."

"Thanks. You smell good."

"A woman well-loved."

"That must be it. Goodnight, honey."

"'Night, Russ." Meg yawned, then closed her eyes. She heard the click as Rusty turned off the light, before she fell sound asleep.

MEG AWOKE EARLY. AFTER she got the coffee started, she hunted through the fridge for the ingredients for omelets. The sound of people moving about, the bathroom door closing and opening, feet on the bare floor warmed her. The guys were awake and would be, like baby birds, begging for food soon. She pulled out a green pepper, an onion, and American cheese.

Singing *I Think I Love You* again, softly, under her breath, she smiled at each male who crossed the kitchen threshold.

"I know, I know. Toast. I'm on it." Charlie said.

"Let's use raisin bread," Meg replied.

"Raisin bread? I've never had that," Tommy said.

"It's amazing." Meg handed a fresh loaf to her son and cracked eggs.

The doorbell rang, followed by a pounding on the door. Rusty entered the room, scratching his chest before sashing his robe. The dog barked. "Who the hell? What time is it?"

"It's nine. You guys slept in."

Rusty kissed her and hugged her from behind. "Maybe if we ignore it, it will go away," he whispered in her ear.

The pounding continued. Meg disengaged from him.

"Wait. I'll go. Might be dangerous," he said, heading for the door.

The boys followed.

"Stay back, guys." He shielded them with his hand.

Coco kept barking as she joined Rusty at the door. He grabbed her collar. "Coco, don't eat anyone until we tell you to. It might be a friend."

Sure doesn't sound like a friend. Meg turned off the flame on the stove and hung back, leaning against the hall wall, where she could see the door.

"Get back, boys," Rusty said. "We hear you!"

"Then why don't you open up? What are you hiding in there?"

He yanked open the door. Stunned, he stepped back.

"Maria! What are you doing here?"

"Checking up on you." She pushed her way in, stepping over the threshold before being invited. The pretty woman with wild, black hair and a ferocious expression marched down the hall, shoving the boys aside.

"Ah, I see. So, this is the slut, the whore you left me for, eh?"

Meg's eyes widened. "What? What did you say?"

"You heard me."

"How dare you come into my house and call me disgusting names. And in front of my son, too!" Meg fisted her hand and stepped closer to the visitor. Rusty scooted between the two.

"You didn't mean it, did you, Maria? Come on. Come with me. Let's talk." He put an arm around her shoulders, but she shrugged it off.

"I did, too, mean it." Maria fixed a murderous stare on Meg.

"Get out! Get out of my house!" Meg gestured toward the door

"Get the phone, Tommy," Charlie said, moving toward the bed-room.

"I'm calling the police." Tommy followed Charlie.

"Now see what you did?" Rusty faced Maria. "Boys! Don't call the police."

"Go ahead. I don't care if they arrest me. I'll take this skinny little thing apart."

"Who you calling skinny?" Meg raised her fist again and approached Maria.

"Meg, stop! Maria! Ladies!" Rusty got between them. "Let's talk about this, calmly and quietly. No need for the police."

The boys returned. Tommy wielded Rusty's phone. "Officer Bolton isn't going to like this."

"Enough! Tommy. Put the phone down. Maria, over there," Rusty raised his voice and pointed to an easy chair in one corner of the living room. "Meg, you go over there." He pointed to an opposite corner, but his voice had softened.

The women took their seats. "Let's talk about this. Maria, you showed up unannounced, and uninvited." Rusty paced the diagonal space between the women.

"You think I'm gonna let you walk out of my life so fast?"

"I thought we'd talked about this. The guidance counselor at Tommy's school said I had to get away and spend time with my son."

"So? What about me?"

"The problem with you, Maria, is you just don't get it. Tommy's my son. My flesh and blood. I'm all he has. He has to come first."

"I don't see why?"

"See? I tried to tell you in New York. You don't get it. You don't. Tommy will always come first with me. And you don't accept it. If you can't live with my choice and support it, then there's nothing between us."

She snorted. "There was a helluva lot between us."

Rusty's face colored. "Never mind. Maria, there are children here. Okay?"

"Oh, oh. Pardon me. Intimacy is forbidden to talk about?"

"This is another thing you don't get. I told you our relationship had run its course before I left New York."

"Maybe for you. But not for me. So, this kid thing. This slut, she does it? She gets it?"

"Look, you've got to stop calling me that."

"Lady, if you call my mother a name again, I'm calling the police." Charlie crossed his arms over his chest.

Gotta love my son.

"Okay, okay. Sorry. Answer my question." She turned her attention back to Rusty. "This, this, whatever. Woman. She gets it?"

Rusty's voice softened. "Yeah. She does. In fact, she's been a better mother to Tommy than his biological mother."

"She's manipulating you!" Maria rose a bit from her chair.

"Nope. No. She isn't. Tommy loves her. Don't you son?"

Tommy nodded; his eyes full. Charlie put his arm around his friend.

"So, what you want is a mother for your son?"

"That's part of it. Yeah. But not all. Far from all."

"What else?"

"I don't think this is any of her business," Meg piped up.

"I don't mind talking about how I feel about you." Rusty put his hand on her shoulder.

"What else? I'm waiting." Maria shifted in her seat.

"I've never met a woman like her. Smart. Beautiful. And loving. She takes care of all of us, without complaining. No whining. Sure she doesn't take any...crap. She gives back as good as she gets. But she's...well, she's like no other woman. She's who I want."

Tears stung the backs of Meg's eyes. Could this be happening?

"And you're sleeping with her?"

"None of your business!" Meg pushed to her feet.

Rusty raised his hand. "It's okay. Yeah. I am."

"And the sons know this?"

"They do."

"And they accept it?"

"They do. It's over between us, Maria. I was stupid to think I could compartmentalize my life. I need a woman, like Meg. Who can love me *and* Tommy. Who knows what a home for a family looks like. And I've found her."

Meg broke down. Tears stained her cheeks. Charlie hugged her.

"I think you'd better go, Maria." Rusty took her arm. She stood up, frowned, and slapped him across the face.

"I'm calling the police. Officer Bolton said hitting is assault." Tommy picked up the phone. He dialed, then spoke. "A woman assaulted my father."

"You'd better go, Maria." Rusty rubbed his cheek.

Rummaging through the pockets of her robe, Meg found a tissue and mopped her face.

"You don't even know how he feels about you, eh? Well, we'll see. When he comes back to New York, he'll be tired of some hillbilly hick girl who's easy. He'll come back to Maria. You'll see."

The sound of a siren grabbed Maria's attention.

"You'd better go," Rusty repeated, escorting her to the door. But it was too late. Officer Bolton was on his way up the path.

"Oh, no. Not you two again?"

"This woman slapped my dad," Tommy said, pointing to Maria.

The officer took out his notebook. "All right. Line up. Let's hear it. One at a time."

Rusty shot Tommy a look, but the boy simply smiled and shrugged.

"I just have one question," the Officer said. "Do either of you have any more significant others who might show up at the drop of a hat?"

Meg and Rusty shook their heads.

"Good. Because next time your kid calls, it had better be good." He put his cap back on and got into his car. He rolled down the window.

"And I mean it. I'll haul you two to jail and put your kids in foster care!" He hit the gas pedal and sped out of the driveway.

Chapter Fifteen

The encounter with Maria and Officer Bolton had disrupted their day. Rusty and Meg took the boys to the lake to swim and out to dinner at Homer's. While the kids fed the ducks off the dock, Rusty ordered iced mocha coffee for himself and Meg. The umbrella over the table offered little relief from the heat. Or was it the tension from the scene with Maria?

The cold coffee cooled him a bit. He glanced over at Meg. She'd been quiet. Too quiet. He needed to know what she was thinking. Maria's last words, before she slapped him, were aimed at Meg. Did she think Maria spoke the truth? It was the farthest thing from the truth ever—like polar bears moving to the Caribbean. But did Meg believe it?

He cleared his throat, getting her attention.

"We need to talk." He spoke up.

"Agreed."

"Maybe not here. The boys'll be back in ten minutes."

"Agreed."

"Tonight? After dinner? Can you read to them early?"

"Yes."

"Why are you giving me one-word answers?"

"Why not?"

"Come on. What's up?"

"We'll talk tonight."

"Okay." Rusty took her hand. Even giving it a squeeze didn't bring a smile to her face. Worry roiled in his gut. This was not a sign she'd be open to the truth. He hoped she hadn't made up her mind about him yet. Not in a negative way, anyway. She slipped her hand away.

"Are we okay?" He couldn't resist the question.

"I hope so."

"Me, too." He took her hand again and she smiled.

"Are you guys holding hands? Gross!" Tommy made a face.

"Can we go? Tommy and I want to read the next chapter."

"Okay, Charlie. Let me get the check." Rusty made a gesture and the waiter brought the bill.

"I wish you'd let me pay."

"Not on your life."

"John left me money."

"Good. Hold on to it."

She frowned. He threw a few bills down on the table and pushed to his feet. He took her hand and the two adults, and two kids marched to the car. At home, Meg cuddled up with the boys on the sofa. Rusty worked on his computer.

"Game tonight. Okay?"

"Got it. No problem."

"How did you know?"

"You mentioned it at breakfast. I'm a good listener."

"Right."

"What time?"

"Five. Still okay?"

"Of course."

He disappeared behind the bedroom door. Before he pulled out some stats for the game, he needed to have some questions ready for his talk with Meg. He fished through his briefcase for a pen and paper. Finding an old notebook, he sat down, poised to write. Maybe this kind of planning wasn't his style, but fumfering around in front of her, searching for words and trying to figure out what questions to ask on the spot wouldn't get him results.

Tonight was too important to leave to chance, to impromptu impulses. Although he'd always been proud of being spontaneous. Things with Meg were too serious to leave to chance. Even the thought set butterflies free in his belly. He'd never made a commitment to a woman before, not one intended to last more than a month or two. Even Angela was all about partying and fun times—until she got pregnant. He figured he'd consider marriage maybe when he was fifty.

Meg had knocked him off his feet. He'd never met a girl like her. Baseball players usually dug through a crowd of groupies or girls out for fun with no commitment for their woman-of-the-week, month or whatever. Then there were the gold diggers. Often, they didn't even remember your name, just the position you played and your annual salary. Those women gave him the creeps. He'd developed a "gold-dar", as he called it, making him able to sniff out a money-hungry miss from across the room.

There were times when he'd put Maria in that category. Every time he'd been ready to walk away because of her spendthrift demands, she'd do something to reel him back in, like treat him to a weekend at a resort.

Meg wasn't silly, money-hungry, or superficial. She'd been a one-eighty from every girl he'd ever dated. And wow! She started out as a snobby, know-it-all, pain in the ass, but then, out of necessity, they pulled in tandem. A chick like Meg, who could love and care for his son as well as she loved him, was a rare bird. He'd probably never meet another like her.

Tonight had to go smooth, like glass. They needed to be on the same page. Although he wasn't exactly ready to propose, the idea had crossed his mind without causing him to have a migraine or a mild seizure.

He'd made some mint iced tea, her favorite, and stashed it behind the milk. Although he hadn't planned this before Maria arrived, perhaps he owed his ex-girlfriend a thank-you for pushing things along. He wrote quietly, thoughtfully until the game got underway.

Putting down his pen, he tuned in to the action and called in on his phone. He'd be doing color commentary tonight. And afterward? The future of Rusty Reisse and Tommy hung in the balance. He needed to hit it out of the park with Meg. And it had to be on the first pitch.

"Rusty Reisse here, joining the New York Nighthawks for their third game in the series against the Boston Bluejays. Dan Alexander's pitching. Can Jake Lawrence keep his five-game hitting streak going tonight? Only time will tell." And the same was true for Rusty.

WHILE THE BOYS RAN ahead to greet Coco, Meg and Rusty sauntered up the front path. Rusty slung his arm over her shoulders, she snaked hers around his waist. She dreaded their planned talk tonight. What if Maria was right and he'd take up with her as soon as they were back in New York? She chewed her bottom lip. Could Meg pull back now and protect her heart, or was it too late?

If Roberta had told her she'd be so in love with Rusty Reisse before she came up here, she'd have laughed her out of the room. No way. Rusty Reisse? A former pro baseball player? Never. She'd hold out for an intellectual, like John. A whiz at math, someone who understood U.S. and foreign markets and would never run around on his wife.

Then there's Rusty. He thinks a foreign market is the bazaar at Casablanca. And running around? Hell, the man had admitted to being a player—and he meant beyond baseball. He could never be the man she'd want to spend the rest of her life with. Nope, never, no siree. Yeah, right. That's exactly who he was, and her heart was in it one hundred percent.

What would he say tonight? If he said once they got back to the city, all bets were off, they'd be free to date others, could she keep it together? She didn't want to date anyone else. Did he? She didn't think so. He'd seemed so wrapped up in her, in the boys, in the little temporary family they'd created. He'd been attentive to her needs, helping out, treating her to meals, and taking time with both boys. And in the bedroom? To the moon and back. Damn. Did it have to end now?

Her eyes wetted, but she held back. *Remember what grandma used to say, 'Don't borrow trouble. It'll be knockin' on your door soon enough.'*

She'd already had a mountain of it, a world of heartbreak. Wasn't it time for some relief, for happiness to come her way? She took a deep shuddering breath.

"I'll keep the boys occupied until bed. Early night."

"Good. See you after the game." He kissed her lightly before heading for the bedroom and closing the door.

The burger from Homer's rolled around in her stomach. She needed to stop thinking about her talk with Rusty or she'd get sick. Focus on the boys.

"Let's do two chapters. Maybe even three, if we have time. Okay?"

The boys nodded and curled up next to her. She put an arm around each one.

"Tonight, Tommy turns the pages. Right?"

"Right. I did it last night," Charlie said.

In light of the "talk" she and Rusty had scheduled, Meg hugged the boys closer. Grateful to have them, she flagged this in her memory. When she lost John, caring for Charlie had provided the greatest comfort. No amount of kind words, flowers or casseroles warmed her grieving heart as much as keeping Charlie close. No expressions of sympathy soothed her as much as tending to her son's broken heart.

Tommy had taken to Meg quickly. She'd picked up on his need for a mother. He'd listened to her, obeyed until he felt comfortable enough not to. He tested her from time to time, and she clamped down on him with a strong, but loving hand—giving him the security he craved.

Would this end? Would she lose Tommy when they got back to the city? She reminded herself he belonged to Rusty, not her. She had no claim on the boy. It saddened her to think in September, he'd move on, along with Rusty.

Forcing herself to focus on reading calmed her. No reason to assume the worst until it happened. What if her fortunes had turned and she'd get to keep Tommy and Rusty, too? The thought made her smile.

"Let's look at the bright side," she said.

"What bright side? Joe Hardy is trapped in a cave," Charlie said.

"And water is getting high," Tommy piped up.

Meg directed her gaze on the printed page again. "You're right. He needs help."

And so do I. Having finally admitted it to herself, Meg resumed reading aloud. Didn't Roberta once tell her admitting you needed help was the first step toward getting it? Meg hoped so. Struggling along alone had worn thin over a year ago. Would tonight's meeting give her a future?

She finished the chapter, tucked the boys in their beds, and kissed them goodnight.

Meg switched off the light and headed for the deck, with her heart in her mouth. It had been forever since she had wanted anyone, the way she wanted Rusty.

Had she picked the wrong guy? Well, she hadn't actually picked him. They'd wandered into the same room in the dark. Totally by chance, unless Fred and Roberta had planned it. Unlikely. Fate had thrown them together. The irresistible force met the immovable object and now, love was on the table.

She opened the door and gasped. Five candles burned on the deck. A tall, frosty glass of something sat at her place, along with a dish of mint chip ice cream, her favorite. Rusty, clad in a bathrobe, sat at his place.

"What took you so long?" He grinned.

She checked her watch. "Isn't the game still on?"

"Rained out."

He rose and pulled out her chair.

She smiled and took her seat. "This is lovely."

"Mint tea. Your favorite."

She nodded. "You remembered."

"I remember everything about you, Meg."

"Do you?" She sipped the tea then picked up her spoon.

"I remember how you took Tommy in right away. How you hold him close when you read to him. I remember how I've woken up to the smell of coffee brewing every morning since you got here. I remember how good you taste, above and below the waist. The sound of your laugh, your questions at the ball game, the way you handled the snake."

"You remember a lot." Heat rose in her cheeks.

"Most of all, I remember how great you make me feel. In bed. Out of bed. All the time."

The sting of tears behind her eyes overwhelmed her. They burst through her control and eased down her cheeks. It had been so long since anyone had said those words to her.

"Don't cry, honey." Rusty brushed her tears away.

"I can't. It's just." Words wouldn't come. She leaned forward and kissed him. Picking up her napkin, Meg wiped her face, then took a deep, shuddering breath. "What about when we're back in the city? I don't want to be pushy, but after what Maria said…"

Her voice trailed off as her gaze met his.

"Forget what she said. She doesn't matter. I want to see you in the city. I don't want to push you, if you're not ready. But I don't want to lose you."

"I'm ready."

"Are you sure? Because I sure as hell am. I'm done with Maria, and all the other Marias, for life." Rusty closed his fingers around the full shot glass in front of him.

"Really?" Meg's voice squeaked.

"Up until now, a family didn't mean anything good. It meant nagging, controlling, bitching, and rules, a straightjacket."

"What changed your mind?"

"We've been living like a family since the beginning. Okay, maybe we weren't sleeping together, but everything else was the same."

"Except we argued and fought all the time."

"Not all the time. Sometimes." Rusty took a slug.

"And?"

"And, after we declared a truce, I liked what we became."

"You mean a family?"

"Right. I had it all wrong. A family doesn't tie you down, it frees you up."

"That's what I've always thought."

"I don't mean to pry, but is that what you had with John?"

"Yeah. We were close, very close. When he wasn't working, we were together all the time."

"Sort of like us?"

"What you and I have is different. Different in a good way." She put her hand on his forearm.

"How so?" He covered her hand with his.

"You bring new things to me. Like baseball. I'd thought it was silly because I didn't know about it. I thought hitting a ball with a wood stick was boring. And anyone could do it. Now I see it requires athletic skill. I like the game. I see the challenges. And then there's Tommy."

"Oh, yes. My son. He's a handful." Rusty shook his head slowly.

"He's delightful. Inquisitive, pushing the envelope, bright, creative, affectionate. Charlie adores him. And so do I."

Rusty's eyes filled. "I'd given up searching for a woman who would want to be his mother."

"He's a good kid."

"I haven't been much of a father. He wasn't planned. I had no clue about raising a kid, being a father. I relied on Angela, but she took off.

I had no help. I think I've probably made every mistake in the book." Rusty wiped his eyes.

"But you love him, and he knows it. That's what counts. Bottom line."

"The second he was born, I was a goner. I fell for him. And have loved him ever since."

"It shows."

"Good. I've learned a shit-ton about parenting from you. You're an amazing mother. Patient, unselfish, all the things I'm not."

She lowered her gaze. "I try. It's harder without John. Charlie looks up to you. Not teaching him about baseball was a mistake. He seems to love the sport."

"I'm not sure he likes me as much as he likes Frank Todd." Rusty smiled.

"Screw Frank Todd."

"I think that's what Todd had in mind."

She laughed. Rusty kissed her.

"I'm not too good with words. I want to be with you. So? What do you say?"

"I say yes."

"No more worries about Maria?" He raised his eyebrows.

"Nope." She shook her head.

"Toast?" He raised his glass and she followed. "To Meg and Rusty, Charlie, and Tommy. May they be happy together forever."

Meg swallowed. Forever is a long time. Was this a marriage proposal? A living together arrangement? Friends with benefits? Or a never-ending dating relationship? Panic made her sweat. She wiped it off her upper lip. Don't question. Say yes and figure it out later, she told herself.

"Happy together," she echoed. They clinked glasses and drank.

NIGHTS GREW COOLER as September drew near. While the trees were still green, it wouldn't be long before their color would turn to gold, orange, even red, as if by magic. The new school year loomed ahead. Did Rusty manage to fix things with his son enough to please the school social worker? She had sent encouraging replies to his weekly emails. He'd be returning a different child to the fancy school and hoped they acknowledged Tommy's progress.

Happiness surged through him. Once they'd sealed their pact, their future, he relaxed. Shaking his head, he didn't understand what had scared him so much about marriage? The answer? He hadn't met Meg.

"How about one more day at the lake?" She buttered a piece of toast.

"Today?" Rusty took a forkful of eggs.

"Yes!" The boys chanted together.

"Works for me." Rusty glanced at the calendar on the wall. "This weekend is Labor Day weekend."

"Charlie and I have to get back on Labor Day. School starts two days after, and I have to be there early."

"We're leaving?" Tommy asked.

Rusty nodded. How could he let Meg go? Sure, they'd agreed to see each other in the city, but it wasn't much of a commitment. Not like if they were engaged. Could you propose to a girl you'd known for only two months? The idea scared the shit out of him. But once she got back to New York, she might meet another guy.

While Meg packed up towels and snacks for the lake, Rusty cleaned up the kitchen. Frowning, he explored his options. Never a man to lack self-confidence, with Meg he shook like a teenager with a crush. Unlike any other women he'd dated, Meg had an independent streak he admired and feared. If she doubted him, she'd walk away without a second thought. Right?

She'd never toss off an engagement so quick. But she wouldn't commit too fast either. He'd have to figure out how to approach it. Once he finished the dishes, there was a tug on his shirt.

"Come on, Dad. Get dressed. We're ready."

Rusty dried his hands, then changed into his swim trunks and headed for the car.

"Coffee at Java the Hut and lunch to go at Cozy?" He got behind the wheel.

"Sounds good." Meg kissed his cheek.

Rusty started the car and drove to the popular coffee house. Once they got to Cedar Lake, he carted the food and Meg took the beach bag with towels. The boys ran ahead.

"Our last day here." He sighed.

"Yeah. I know. So not ready to go back."

"You, too?"

She nodded.

"Same here." His gaze connected with hers. "I think I'm in love with you," popped out of his mouth before he could stop it."

"Really?"

His cheeks heated. He'd said it. No taking it back now.

"Yeah. I am. You're amazing."

"Me, too."

"You think you're amazing, too?" His eyes widened.

She slapped him lightly on the shoulder. "No, silly. I'm falling for you, too."

His heart leaped into his throat. "You are?"

"Yep."

Rusty dropped the bag and grabbed Meg. He pulled her into a bear hug and kissed her soundly. She wound her arms around his neck. Her softness melted against him, urging him to take their smooch to the next level. He exerted self-control and stepped back. Her eyes glittered, and her smile beamed with warmth.

"Then marry me."

Her mouth fell open. "What?"

Boy, his mouth was sure working overtime without consulting his brain, wasn't it?

"I said, marry me."

"Oh my God. This is so, so..."

"Sudden?"

"Yeah."

"We've been living like we're married for a couple of weeks now. I like it. Don't you?"

"I do."

"Ah, those are the words I wanted to hear."

She laughed.

"So? Will you?" His pulse jumped, and his breath caught for a second.

"You're right. We are. I like it, too, so, I guess my answer is, yes, I will marry you."

Bells, whistles, and cheering crowds war-whooped in his head! He couldn't believe it.

"You will? Really?"

"Yes. Didn't you want me to?"

"Oh, I do. I did. Baby. Honey. Meg. I do."

Rusty hugged her, twirling her around. The boys stopped to stare.

When he put her down, she faced them. "We're getting married!"

Charlie and Tommy did high fives and laughed, running to their parents for a group hug.

Rusty glanced at the sky.

"Clouds are rolling in. Let's swim before it rains. Last one in is a rotten egg." And he took off, to the sound of Meg's laughter behind him.

Chapter Sixteen

Meg sorted laundry in the mudroom.

"I think this is Tommy's shirt. And isn't the green one yours?"

Rusty cleared dishes off the table. "I hate this."

"What? Laundry? Everyone hates laundry. It's universal."

"Packing. This is yours, that's mine. Nothing is ours." He dried his hands on a dish towel.

"Someday things will be ours."

"Not soon enough for me."

"You're in a hurry to get married?" She faced him.

He eased his hands around her waist. "In a hurry to stake my claim."

"Your claim? What am I, a gold mine?"

"Perfect. You are. My gold mine."

She shoved him gently. "I don't belong to anyone, except Charlie."

"After you're married, you'll belong to me."

"And you'll belong to me, Mr. Player." She rested her hands on her hips.

"I will."

"You're okay with that?"

"It has to be a two-way street, doesn't it?"

"I think so. But I wasn't sure about you?"

"Yet you agreed to marry me?"

She lowered her gaze, hiding her feelings. "I know. Dumb, huh?"

He pulled her closer. "Not dumb. Smart as a fox. We belong together, Meg. Even our kids know it."

His words warmed her. "True." She raised her eyes to his, happy to see the glow of love shining there. Running her hands up his chest, she joined them around his neck.

"Are you starting something?" He cocked an eyebrow.

"Not with the boys up. What are they doing?" She pushed away.

Coco ambled in and sat at attention at her treat jar. Meg opened it and gave two to the dog.

"They're watching a movie."

Meg glanced outside. "Rain's getting heavier."

"According to the radio, a big storm is coming our way." Rusty joined her at the window. He draped his arm around her shoulders.

Her brows knitted as she watched the clouds darken and the rain pelt the deck.

"Doesn't look good."

"We're okay, right? We have food, batteries, and stuff in case the electricity goes out?"

"Let's check."

The adults scattered. Rusty examined the fire extinguisher and the flashlights. Meg opened the fridge and cabinets, making a mental inventory.

"We have food. Gas stove should work even if the lights go out."

"Candles?" Rusty raised his hand high before opening every drawer in the kitchen until he found a small supply. "Got 'em." He scooped up a handful.

Charlie and Tommy stopped in the kitchen doorway. "Movie's over."

"Let's make popcorn and watch one together. Did you bring any movies, Tommy?"

"We have Homeward Bound. Ever see it?"

"I haven't. Charlie?" Meg turned to her son. He shook his head.

"You get the popcorn, I'll get the movie," Rusty said.

Meg gathered a couple of blankets, too, as the storm brought a chill to the air.

The Rusty and Meg snuggled with their children as the wind whipped leaves and branches into the air and against the house. Rain drummed on the windows so hard, Meg thought it was hail. The boys fell asleep in front of the television. Rusty carried them to their beds, and Meg tucked them in.

"We still have some dry wood. A fire, milady?" He bowed.

"Oh, yes. It's getting really cold." She spread extra blankets over the boys.

When Rusty lit the wood, the lights went out. Meg jumped at the sudden darkness.

"Perfect timing." Rusty pushed to his feet. He tried the light switches in the room and the one for the light above the front door. "Darkness."

Meg held her palms to the fire. "It's cozy."

"You're not scared?" He joined her on the sofa.

"Nope. Just a storm." The leaves of a branch flying by the picture window brushed the glass. Rusty stood in the doorway.

"There's a lot of stuff flying around. The wind is brutal."

Meg joined him, slipping under his arm and snaking her arms around his waist. He hugged her.

"I love a good storm." Meg smiled.

"You do? Is there such a thing as a good storm?"

"If I don't have to go outside. And I'm safe and warm. I like to watch nature rage sometimes."

"You're funny. Most women would be afraid."

"Once you've been through what I've been through, not much scares you anymore." She sighed.

He nodded. "How about spiders?"

"Spiders? Terrified. Hate those things. Geez. Spiders are a completely different story." She shuddered, making him laugh.

He squeezed her shoulder and kissed her head. The overhang kept them fairly dry. But rain still gusted in their faces as the wind blew first in one direction, then another. Pine trees bent practically in half as Mother Nature had her way with them.

It struck Meg as fitting that their time in Pine Grove would end with such force, the elements tearing through the land and across the lake with a ferocity that forced plants and animals to bow in reverence.

"COME ON. THE BOYS ARE down. Let's fool around." Rusty took her hand and led her back to the sofa.

"Here?"

"In front of the fire."

She nodded, chuckling, as he threw the sofa cushions on the floor just a few feet from the flames. He ripped his sweatshirt over his head and lay down.

"Now, you." He watched her with hungry eyes.

Meg took her time. But as soon as she was down to her panties only, she shivered. The bluster of the storm had brought a taste of fall to the house. She grabbed the blanket and joined Rusty.

He eased her shoulder back on the pillows and pushed up. Hovering over her, he kissed her. Seeking the warmth of his body, Meg held on. She opened her legs and he rested between them. Closing her arms around his neck, she parted her lips. Their tongues danced. He explored her mouth as she flattened her hips to his. Meg wrapped her leg around his, digging her toes into the cushion.

Heat from the fire added to the warmth from his body. He raised a hand to her breast and tweaked the nipple. She arched her back. He sat back on his haunches, staring.

"You're beautiful when you're horny." He squeezed and stroked her breasts, bending his head to make contact with his tongue.

"Damn. When you do that." She made a soft, hissing sound.

"Yeah? Like it?"

"Love it."

She reached down, searching for his dick. He shifted and she found her target.

"Like steel. I'm gonna call you the Man of Steel." She brought her gaze to his.

He laughed. "You make it like that."

"Really?"

"Of course. Even the memory of you, naked, gets it started."

She smiled at him. Such an honest guy. Could he really have been the player the Internet claimed he'd been for years? She combed her fingers through his hair and kissed him.

"You'd better stop." He gently removed her hand.

"But I like it."

"Yeah, well so do I. But not if you want this to last."

She drew her lips down in a pouty expression. He glided his hands down her body, palms riding over the hills and valleys. When he got to the top of her thigh, he gripped her, closing his fingers around her flesh. With his thumbs, he invaded her core. He kissed his way down her abdomen and met his hands at her sex, where his eager tongue made contact. Her hips bucked as he wove his magic, ratcheting up the sexual tension inside her.

"Oh, God. Rusty."

A small chuckle escaped his throat.

"I'm gonna come."

"Go ahead." He kept at her, slipping two fingers inside while his tongue swirled over her.

Meg tried with everything in her to hold back, but she couldn't. The intensity climbed to the breaking point and crashed over the top. Her muscles clenched and her hips undulated on their own.

"Shit!"

"Shhh. Don't wake the boys."

"I tried."

"I wanted you to."

"But I wanted to with you inside me."

"We can do that, too. No rush."

She glanced out the window. The storm still raged, and the fire burned as she ran her hands up and down his chest. The feel his of skin and muscle and the soft coating of hair excited her all over again. Damn. She wanted him.

"I could do it to you, too, you know."

"Oh?" He arched an eyebrow. "An offer?"

She bolted upright and shoved him down. Meg straddled him and took him in her mouth.

"What are you doing?" He attempted to get up, but she pushed him back.

"Quiet. I know what I'm doing." She shot him a look, and he closed his mouth.

"If you're sure..."

"Shhh!" She slid off him and folded her legs beneath her. Taking her time, she got a firm grip and went to work. After swirling the tip with her tongue, she eased him all the way in her mouth. She smiled at his groan. Meg had him right where she wanted him, in her power.

She took her time, sliding up and down his shaft, increasing and de-creasing the suction as she saw fit. He lay still, except for the few sounds of pleasure emanating from his mouth. His eyes closed, he combed his fingers through her short hair as she worked on him. She sensed him tighten so she increased her pressure. He spoke.

"Don't. Stop. I'm gonna. I'm warning you. I'm gonna."

She wanted to take him to completion. Sure enough, within a minute, he came, filling her mouth with his seed. She swallowed, licked him off, and sat back on her haunches.

"I told you." He opened his eyes.

"I know. I wanted you to come."

"You're amazing. Where did you learn to do that? No!" he raised his palm. "Don't tell me."

"Let it forever be a mystery," she replied.

"To look at you, one would never suspect. A schoolteacher. Coulda fooled me." He shook his head.

"Suspect what?" She tilted her head.

"You knew so much about sex."

She laughed. "I was married for ten years."

He took her head in both his hands and drew her face to his for a kiss. "That was fantastic. I love you."

As tears blurred her vision, she smiled. "I love you, too."

What was she saying? How could she love anyone but John? A sense of betrayal rumbled in her belly. But he had been a practical man. John wouldn't want her living alone forever. He'd want her to be taken care of, and Charlie, too. She'd already agreed to marry Rusty and now she told him she loved him, which she'd known for ages but never admitted before. The words tripped off her tongue as if she'd been saying them every day.

He rested his palm on her cheek. "Say it again."

"I love you."

"Do you mean it? Really?"

"I don't say what I don't mean."

He sighed. "I'm the luckiest man in the world."

A loud boom interrupted their intimacy. Meg cringed. "What the hell was that?"

"Something fell on the roof. I'll take a look." He pulled on sweats and padded to the front stoop. After a few minutes, he returned.

"A big branch fell on the roof. I don't think it punctured it, though."

"Good. A flood in the house is the last thing we need."

Rusty undressed, took her hand, and pulled her close. "Doesn't look like the storm is winding down. Let's get some shut-eye."

He lay down and tucked her into his side. Rusty pulled up the covers as she rested her arm across his waist, and they drifted off.

MEG AWOKE FIRST. THE fire was out and the house had grown cold. Shivering, she wrapped a blanket around them, and they scurried into the bedroom.

She pulled on sweatpants and slipped on a sweatshirt. A strange howling sound drew her to the front door. Coco barked. Outside, the rain had subsided. A small river of water cascaded down the street, flooding everything in its path. Water had risen to the bottom step. She watched as the wind raged. Peering out to the left, the sky was almost black. Angry clouds swirled. She saw a small funnel.

"Tornado? Here?" Her eyebrows rose and her mouth hung open.

The darkness approached. Helpless, Meg stood and watched as it rose up and skimmed over the tops of houses. Debris flew in circles. The wind threw small branches and twigs against the house. Dirt pelted her, forcing her back. She closed the door and went to the window.

A larger branch came right at her, crashing in and breaking the glass. Meg jumped back in time to avoid being hit by flying shards. She looked up as the funnel cloud hit a giant tree with two main trunks.

She heard a loud crack, then a huge boom, shaking the entire house. Thrown to the ground, Meg pushed to her feet. The boys shrieked. Rusty cried out. Meg ran to the children's room where a branch stuck through one of their windows. Charlie and Tommy bounded out of bed.

"Dad!" Tommy raced to his father but came to a screeching halt at the door. Rusty, wrapped in his robe, had flattened himself against the wall.

Meg's hand flew to cover her open mouth. One of the trunks from the large tree next to the house had crashed through the roof. Some branches hung down over the bed.

"Are you all right?" she choked out.

"Yeah. Barely. What the Hell?"

"It was a tornado. I saw it."

"Jesus H. A tornado?" Rusty faced her, tightening his sash.

After a few moments, Meg got over the shock. "Boys! Back to your room. Pack up everything. We can't stay here."

"I'll call Fred."

"And the fire department," she added.

The boys ran off. Rusty grabbed her arm. "Are you okay?"

She hadn't realized she was trembling. "I think so."

He hugged her. "I've gotta get dressed. We need to get outta here before the whole house caves in."

Rusty dressed in two minutes and picked up his phone. Meg called the fire department. Within minutes, a siren drew near. Tommy and Charlie dressed themselves in record time and threw the rest of their belongings in their suitcases.

Rusty loaded their stuff in the car.

"Mom! What about the salamanders?"

"Time to release them back into the wild. Come on. While the fire department is looking things over, we'll go out back. It's not raining. Charlie, can you carry the tank?"

"I'll take it." Rusty joined them. "Cars are loaded." He turned to the firemen. "We'll be back in a few minutes."

They opened up the back door and headed for the woods. Meg held Coco on the leash.

"I remember where we found them." Charlie led the way. Tommy followed.

"Here!" Charlie pointed.

In the deluge of the last few days, the once gentle little stream had grown. It now flowed steady.

"Mom. Can they do okay? Look at the water."

"Put them down next to it. They can decide whether to get in or stay on land."

The boys nodded.

"Who wants to go first?"

Tommy raised his hand.

Not convinced the boys knew the salamanders apart, she respected their wishes. Rusty put the tank on the ground.

"Tommy, take Hardy out and put him down. Be gentle. Remember, salamanders are fragile."

Tommy followed instructions. The minute Hardy hit the dirt, he took off, waddling away as fast as his little legs could carry him.

"Be free, Hardy," Tommy said, brushing a tear from his cheek.

"Now you, Charlie. Take Frank."

"Not Frank. Rusty," Charlie corrected.

Meg glanced at Rusty. A lump formed in her throat and tears stung her eyes. "Okay. Frank. Rusty. Whatever. Gently now, Charlie."

The boy moved up and put the other salamander near the first one. "They're friends. They need to stick together."

Meg nodded. Words stuck in her throat. How could she ever doubt Rusty and what he meant to her and Charlie?

The boys said their farewells to their pets. Meg draped an arm around the shoulders of each boy and steered them in the direction of the house.

Rusty picked up the tank. "Are you taking this home?"

"Sure."

It had almost been time to head back to the city anyway. Maybe, instead of checking into a motel, they should simply go home? Meg's heart squeezed. She didn't want to leave. And definitely not early. There was nothing they could do. The fire department had already declared the house uninhabitable. She sighed.

"Don't want to leave?" Rusty glanced at her.

"You read my mind."

He took her hand. "Makes two of us."

"I think it makes four of us."

AS THEY APPROACHED the house, they could clearly see the tree lying across the roof. Rusty carried the tank back and put it in the trunk of her car.

"How did Fred take it?"

"Not well. He said he and Roberta have reconciled and want to keep the house. But they spent so much money on divorce lawyers, they don't have the bucks to repair it. So, they have to sell. Who's going to buy a house with a giant hole in the roof?"

"No insurance?"

Rusty shrugged. "Dunno. It's Fred's headache now."

They finished packing.

"One last lunch at Homer's?" Rusty closed his trunk.

"Sure."

"I want to ride with Tommy and Rusty."

"Go ahead, Charlie."

Alone during the short ride to the restaurant, Meg wondered what would happen now. Would they still be engaged? She had no ring, but she'd said yes. Would she be able to get over her guilt? She did have Charlie to consider. He needed a father and he adored Rusty.

Homer had a fire going. Rusty slipped him ten bucks for the table closest to the blaze. They ordered burgers. Even though it was cold out, the boys had brought bread and scooted outside to feed the ducks. While waiting for their food, Meg faced Rusty.

"Where do we go from here?"

"Back to the city, right?"

"No, you and me. What's next?"

"Dating. Ring shopping. Setting the date?"

"Really?"

"Why wait? We know what we have is good. It's solid. Let's get married." He shifted in his seat.

"You're hilarious. Biggest player in the world and now you want to rush into marriage?"

"If we agree it's the right thing, I don't get why we should wait." He picked up a roll from the basket on the table.

"Because two months is beyond whirlwind. It's crazy."

"But we've been living together. It's not like we started on a blind date. Well, actually we sort of did start that way, didn't we?"

"Back in the real world. How can we make it work?"

"We get married. You get rid of your place and move in with Tommy and me."

Meg's eyebrows shot up. "Me? Move?"

"Of course. I bet my place is bigger."

"Maybe."

"Oh?" He looked up.

"You thought I was a poor schoolteacher? John was a Wall Street wizard. We're okay."

"Great. But my place is a three-bedroom in a high rise. We're on the thirty-fifth floor with a view of the park."

"Nice."

"Come on, Meg. Take the plunge. Move in with me."

The boys joined them.

"Hey, Tommy. What do you think if Charlie and Meg moved in with us?"

"Awesome!" Tommy grinned.

"But what about my school? My friends?" Charlie's eyebrows knitted.

"Let's not jump the gun." Meg chewed her lip.

The food arrived. They ate in silence for a while. Charlie popped a French fry in his mouth, then faced his mother.

"I don't want to leave Pine Grove."

"What?"

"I don't want to leave Pine Grove."

"We can't stay, Charlie. The house is going to collapse." Meg wiped her mouth with her napkin.

"I don't care. Find another house. I want to stay!" He got louder.

After each response from his mother, the timbre of Charlie's voice rose. His eyes filled and he kept repeating, "But I want to stay."

Anger rose in Meg's chest. "We have another life. We have to go back."

"Why? I like it here. I want Rusty to be my dad. Tommy to be my brother."

Silence hung in the air.

"That's what we've planned, son." Rusty's voice softened. "But your mother's right. We have to go back. They're expecting her at school. And you, too. Tommy has to go back to his school, and I have to go back to my job."

"I don't want to," Charlie said, sobbing. Rusty hugged the boy. Tears wetted Meg's eyes. Out of reasons to go home, she kissed Charlie's head.

"It's just the way it is."

"She's right. We'll see you in the city. Soon, we'll be living together again." Rusty released the boy.

He wiped his face with a napkin. Rusty paid the bill and the four made their way to their cars in silence. Rusty opened her car door.

"I'll call you tonight, okay?" He hugged her.

She nodded. As she went to enter, he took her arm.

"Wait. Let's make one definite date. The World Series Ball. There's this gigantic party at the Waldorf every year after the Series. It's black tie. Will you go with me?"

"I'd love to. But, wait!"

He stopped.

"Only if you come to the Harvest Festival at my school."

"Wouldn't miss it. Text me the date. I'll give you the one for the Series bash."

She smiled. Two dates. No matter what happened, they had those two connections planned.

"Great."

"Love you," he said, kissing her.

"Love you more."

"Yuck!" Charlie and Tommy made noises. The two boys shook hands. Rusty hugged Charlie and Meg embraced Tommy.

"Will you be my mom?" he whispered.

"Of course."

He kissed her cheek and stepped back.

Meg shut her door and turned on the ignition. Charlie flattened his hand against the window. Fighting tears, she pulled out of the parking lot and headed for the highway.

She and Rusty were engaged, weren't they? Then why was leaving so hard? Why did a lump of emotion settle in her chest? Did it have to hurt so bad?

"Mom, Rusty said he'd get us Nighthawks tickets. Can we go to a game?"

"Sure." Meg sighed. Back to her empty home. She had to have hope they could keep the fire between them burning, didn't she? Hell, hope was her middle name.

Chapter Seventeen

Rusty strode with confidence into the social worker's office. They shook hands and he took a seat opposite her.

"Mr. Reisse, I see we have a good report on Tommy so far. Of course, it's only the first three weeks, but he's much improved." Sylvia Kaplan lowered her gaze to a folder on her desk.

Rusty smiled. "I took your advice."

"Says here, Tommy's expecting to get a new mother soon."

"Right. I'm engaged."

"Quick, wasn't it?"

"When you meet the right woman, why wait?"

"I suppose I should congratulate you, but it does seem hasty."

"Look, Mrs. Kaplan. I'm thirty-nine years old, not twenty-two. I'm no rookie. I know something about women. Meg Gunderson is perfect for both me and my son. I don't need you, or anyone else second-guessing my choice."

"I'm sorry. You're right, Mr. Reisse. Mazeltov. Congratulations. I hope you and Tommy will be very happy."

"We had a great time together this summer."

"Glad to hear it. I'm sure Tommy will have his best year ever at school."

"Thank you." Rusty rose. "I appreciate your concern for him."

"It's my job. Besides. Tommy's very charming." She smiled.

"Takes after his old man." Rusty grinned.

He left her office puffed up so much he practically strutted down the hall. Checking his phone, he noticed several messages. Two from the Nighthawks Director of Publicity, Nathan Rocking. And one from the studio engineer. Rusty frowned. The whirlwind he called his life had kicked into gear.

He needed to get his schedule set and call Meg. They'd have to fit dinners and family activities into his craziness. On the road for three days, home for two, back on the road for nine days, home for a week.

He'd never worried about it before. Now his traveling was about more than just childcare for Tommy when he was on the road. He had a family. Well, an almost-wife and an almost-second son to take into account. He took a deep breath. Never a planner, Rusty had to learn. Compartmentalizing his life had been his priority for years. Adding Meg and Charlie to the mix only complicated an already near-impossible schedule.

Rusty returned to his apartment. He packed his suitcase and called Meg.

"Dinner tonight? Let's go to Le Mignon."

"French? With the boys?"

"They'll love it."

"I was thinking more along the lines of Angelo's."

"Pizza?"

"Italian food. Better for the boys."

Rusty put the end of his pen in his mouth. "Okay. I'll make a reservation."

"Six?"

"So early?"

"The boys?"

"Okay. Six. Love you, babe."

"Love you back."

Rusty plopped down at his computer. After making the reservation, he moved to the sofa. Stretching out, he stared at the park. Leaves were just beginning to change. The Nighthawks first playoff games would start tomorrow, Saturday. Rusty's contract required him to broadcast all the playoff games. He prayed the Nighthawks would win quickly, so he could get his life back and enjoy the offseason. Maybe plan a wedding at Thanksgiving?

He finished packing and took a shower. He planned to ditch the team plane and fly out Saturday morning on his own instead of Friday night. He'd spend the night with Meg, instead of sweaty, nervous ballplayers. So he'd have to pay for his flight and leave early to be there on time. One night making love to Meg was worth every penny.

Dressing for dinner, he tied his tie, combed his hair and threw a few last-minute items in his suitcase. He leashed Coco, who was spending the weekend with Meg and Charlie, too, and headed for school to pick up Tommy.

"Remember, be polite. Do everything Meg asks you to do. Right?"

"Right." Tommy took the leash from his father.

"Go to bed on time. No fussing."

"Right."

"Play nice with Charlie."

"Right."

"Help walk Coco."

"Right."

They walked on in silence.

"When are you coming home?"

"Tuesday or Wednesday. As soon as I can."

"When the season is over, you won't go away anymore?"

"Right. Meg and I'll get married when the season's over. We'll begin our new life."

"I can't wait."

"Me, too. I miss Meg and Charlie."

"I'll be eating her pancakes while you're away."

"Don't rub it in."

Tommy grinned. No taxi would take a big dog like Coco, so the guys hoofed it to Meg and Charlie's place. It was a long walk, but they talked while they crossed to the West Side. Rusty could hardly wait to get on with the marriage.

THIS WOULD BE THE THIRD sleepover for Tommy. Meg had hired a mother's helper to take care of the dishes, help with food preparation, and walk the dog. Meg had work to do for school over the weekend preparing projects and there was Charlie's soccer game.

She crammed as much as possible into the weekend. Being too tired to miss Rusty helped. At night, she'd toss, rolling around in the empty bed. She longed to snuggle up to him. Going without mind-blowing sex drove her crazy. Where was the warm body she'd grown used to?

For months after John died, she couldn't sleep in their bed. Wrapped in a blanket, Meg had squished herself against the sofa back. She'd be so weary she'd drop off into a deep, dreamless sleep quickly, but wake up still exhausted. Once she got used to sharing her bed with Rusty, she slept like a rock.

Falling into the recliner by the window, Meg checked her weekend list. She'd written down the activities planned, meals, and necessary food and supplies. She checked it over again. She expected Debbie, the girl who lived next door, to arrive at nine on Saturday morning to walk Coco while Meg and the boys headed for Charlie's soccer game.

Meg pushed to her feet. Time to change for dinner. She took a brief shower then pulled on snug jeans, a white blouse, and orange blazer. While she applied makeup, the boys watched television. Meg didn't rush. Rusty came across many famous women in his broadcasting work. Glamorous women brushed elbows with him every day. Conscious of her looks, Meg added more eye makeup than usual, brushing and dusting to make it appear natural.

A knowing smile curled her lips. Rusty would spend the night. Damn, she needed him. She'd become addicted to his lovemaking.

Soon the season would be over. He'd mentioned getting married at Thanksgiving, but she wasn't sure. Would her life calm down, even for a few days, so she could think?

At five forty-five, Meg fed Coco and ushered the boys out the door. They strolled up Amsterdam Avenue to their favorite family restaurant. When they entered, Meg spied Rusty at the bar. She took a second to look over the handsome athlete, standing so straight and tall with a glass of beer in his hand.

His broad shoulders tugged a little at the fabric of his sports jacket. He wore a light blue button-down shirt—a perfect color to match his eyes. His hair lay neatly combed. He'd shifted his weight to one leg which made his hip jut out a bit. And his butt? Damn, it looked fine, perfectly outlined by the tailored khakis he wore. Easily the most handsome man she'd ever dated, she'd noticed his physical assets even during the early, angry weeks in the house. Though she hadn't admitted it to herself, she'd been deeply attracted to him from the moment she'd laid eyes on him. Fighting it had done no good. The minute he turned on the charm, she'd fallen. And when he punched Harold, she was a goner.

As if he could feel her stare, he turned and shot her a loving smile. His whole face lit up, warming her heart. How could she doubt their relationship?

"Howdy!" His gaze traveled her length, heating her body. What sexy Rusty could do with simply a look made her shiver.

Charlie ran to him, flinging himself against the man, who caught him in his arms for a hug. Then, he stepped over to her, embracing her.

"She yours?" One of the men at the bar who'd been standing next to Rusty looked her over.

"Yeah. Keep your jealous eyes off her."

The man chuckled. "Lucky dog."

"Mr. Reisse? Your table is ready."

Rusty took her hand and followed the maître d. Meg sighed. Damn it. Rusty was right. It sure felt like a family.

"LET'S GO SHOPPING TOGETHER," Roberta called Meg.

"For what?"

"Dresses for the Walldorf World Series bash, silly."

"You and Fred are going?"

"Of course. I need a new dress. It's black tie and I hate all my long dresses. Come on. Let's go shopping. Bring Charlie."

"Charlie? He'd hate it."

"But he'd come to be with you, right?"

"Actually, he's got a playdate with Tommy tomorrow after school."

"He goes there without you?"

"Uh huh. Charlie's made a lot of progress."

"Great! Then let's go, okay?"

"Okay. I don't have a long dress, either."

"Good. I'll meet you at school."

Meg waited in the school vestibule. Even the sun shine didn't warm the chilly late October day. She had a million questions about the little house in Pine Grove. If they'd repaired it, could Meg and Rusty rent it for Thanksgiving?

A blast of cold air startled Meg from her thoughts.

"You look good. Love agrees with you. Let's go."

"Where to?"

"Bloomies, girl. Let's start there. Then we can go to Bergdorf's if we don't find anything."

Roberta linked her arm with Meg's and the two women headed for the subway.

"Have you repaired the place in Pine Grove yet?" Hope burned in Meg's chest.

"The house? Oh, no. Too expensive. We unloaded it. Sold it to some schmuck. Fred said he's fixing it up and planning to live there himself."

Meg's heart sank. Disappointment dampened her spirits. Looked like there would be no repeating the happy days she'd spent there with Rusty. She sighed.

"You liked it, didn't you?"

Meg nodded. "It was perfect."

"Pretty funny the way I hooked you two up."

"Not at the time. I was ready to kill you."

"Fred yelled at me when he found out. He said we shouldn't do it. But I didn't listen. Knowing you two were there kind of rekindled things for us."

"Those first weeks were rough. You did it on purpose?"

"Yeah. My idea, but Fred takes credit."

"How'd you know?"

"We didn't. But took a chance. Hell, if it didn't work, one of you would leave and we'd refund your money."

"It was pretty crazy in the beginning."

"Maybe. But look where you are now. In love and happy."

Meg bounced back and forth between happiness and worry. When they were together, she didn't have a single doubt about their relationship. But nights when she was alone, Meg wondered if their love would last. What did she really know about Rusty? Could he commit and stay faithful to one woman?

She eyed her friend, who seemed oblivious to Meg's discomfort at being characterized as in love and happy. Sure, she was in love, but happiness? It only came to call on days when she was with Rusty.

Meg hadn't bought new clothes since John died, especially not a formal dress. Pumped by the reason for shopping, Roberta's enthusiasm surpassed her usual bouncy self. Meg examined dress after dress, unsure of what to select.

"You need to look sexy. There will be a lot of movie-star types there. You need to hold your own, Meg. No high necks and long sleeves. Let's find something strapless."

"I don't think so. I don't want to spend the evening yanking up my dress every five seconds."

"Okay, okay. Hmm. What color? Silver? Gold?"

"Midnight blue? Pink?"

"Pink is a little girl color."

"I love pink." Meg jutted out her chin.

"Okay, okay. Pick what you want."

Weighed down by dress after dress, slung over their arms, the women traipsed to the dressing room. When the smoke cleared, Roberta had purchased a bright red dress with short sleeves. Meg had decided on a pink sleeveless chiffon gown. While the neckline did reveal some cleavage, the garment wasn't daring. It fit right into her comfort zone, elegant and feminine.

"Shoes and bags are next," Roberta said, over lunch.

Meg returned at six thirty. Rusty arrived at seven with the boys.

"You look tired. Let's order pizza," he said.

She smiled. "Okay."

"Who wants meatball and who wants pepperoni?"

"Add green pepper, too. We need veggies." Meg sank into a chair and watched the guys get dinner planned and ordered.

When the food arrived, the boys set the table. Meg joined them and pulled a slice onto her plate. "Roberta and I got dresses for the World Series thingy."

"You mean the bash?"

"Yeah."

"Can I go?" Charlie raised hopeful eyes.

"It's a dance, Charlie. At night. With booze. No kids. I'm sorry." Rusty took a second slice.

"I'm sorry, guys. Once in a while, we have to do some grown-up stuff." Meg bit into a meatball.

"Can Tommy spend the night?"

"Yes. Debbie said she could stay with you guys. How's that?"

"Can we have pizza?" Tommy asked.

"Sure. Why not? You can have your own World Series celebration here." Meg ruffled Charlie's hair.

"I hate when you do that."

"I'm sorry. Guess you're too old now."

"Yeah."

Meg sighed. Her son seemed to grow up overnight.

Rusty wiggled his eyebrows at her and grinned. "Don't tell me what the dress looks like. I want to be surprised."

She put the last piece of crust in her mouth. "Saturday is the Harvest Festival at noon, and then the World Series party. You're coming to the Harvest Festival, right?"

"Absolutely."

"You're coming to the Harvest Festival?" Charlie's eyes widened.

"Wouldn't miss it."

Meg hoped Rusty would love it as much as she did. Gazing around the table at the noisy guys warmed her heart. They made fast work of two pizzas, leaving only one slice. Coco barked.

"I'll take her." Rusty pushed away from the table.

The dog licked Meg's hand. "If you clean up, I'll take her."

"Done!"

She leashed the dog and shrugged on a jacket. Life was good.

SATURDAY MORNING, MEG slept late, rising at nine o'clock. Panic set in. She threw down the covers and grabbed her robe.

"Wake up. We have to be there in an hour!" She headed for the bathroom.

Brushing her teeth with vigor, she replayed the hot scene from the night before. Rusty had been in rare form as he took her twice. Thinking about it jumpstarted her motor. No way did she have time for heavy breathing. She turned on the shower and stepped in. The hot water soothed a few aching muscles. Before she finished rinsing off, the door opened. Rusty entered, scratching his face, then his belly.

"Hurry up there, lady."

"Oh, go ahead. I'll turn my back."

"If you say so." He took a leak.

She turned off the water seconds before he flushed the toilet. "Good timing," she muttered, snatching a towel off the rack. "Your turn. But make it fast."

"Why don't you go on ahead with Charlie? I'll get Tommy up and ready and we'll join you as soon as we can."

"Really?"

"I don't want to make you late."

"You don't want me yelling at you."

"Exactly."

"Okay." She moved toward her son's room. "Charlie! Time to get up."

Charlie hid under the covers. "Do I have to?"

"Were you two up late playing games?"

A sheepish Charlie pulled the covers down to reveal his face. "Tommy was beating the game."

Meg huffed, hands on hips. "I told you not to do that, didn't I?"

He smiled weakly.

"It's Harvest Festival. We have to get there early, Charlie. Come on. Time to get up." Meg ripped the covers down on his bed.

"Me, too?" Tommy asked.

"You, too. Your dad's up already. Let's go, boys. It's going to be a great day. See? The sun is shining." Jerking open the top drawer in Charlie's dresser, she pulled out underwear. Then she hit the closet, yanking out jeans and a sweatshirt. "Here you go. Get dressed. Breakfast in five."

Running back to her room, she threw on underwear, a sweatsuit, and socks. Fresh from the shower, Rusty stood back and let her race around the room.

"You're amazing. It's like fast forward, watching you."

"I'm late. I'm throwing some eggs in a pan. Okay?"

"Let me make breakfast for Tommy and me."

"Nope. It'll take too long. I want you to be there. This festival is my biggest event all year. I'm the faculty chair."

"Okay, okay. I get how important this is for you. Don't worry, babe. It'll be fine." He kissed her cheek as it flew by. She was in the kitchen in a heartbeat. After turning on the stove, she whipped out a carton of eggs and a half gallon of juice. Reaching up into the cabinet, she grabbed four paper plates from her stash.

Within five minutes, eggs were frying. The guys joined her. Charlie's hair needed combing but, otherwise, he was dressed. Tommy, too. Rusty pulled his sweatshirt over his head as he entered. Meg's gaze lingered on his chest, so nicely outlined by his T-shirt. She'd never get tired of looking at his body.

"Eat up. We can be there by nine forty-five."

Walking so fast she was almost running, Meg got to the schoolyard before the guys. Of course, Harold was there. They needed a member of administration at every major event. His frosty nod would be his only greeting. *Damn. That asshole Harold is here. Forget him and do what you have to do.* She joined Mary Partlin, a single mom and president of the PTA, in the middle of the yard.

"Sorry I'm late, Mary. What do you need me to do?"

"No problem. Here's a list. Okay?"

"Great."

"Oh my God. Who's the gorgeous guy?"

"Where?" Meg looked around but only saw children, Harold, and Rusty.

"Him." Mary pointed right at Rusty.

"Oh. He's with me. Rusty Reisse."

"*The* Rusty Reisse?"

Meg nodded. "I'll find something for him to do."

"I've got something for him to do but not here," Mary snickered.

"Down girl. He belongs to me."

"Really? I thought you and Harold were a couple."

Meg shook her head. "That's history."

"Hell, if I had to choose between Rusty Reisse and Harold, it would a slam dunk for me. You go, girl" Mary smiled.

"Charlie, Tommy, Rusty! Over here." When they gathered in the center of the yard, Meg handed out work assignments. Charlie took Tommy over to the game booth section.

"A haunted house? Me?" Rusty pointed to himself.

"They always need help setting up."

"Whatever you say, babe."

She gave him a brief kiss and strode over to the grills.

Chapter Eighteen

Rusty scratched his head. Why did women think every man was mechanical? Rusty knew zip about building stuff. He was lucky to know one end of a hammer from the other.

"Hey, you!"

Rusty turned.

"Yeah. You. Buddy. I need a hand over here, setting up the haunted house. Got a minute?"

"Sure."

"I'm Ralph," the man said, extending his hand.

"Rusty." They shook, then headed to the section earmarked for the haunted house.

"We build it in the stairwell every year. Easiest place. Come on. We need tall guys."

Rusty followed, pretending not to be miffed Ralph didn't recognize him. Ralph shoved some supplies at him. "You know how to do this, right?"

"Wrong. I've never done this before."

"Are you a father in this school?"

"No. My fiancée is a teacher."

"Oh. No kids?"

"I have a son."

"Then you should be doing this stuff. At his school or this one. Figure it out. You look pretty smart." Ralph walked away.

Rusty juggled the wood and looked at the staircase. The wood had things painted on it. Ghoulish faces, witches on broomsticks. He had no clue where to put what or how. He grabbed another man walking by.

"Hey, buddy. What do I do with this?"

"I'll show you."

With the man's help, he got the pieces in place and quickly left the area. Looking for Meg, he was flagged down by a little girl.

"Look, mister. I can tie my shoe."

The kid must have been five. "Sorry, little girl. But I have to find someone."

"Look!" she yelled.

Rusty froze. People stopped and stared at him. He shrugged and held up his palms. "Okay, okay. I'm watching." He stood, shifting his weight from foot to foot, while she accomplished the task at a snail's pace.

"Very good. Very good." He turned away.

Meg joined him. "What's going on?"

"Nothing. What do you want me to do next?" He gritted his teeth to keep his tone civil.

"Boxes. Can you help unload boxes of books? We got a surprise donation from a publisher."

"Sure. Where?"

"There." Meg pointed to a van parked at the curb. Rusty nodded and headed over and received more instructions. Checking his watch, he noticed it was eleven. Some of the booths had opened up. People were arranging second-hand books on tables and families were arriving. Rusty toted box after box of heavy books to tables set up near the street.

He smelled something burning. Looking up, he saw smoke rising from the grill area. Great, burnt hamburgers for lunch. The sun grew hot for October. He mopped sweat from his forehead and neck. A parent volunteer directed where each box should go. No one recognized him. No one asked him for his autograph. He'd become invisible, a new experience for former major league hot-shot, Rusty Reisse.

When he finished, he plopped down on a bench. Tommy and Charlie raced over.

"Dad, can I do the games?"

"Sure."

"Money?"

"And food. Hot dogs and brownies," Charlie said.

Rusty peeled off two twenty-dollar bills and gave one to each boy. "Here you go. For games and food. Make it last."

"Wow! Thanks, Dad."

"Thanks, Rusty."

In a flash the boys took off toward the smoky area. Rusty shook his head. Which would be better? A burnt hamburger or an overcooked hot dog? He grimaced.

"You're off duty for a while. Do you want to check out the booths?" Meg joined him.

"What's that?" He pointed to what looked like a bench over a large tank of water.

"It's the dunking booth."

"Really?" Rusty raised his eyebrows.

"Yes. Like to volunteer to take a seat there?"

"No way!"

"Oh my God." Meg covered her mouth with her hand.

"What?"

"Look." She pointed. "Harold is getting on the dunking booth thingy."

A slow grin spread across Rusty's face. "Well, well."

"Oh no. You can't. You're a professional."

"I don't see where it says professionals can't have a crack at the asshole."

"Don't Rusty. Please."

"Aw. Come on. I've done everything you wanted. This one is for me." He rose and strolled over to the booth. Meg followed. At first, Harold didn't recognize him.

"Oh, no. No pro ball players allowed."

"I don't see any signs. That's discrimination. You don't want to teach discrimination to the kids, Harold, do you?"

"No. No. I'm outta here."

Rusty dropped a ten on the desk in front of the child running the booth.

"Wow, mister. You get ten balls for ten bucks." The boy put the money in a cigar box.

"I'm not gonna need ten."

The boy handed Rusty three tennis balls.

"No, you can't!" Harold held his hand over his face.

"Oh, yes I can." Rusty fingered the ball until he got comfortable. He drew a bead on the circle he had to hit to release the mechanism holding the bench above the water. Bringing back his arm, he rifled the ball at the target. Boom! Direct hit on the first ball. It made a loud sound and—*splash*—Harold hit the water. Rusty grinned.

"You're a good shot, mister. Do you want change?" The boy at the desk offered seven bills to Rusty.

"Keep it, kid. It's for a good cause."

Harold sputtered and flapped his arms like wings. A woman helped him out of the tank.

"Be good, Harold, or I'll do it again."

MEG DIRECTED THE BOYS to the line for hot dogs and hamburgers. Smoke billowed off the grill as school fathers sweated and cooked. Rusty joined her.

"Do I have to eat one of those?"

"One of what?"

"A burned hamburger?"

"Don't be a baby. It's for a good cause." She patted his cheek.

"I know, but geez. A man's got his limitations."

"I know how you are about food, but suck it up, dear. Why don't you join the boys? I'm sure they'll let you cut in line."

Rusty grimaced and loped off to meet up with Tommy and Charlie.

Meg bit her lip. Although she'd been busy directing people and making sure the festival ran smoothly, she'd managed to keep an eye on her beloved. Things had not gone well for him. He worked, toted, helped, carted, and sweated his way through the morning, frowning. She'd hoped he'd get in the spirit of things, get in touch with his inner kid and find something fun. Or at least enjoy helping the parents.

She did chuckle watching him dunk Harold. But that didn't erase the nagging feat her man did not have a good time. She sighed. Maybe you had to be part of the school or know more people there to have fun. Surprised no one recognized him, she was equally impressed he didn't run around telling everyone. If he'd been bragging about who he was, it would have embarrassed the hell out of her. Thankful the man had showed humility, she could see the Harvest Festival wasn't in his wheel-house.

Silently she thanked him for putting up with it and pitching in. Rusty and the boys sat at one of the long tables and chowed down. Yep, it could be damn hard to swallow one of those overcooked burgers, un-less you had a giant bottle of water or iced tea. She guessed he did it out of love for her. She sighed. He was a good man, even if he didn't get the whole Harvest Festival thing.

At three, the event slowed down. By four, booths were packing up. Rusty approached her.

"I'm gonna go. Do you want me to drop the boys home?"

"I'll take them. What time do I have to be ready for tonight?"

"I'll pick you up at seven forty-five, okay?"

"Pick me up?"

"I've got to go home and change. Grab a snack because there's a cocktail hour before the dinner."

"Okay. Thanks for doing this."

"It's a real handful to manage."

"Yeah. I know it's not your thing. I appreciate you doing it anyway."

"It wasn't happening for me. I'm sorry."

"I get it."

"See you tonight." He bent to kiss her quickly before heading for the exit. She saw Harold with a towel wrapped around his head. He shouted some words after Rusty, who ignored him. She laughed. What a doofus. How could she ever have dated him?

"Can we play two more games each before we go?" Charlie asked.

"Sure." Meg pulled out two five-dollar-bills and handed them to the boys. "Then we have to go."

"Okay." Tommy smiled. "Come on. Let's do the milk carton game."

The boys ran off. Meg made the rounds, helping the PTA president gather and count the money. A new crew arrived to help clean up the yard and pack away booths for next year. A van showed up to cart off the leftover books.

Meg and the boys returned home by five. Debbie rang the doorbell fifteen minutes later. Charlie and Tommy were melted on the sofa, watching a movie. Meg handed Coco's leash to Debbie, then stretched out on her bed for a nap.

Excitement filled her veins. She'd be going to a major party tonight. The media would be there, interviewing people. She expected to brush shoulders with a ton of celebrities. Although she closed her eyes, she couldn't stop smiling. Like a schoolgirl, giddiness at her invitation to such a magnificent event sent a tingle up her spine.

She and Roberta had giggled about it, teasing each other over which celebrity they would most like to meet. Of course, there would be ballplayers there, too. Unfortunately, Frank Todd was too small potatoes to be invited. But Rusty had given her a rundown on his favorite players who would be there. He'd planned to introduce her to everyone. Meg could hardly wait.

After an exhausting day, she slipped off to sleep, dreaming about her Cinderella moment at the ball yet to come.

"MRS. GUNDERSON, MRS. Gunderson."

A voice came out of the haze of deep sleep. Meg cracked an eye. Debbie stood at her bed and gave her a shake. "It's time to get dressed, Mrs. Gunderson."

Meg yawned and checked the clock. Damn! It was six thirty! She swept the covers down and swung her legs over the side.

"Can I help?"

"I can do it. Shower first."

"Okay. But if you change your mind, I'll be in the kitchen heating up the boys' dinner."

Meg nodded. She turned on the spray. The hot water soothed her. A smile spread across her face. How her mother would laugh if she could see her thirty-four-year-old daughter giddy as a teen getting ready for the prom.

She scrubbed all over, preparing for a steamy night with Rusty after the festivities. After she dried off, she opened the closet door and gazed at the dress. How much makeup? What color eyeshadow? Sudden insecurity gripped her. Meg had not dressed up since John died. Not with full makeup and sexy lingerie.

She pulled out a lacy bra-and-panty set she'd bought to tease John with but never got to wear. The push-up bra increased her cleavage. She pranced in front of the mirror for a moment before sitting down at her dressing table. She'd swear cobwebs covered the surface. Plucking a tissue from a box, she dusted off the tubes, vials, bottles, and sticks.

She heard a knock on the door followed by "It's me, Debbie."

"Come in."

"Do you need help?"

"What do you think?" Blinking her eyes rapidly, Meg turned to face the young woman.

"Seriously?"

"No, yes. Okay. I'll be still." She stopped.

"Pretty good. What do you have here?" Debbie stepped closer. She glanced over the paltry array of sticks, cremes, and powders.

"Let's take a little bit of this."

Meg sat quietly, letting Debbie tweak her makeup. When she looked in the mirror, her eyes widened. "Wow. You sure know what you're doing."

"Let's see your dress."

She slipped the pink confection over her head. Debbie zipped her up. Meg stepped into satin slippers and twirled once. "So? What do you think?"

"I think Cinderella had better move over."

"That good?"

"That good."

The boys burst through the partially open door, then screeched to a halt.

"Wow! Mom. You look beautiful." Charlie's eyes got as big as saucers.

"What he said," Tommy stammered.

"Thank you, boys." Meg fastened a pearl necklace around her neck, then put on the matching earrings. As she spritzed herself with lilac perfume, the doorbell rang.

She checked her watch. "Can't be Rusty. He's not due for half an hour."

"I'll get it," Charlie said, flying out the door with Tommy right behind him.

"You look gorgeous, Mrs. Gunderson." Debbie clasped her hands over her heart. "Like a fairy princess."

"Like a girl going to the prom?"

Debbie nodded.

"Your date is here," came a deep voice. Rusty entered the bedroom. Meg's mouth fell open.

Dressed in a perfectly fitted tuxedo, Rusty looked like a handsome prince.

"Look at you." Meg's voice faded. The boys crowded the doorway. Debbie moved back.

"Something wrong?" He checked front, back, his zipper.

"Everything's perfect. You look...amazing."

"Me? You're the queen here. You'll be the prettiest girl in the whole place."

"Thank you."

"But there's one thing missing?"

"Missing? What?" Her eyebrows knitted.

"This." Rusty dropped to one knee and reached into his pants pocket.

Meg covered her face with her hands. "Oh, no. You didn't."

"Of course, I did. Can't tell everyone we're engaged without this."

He opened the black velvet box to reveal a three-carat emerald-cut diamond ring.

"Meg, will you marry me?"

"You already asked her, Dad."

"And I'm asking her again."

She dropped her hands. Her eyes filled. "You're such a...such a..."

"A romantic? Yep. Guilty. So? Will you?"

"Yes." She nodded.

He pushed to his feet and slipped the ring on her finger.

"Now we're official."

A tear escaped down her cheek. Rusty brushed it off, then kissed her.

"Yuck!" Charlie made a face.

"Come on, boys, I think there's an Abbott and Costello movie on. Let's go."

Debbie shooed the boys out of the room. "It's the most beautiful ring I've ever seen." She smiled at the couple and closed the door behind her.

"Rusty, it's too much. Too big." Meg spread her fingers and stared at her hand.

"It's smaller than I wanted to get, but I knew you wouldn't like anything bigger. What do you think?"

"I think it's the most beautiful ring in the entire world." She threw her arms around his neck and kissed him hard.

"You keep doing that and we'll never make it out of this room," he whispered, hugging her tight. "Are you ready?"

"Just have to get my bag."

When he released her, she scurried around, shoveling makeup, comb, mirror, and tissues into a small, beaded bag. She ran a brush through her hair, replenished her lipstick and faced him. "Ready."

"You're gorgeous."

"I feel like I'm going to the prom."

"Wait until the press gets a load of you. Wow." Rusty shook his head and chuckled.

"Let's go, my prince. I'm starving."

They kissed the boys goodnight. Meg scooped up a stole and left the apartment.

A limo waited outside for them. The chauffeur opened the door and Meg got in. Every nerve in her body tingled. She'd never been to anything like this.

"You're gonna love it. My old buddy Cal Crawley is gonna be there. I was a rookie his last year playing. He mentored me. And Nelson Hingus. Team owner. He's a great guy. You're gonna love them. And they're gonna flip over you."

"I'm not the first woman you've taken to this thing, right?"

Rusty shifted in his seat and looked away. "Of course not. But you're different."

"You mean I'm not a model or a movie star?"

"You're real. And I love you. Big difference."

She smiled and sat back in the luxurious leather seat. She had this. No worries.

Chapter Nineteen

Their limo pulled up behind five others. They waited as each couple alit and posed for television. Meg spied a man with a mike standing next to blinding lights and cameras. She caught a glimpse of each woman as they stepped out of their vehicle and into the spotlight. The dresses, wow, the dresses! Most were so revealing they'd be censored on broadcast TV.

"Boobs are hanging out everywhere," she mumbled.

"What about boobs?" Rusty faced her.

"The women. The dresses."

"Oh, that? Just movie stars showing off. Pretending theirs are real."

Meg smacked him lightly on the arm. He laughed. "I'm glad you're not showing so much skin. They need to advertise. You don't."

Meg swallowed. Suddenly she'd gone from Cinderella to Little Red Riding Hood. Then they were next. The doorman at the hotel opened their door and Rusty got out. He extended his hand to her.

"Rusty! It's Rusty Reisse, folks! Rusty Reisse, home-run king of the New York Nighthawks! Hey, Rusty!" came a strange, male voice.

Clutching his hand, Meg managed to get out of the limo without falling. But you couldn't exactly call her exit graceful. Blinding lights shined in her eyes. She held up her hand to shield them.

"Put your hand down, Meg. Let the people see you," Rusty whispered.

"And who's this pretty little lady?" the voice asked.

Meg couldn't even see the man as he stood backlit in the shadows. Rusty straightened to his full height, his voice easy and confident. "This is my fiancée, Meg Gunderson."

"Fiancée? You're taking the plunge?"

"Yep." Rusty beamed right at the camera. Meg hugged his side.

"Retired from baseball, you're retiring as a player with the ladies, too? Awesome."

When the mike was thrust into her face, Meg fastened a death grip on Rusty's hand.

"And what do you do, Meg? Act? Sing? Model?"

"I'm an elementary school teacher."

"Okay. Great. Teachers are important." The man whipped the mike away from her as fast as he'd shoved it in her face. "Say, Rusty, what are you up to these days?"

"I'm still broadcasting, Bart. And lovin' it."

"When's the wedding?"

"Could be any day now."

"Oh, wait. Look who's here? It's Mariana Capelli. This Italian movie queen is some bombshell. And who's she with? Why it's Scuddy Figueroa, star pitcher for the Boston Bluejays!"

The man gave Meg a little push toward the door. She and Rusty headed inside. Her heart beat so fast and loud she was sure he could hear it.

"Glad it's over?"

She nodded. He patted her cheek. "You were fine."

"I didn't do anything."

"At least he wasn't staring down your dress. Bart likes to do that. See whatever he can, while he has the chance."

"Gross."

"Yeah. He's a nasty guy with an evil mind."

"But you were so nice to him? Like you were old friends?"

"Politics. Showmanship. Whatever you want to call it. I'm a public figure. I can't afford to make enemies."

It was as if Meg had gotten on the biggest roller coaster in the country and she'd barely weathered the first steep drop. Would this be the toughest ride of her life?

"Let's get some food. You'll need it to handle the wolves coming our way." Still holding her hand, he led them to the ballroom. "If you'd loosen your grip a little, I could feel my fingers again."

"Oh! I'm sorry." She let go.

"Don't let go. I don't want some Casanova stealing you away. Buffet's over here. And the bar. Damn. I need a drink."

"Me, too." A drink? *How about let's start with three and work our way up?* Meg looked around. All the women were models or movie stars. Their dresses were practically topless, or see-through, or slit up to the waist and no panties peeking out. *Am I overdressed?* When she looked down at the demure dress, it seemed dowdy in comparison. So many were shiny, silvery and gold, glittery. Her simply pastel chiffon paled next to the gaudy, "look-at-me" outfits the women wore.

"Well, well, well. You brought the little wren." A female voice behind her startled Meg.

"Maria," Rusty said, slipping his arm around Meg's shoulders.

"I'd rather be a wren than a noisy, obnoxious, delusional parrot who doesn't know when to shut up," Meg blurted out.

Maria stepped back. "So she can talk."

Meg fiddled with her hair, flashing her ring.

"A diamond? Oh no. Please tell me you're not engaged. Rusty, come on. You can do so much better." Venom dripped from her tongue.

"Maria, I think you'd better take off before Meg flattens you. Not that I wouldn't like to do it myself, but a gentleman never hits a lady. No matter how unladylike her behavior. Meg is a thousand times the woman you'll ever be. So just go away, okay?" He made a shooing motion with his hand.

"You'll regret this."

"Marrying Meg? Never."

"Talking to me like that."

"The only thing I regret is that I didn't do it sooner."

"You moronic pig."

A tall man wearing a tux grabbed Maria's arm. "Stop it. Time to go, Maria."

Rusty ushered Meg to the food line. Her stomach tied in knots, her appetite went south.

"I don't think I can eat."

"Don't let her get to you. She's just jealous. As well she should be. She can't hold a candle to you."

Meg squeezed his hand.

Strangers to Meg greeted Rusty with a handshake or a brief hug. He introduced her. The men she met glanced quickly over her conservative dress. Some stared at her cleavage for a nanosecond. Why try to imagine what was concealed when there were so many breasts brazenly on display? For those, they didn't need to watch their manners, only keep their libidos under control.

They gave Meg a polite nod. Some bothered to ask if she was an actress. When she corrected them, their eyes glazed over, and they moved on.

The women were worse. Meg figured most of them were old girlfriends of Rusty's. Gorgeous, made up to perfection, confident, smiling, they sashayed over, kissed and hugged him. He introduced her, but the women either ignored it or nodded once and went back to talking to Rusty. They sat at a table with eight other people, none of whom talked to her. Her throat constricted. She ate what little she could stuff down. So, this is what it felt like to be invisible?

Rusty shook hands, kissed women, laughed, joked, and carried on with all who came his way. Meg watched fascinated and repulsed. This was Rusty's world. He had a reputation, he mattered. He was a star and still in the public eye as a broadcaster. Meg was nobody. Although he kept her close, she drew further and further away, emotionally, as the evening wore on.

Who was this man who thought these people worthy of his attention? Did she even know him? There seemed to be little resemblance to the man she'd grown to love in Pine Grove. Sure, he'd been arrogant at first, until she stood up to him.

Roberta and Fred came over to the table. She jabbered on about the dresses and "Did you see so-and-so? And doesn't so-and-so look like she's had plastic surgery? So-and-so is drunk." Never a gossip, Meg stared at her friend. Roberta belonged there, too.

Rusty finished his food. Meg simply picked. She ate a couple of cold shrimp, then pushed her plate away.

"Dessert? Did you see the dessert table? The boys would go nuts." Rusty rose and offered his hand.

"I don't think I can eat anything."

"You don't have to take anything, come with me. I don't want to leave you here to become shark bait."

Her gaze connected with his. He got it. He could see what was happening. She sighed in relief. Thank God she didn't have to explain it to him later. She'd pictured an ugly argument of her trying to make her point and him denying everything. She got up and accompanied him to the dessert table. He'd been correct. The table dazzled with the most divine, decadent desserts, from gooey chocolate lava cakes to tiramisu to elegant raspberry cheesecakes to plates of brightly colored macarons—everything to tempt the sweet tooth.

Rusty took three items, grabbed two forks and steered them back to the table. An older gentleman wandered over. Rusty rose from his chair.

"Mr. Hingus. How nice to see you." They clasped hands.

"And who's this pretty young thing?"

"This is my fiancée, Meg Gunderson. Meg, Nelson Hingus, owner of the New York Nighthawks."

Nelson took Meg's small hand in both of his. "Mighty nice to meet you, little lady. So you've bagged this guy, huh? He's a lucky man. I wish you both much happiness."

"Thank you, sir."

"You gonna say a few words tonight?" Nelson asked.

"I thought so. Maybe just two minutes of introduction."

"Good. I always enjoy his speeches, Miss Gunderson, even if they are a little off-color sometimes. Keep it clean, Rusty. By the way, I approved your new contract."

"Thank you, sir."

"Nice to meet you." Nelson released her hand.

Meg found her tongue. "Thank you. Same here."

Nelson Hingus wandered off.

"You didn't tell me you'd be speaking."

"Didn't I? I always do a few minutes of silly intro. It's nothing."

But it didn't seem like nothing to Meg. No wonder everyone bowed at Rusty's feet. He was still a player in the world of pro baseball and professional glamour.

The lights dimmed. The man who had been interviewing outside went up to the mike and introduced Rusty.

"Wish me luck," he said, standing up.

"Break a leg," she replied, trying to smile.

Meg took two forkfuls of Rusty's cheesecake—a big mistake. The rich food did not sit well on her tense stomach. She managed to sit through Rusty's funny introduction of Nelson Hingus, who would present awards. Rusty returned to the table with the spotlight following him.

"I'll be right back." Meg pushed to her feet. Her stomach churned as she headed to the ladies' room. Fortunately, it was empty. She knelt over the bowl and emptied the contents of her stomach. When she was done, she rested her head on the porcelain. Weak and upset, she lingered for a few moments longer at the fancy sink, before splashing water on her face. An older woman stood next to her, replenishing her lipstick.

"Pregnant?"

Meg stared at her. Such a rude and impudent question.

"At least you got the ring, honey. Nice rock. Guy must have bucks."

"If it's any business of yours, I'm not pregnant."

"Oh. bulimic. I get it. Your secret's safe with me." The woman exited the restroom before Meg could think of an answer.

"People like you make me sick," Meg muttered to herself. She rinsed her mouth out, popped a mint and reapplied her lipstick. Returning to her table, she tapped Rusty's shoulder.

"I'm not feeling well. I'm going home."

"Really? I'm sorry. We'll leave."

She rested her hand on his arm. "You stay. It's your night. We haven't even run into your manager yet. I don't want to ruin the party."

"I can't let you leave alone."

"I'm a big girl. I'll be fine."

"Are you sure? How sick are you? Do you need an ambulance?"

"All I need is my bathrobe and a cup of tea. Really. It's okay."

"I might be home late."

"Fine. I'll be asleep."

"I'll try not to disturb you."

"Shhh!" came at them from a nearby table.

Rusty kissed her. As Meg stood at the coat check, Nelson Hingus approached.

"Are you all right? You look a little pale."

"Have you finished giving out awards?"

"They only save one or two for the old man here. I'm done. Are you leaving?"

"Yes. I don't feel well."

"How you getting home?"

"Rusty offered but it's his night. I'll catch a cab."

"Nonsense. Come with me, little lady." Mr. Hingus took her arm and escorted her out to the front. He spoke to the doorman. "My limo, Jerry."

A minute later the biggest limousine she'd ever seen pulled up. As the driver got out, Nelson Hingus spoke.

"Harry, take this little lady home. Then come back."

"No, really, this isn't necessary." Meg protested.

"How could I let Rusty's sick future wife find her own way home when I have a car here that's idle? Please, allow me."

Harry held the door open. Meg kissed Nelson on the cheek, then got in the back of the luxurious vehicle. The man closed the door and got behind the wheel.

On the ride home, Meg twisted the ring on her finger and stared out the window. Tears streamed down her face.

RUSTY OPENED THE DOOR to Meg's apartment as quietly as he could. An hour after she left, he'd cut out. Without her at his side, the event lost its appeal. He undid his tie and unbuttoned the top buttons of his fancy shirt.

"Stupid penguin suit," he muttered, shedding the jacket and draping it across a chair. Piece by piece, he got undressed down to his boxers. His mind replayed the evening. He'd witnessed each slight directed at Meg. He kicked himself for not expecting it. He thought she looked fantastic, dazzling, so elegant and sophisticated, not cheap and gaudy like the other women.

Why had he thought bringing her was a good idea? Why hadn't he thought ahead? He'd expected his old acquaintances to be nice to Meg, to be happy for him. Instead, their disapproval was palpable. So the rest of the entertainment world expected him to marry some vapid, glamorous airhead? Not Rusty Reisse. He wasn't that stupid. He knew class when he saw it and Meg Gunderson dripped class from every snake-loving pore.

Sure he'd slept with those women. Who wouldn't take what was offered? But that's as far as it went. After Angela, he'd never bring a woman into his house who couldn't be a good mother to Tommy. He didn't want only a bed partner, he wanted—no, needed—so much more.

It had been a rough night for her. Could she take it? Would she put up with the downside of his life? She'd looked stricken when she left. He also kicked himself for not going with her. Damn, couldn't he see she was hurting? Was he that callous and selfish a bastard he'd let her find her way home alone?

Once he'd finished disrobing, he headed to the kitchen for a glass of water. Dehydrated from all the alcohol he'd drunk, his mouth was as dry as a January wind.

"What took you so long?" a feminine voice startled him.

"You're up?"

"Yep." Meg sat at the kitchen table, wrapped in a robe, drinking tea. Her eyes were puffy and her nose slightly red. Obviously she'd been crying. Rusty swallowed. He had a feeling this wasn't going to go well.

"I'm sorry. I should have taken you home."

"I meant from coming in the door to here."

"Oh. I decided to undress in the living room so I wouldn't wake you."

"Very considerate."

"I try." He padded to the cabinet, took down a glass and filled it with water. Then he joined her at the table. "Are we good?"

He looked down. Holy shit! She wasn't wearing his ring.

"Where's your ring?" He took a gulp of water. Silently he prayed it had gotten lost.

"Here." She pulled the little black box out of her pocket and set it on the table.

"Why aren't you wearing it?" His heart sank, but he grasped at a last hope.

She cast her gaze down at her hands, her fingers played with the box. "I thought you'd have figured it out."

"I know tonight wasn't exactly ideal—"

"Ideal? It was a damn disaster!"

"I wouldn't exactly call it—"

"But I would. That's your world. You're used to it. I'm not. And I don't want any part of it."

"So you don't have to go to events with me anymore, if you don't want to."

"Meg pushed to her feet. You weren't any happier at the Harvest Festival, were you?"

"Well, that kind of thing, with tons of kids running around, and stuff."

"Admit it. It's okay. I saw how uncomfortable you were."

"It wasn't my fault."

She placed a hand on his arm. "I'm not saying it was. I realized that mine isn't your world, just as yours isn't mine."

"What are you saying?" He stood.

"I'm saying, we don't belong together. Not here. Not like this."

"Are you breaking our engagement? Are you saying you don't want to marry me?"

She shook her head. "It wouldn't work."

His mind still clouded with a bit of alcohol, Rusty could swear he'd heard her say she didn't want to marry him. He must be dreaming. "You don't want to marry me?" He repeated his thoughts out loud.

"I love you. I do. But our worlds clash. We'd either be fighting all the time, trying to get each other to accept what we don't want to accept. Or we'd be doing everything alone, slowly drifting apart. Then you'd cheat, maybe. Or I'd find someone more my speed. And it would be over. With a shit-ton of pain, accusations, anger, and soul-crushing heartache."

"You paint a bleak picture. How do you know all that?"

"It became crystal clear tonight."

He fell back onto the chair, the wind knocked out of him.

MEG'S HEARTBEAT QUICKENED. She hadn't meant to break up, but the more she sat at the kitchen table the more inevitable it seemed. Was there any way they could live together, orbiting in two different worlds? Not and stay together. And the end would be ugly, she guessed.

Unable to sleep, she'd made a cup of tea to settle her stomach and waited for him to return. Pain seared through her. She'd put the pieces together on the ride home. Although she'd kidded herself that afternoon, she came clean and admitted Rusty'd had a lousy time at the Harvest Festival. He'd stuck out like a sore thumb. Although she loved him for trying and refusing to admit how much he'd hated being there, she had to be honest with herself. It hadn't worked for him, like his glitzy world hadn't worked for her.

She'd heard him come through the door. Perspiration started. The thumping of her heart in her ears, the sweat on her forehead shook her. Was giving him back the ring the right move? Just because they weren't engaged didn't mean they couldn't see each other, right? They could date. See if they could find common ground.

Meg chewed her lip. Common ground. Was that what they had in Pine Grove? She'd had her nature stuff and he'd had baseball. Whatever it was, magic had taken place in the small house. They had come together as strangers and fallen in love—knowing little about each other's worlds. And it had worked.

Damn—a near-miss as her mother might say. If it wasn't right, why was she so upset? Shouldn't she be relieved, like she felt when she dumped Harold? Getting rid of him had produced no wild pulse, no sweat. It had been simply the right thing. But not with Rusty. She wasn't dumping him, only stepping back. At least she wanted to believe it. How would he take it? Would he be mad? Confused? Accepting? She hoped not accepting.

The silence between them grew loud. Why didn't he say something?

"You don't want to see me anymore?" Rusty raised his gaze to hers. She saw hurt there.

Meg placed her hand on his arm before speaking. "I didn't say that."

"No, giving me back the ring says it for you." He twirled the small box between his fingers.

"I love you. That hasn't changed."

"Coulda fooled me."

"You can't say you don't see it."

"Okay, yeah. I get it. You're right. We don't fit into each other's worlds. Not right now. But we might. In the future. I don't want to stop seeing you."

"Me, either." Her voice softened.

"So, you don't want me to leave tonight? I'm confused."

"Please don't. Please stay."

"What'll we tell the boys?"

"Nothing. Can I take a week or two breather? Tommy and Charlie can continue to have sleepovers."

"They'll notice I'm not sleeping over, too."

"We'll make excuses. I just need time."

Rusty took her hand in both of his. "I know they were rough on you tonight. I'd never want you to be treated like that."

"I'm not a celebrity. I get it."

"That shouldn't matter. There was no respect."

She lowered her head. He did get it. She pushed to her feet. "I'm tired."

"Me, too. Do you want me to sleep on the sofa?"

She shook her head. God, how could she ever want him out of her bed? Never. "Please come to bed." She held out her hand.

Rusty pulled down the covers and Meg got in first. He settled a foot or two away from her.

"Hold me. Please?" Her voice a mere whisper.

"Sure."

He slid over and took her in his arms. Tears dripped down her cheeks and onto his chest.

"You're crying."

"I know." She wiped her face with her fingers.

"If you're so upset, why are we breaking up?"

"We're not breaking up." She combed her fingers through his chest hair.

"Seems like it to me. I love you, Meg. Please, don't rip us apart."

"Can we date?" She snaked her arm across his waist.

"Seems a bit ridiculous."

"Please?"

"Okay." His response was deep and low. "As long as I can see you."

"We'll try it the regular way. Like other people do. Dating first."

"Instead of living together first?"

She chuckled. "You always make me laugh."

He kissed her and settled her against his side. She rested her hand on his chest. His scent mixed with a little sweat met her nostrils. Forcing her mind to shut off, she allowed her senses to rule. Warmth and love flowed through her as he snuggled her close.

Rusty was a good man. They'd figure it out. She wanted him but wanted him back in Pine Grove. Why did she wish for things she couldn't have? Meg sighed and let sleep come.

THANKSGIVING MORNING

Meg closed her suitcase and rolled it to the front door.

"Where are we going?" Charlie called from the kitchen.

"I don't know."

"Why not?"

"Rusty didn't tell me."

She stopped yelling and leaned against the archway leading to the kitchen.

"Did you ask?"

"Numerous times. He said we'd agreed to have Thanksgiving together and he wanted to do it out of town. Go away somewhere for the whole four days."

"Why aren't you marrying him?" Charlie took another spoonful of Cheerios.

"It's complicated. Let's see how things go this weekend."

"I can't wait. It's like a Hardy Boys mystery. We're going away somewhere secret."

She laughed. "I love your imagination. Did you finish packing?"

"Tommy agreed to bring Rummikub. I'm supposed to bring Monopoly, but I can't find it."

"Finish up and I'll look for it." She padded into his room and checked under the bed. There it was. She added the game to his suitcase and shut it. She wheeled his to the front door. Staring out the window at the cold, gray November day, she shivered.

This would be her first time back with Rusty since their parting three weeks ago. Her heart ached for his touch, his laugh, the way he filled up a room. Her mood mirrored the weather, drab, gray, and cold. Moping around on weekends, she complained about life at school to Roberta and Charlie. Harold got in her way whenever he could—disapproving her plans, cutting her budget. He'd made working at P.S. 14 as difficult as possible. Each day, she'd drag herself out of bed, more tired than the night before.

She could swear Charlie's demands increased, making life at home exhausting. Not like it wasn't bad enough being his mother and father, but the cooking, the homework, and her job sapped her meager energy.

"You're depressed because you broke up with Rusty," Roberta had said on the phone.

"We didn't break up."

"Haven't seen him in three weeks."

"So? Sometimes people do other things or take some time away."

"Bullshit. Face facts, Meg. You've thrown away the greatest guy in the world and now you're sorry."

Meg had made an excuse and ended the conversation. Was Roberta right? A nagging doubt had entered her head when he'd called to invite them to Thanksgiving.

"We agreed to spend it together." He'd reminded her.

"That was weeks ago."

"Don't you want to?" His voice sounded sad.

Her heart lurched. "I do. Yes. I do."

"Good. I'll send a car for you Thursday morning. Pack clothes. Don't bring food. Okay?"

"That's it?"

"It's a surprise. We're going away for the holiday. I've made arrangements. Okay?"

"Sounds great. Can't wait to get out of here."

"Me, too. See you Thursday."

"Love you," she'd said, but he'd already hung up—without saying it first. She sighed. Roberta was right. Meg had thrown away the best man she'd ever meet. Foolish, very foolish.

"Mom. There's a car outside and it's honking." Charlie broke into her daydream.

Meg snapped to. "Okay, okay. Take your suitcase. I'll take mine."

Charlie went outside. The driver put the luggage in the trunk. Meg locked up. He held the car door, while Meg and Charlie scooted inside.

"Shall I turn up the heat, miss?"

"Please. Where are we going?"

"Sorry. I'm not allowed to say."

"How long will it take to get there?" Meg had a million questions.

"I'm sorry, miss. The mister said with your command of math, you'd figure out our destination if I told you the estimated travel time."

Meg chuckled. Rusty thought of everything.

"Sit back, miss, and enjoy the ride."

"Come on, Mom, chill out."

"Okay. You're the boss, Charlie."

She sat back and shut her eyes. Visions of Rusty danced through her mind.

Charlie chattered away about his plans with Tommy. Meg listened with half an ear. Recollections of Rusty tromping through the woods, complaining, looking so handsome in his T-shirt and jeans, and Rusty swimming at the lake, wearing snug trunks, or dancing at the corn barbecue came to mind.

She laughed recalling his line about making her sweat behind the shed. Damn, she should have called him on it. The best memories of all were she and Rusty sharing their sweat and passion between the sheets.

RUSTY CHECKED THE TURKEY for the millionth time.

"Dad! If you keep opening the oven, the turkey won't cook!"

"I know, I know. Everything has to be right."

Tommy placed his hand on his father's arm. "Everything is right. It's going to be okay. You'll see. Meg'll love it."

"I hope you're right." Rusty paced in the living room, then went to the window. Angry clouds darkened. Would they have rain or snow for their holiday? He let the curtain swing back into place and headed for the kitchen. Grabbing a handful of ice, he poured himself a scotch on the rocks and tried not to think about what he'd done.

"I'll watch from the living room and tell you when they get here." Tommy grinned and Coco barked.

"Okay."

He needed to do something. "Maybe I should vacuum?"

"Dad!"

"All right. I know, I'll take Coco out."

At the mention of her name, the giant dog lumbered into the living room.

Tommy handed his father the leash. Rusty shrugged on a heavy jacket and opened the kitchen door. Coco pushed through ahead of him. As they walked, he talked to the beast.

"I don't even know if Meg likes surprises. I'm not sure she does. She likes to be in control, know what's coming, ya know? I mean, like her husband dying. That was one big nasty surprise."

Coco stopped to pee, then looked at Rusty and continued on her way toward the woods. A shaft of light warmed his back. He glanced up at the sky. "Look, girl. The clouds are drifting away. There's an opening. I see some blue sky and a little sunlight."

Coco stopped to lick his hand. He petted the canine. "She said we should be apart. Well, we have been. For three weeks. It's been hell. That should be enough, right? I'm going nuts. Don't you miss her, too?"

Coco glanced back with an affirmative woof.

"Exactly!" Rusty ran his fingers through his hair. "This has to work, Coco. It has to. We need her."

Again, the dog responded. When they hit the edge of the woods, Rusty heard *Dad*. He and the pooch turned to face the house. Tommy stood at the back door, his hands cupped around his mouth, yelling.

"They're here!"

Rusty dropped the leash and took off. He ran like Will Grant was rifling a ball from center field at him as he slid into home. Coco bounded after him. As he got into the kitchen, he heard the slam of car doors.

Tommy ran outside. Rusty bounded through the house, stopping in the doorway.

Meg, hands on hips, stopped cold. "What's this?"

"Our house."

"But the roof. It was caved in. Roberta said they sold it." She quirked her head slightly as her gaze connected with his.

"They did. I bought it. I had it repaired, strengthened. Took a couple of months."

"Months?" Her eyebrows rose.

"Come inside. It's cold," Rusty said, picking up her suitcase. With his other hand, he slipped the driver two twenties.

"Is my room the same?"

"You bet it is, Charlie." Rusty grinned as the boy ran to the back of the house.

"Why? What? I'm confused."

"I bought the house and fixed it up. I thought we could use it as a weekend getaway."

"Really?"

He nodded. "But then, three weeks ago happened. We had *the talk*. I got another idea."

"Another idea?"

"Come inside. Have a drink."

They stepped into the living room. "Something smells good," Meg said.

"Mrs. MacDougal made everything. She told me how to cook the turkey. She did everything else." He checked his watch. "Dinner should be ready in two hours."

Meg looked around. The living room was the same, but the walls were freshly painted. She ran from room-to-room. All the ceilings were intact, and the rooms sported fresh wall color.

"This is your house?" Meg's eyes widened.

"Our house. Wine?"

She nodded. Rusty handed her a glass of cabernet.

"Come. Sit down."

She joined him on the sofa.

"I listened to you three weeks ago. When I got over the shock, I realized you were right. Where were we good? Right here. In Pine Grove. Not New York City. So I made a change. My contract with Hingus and the station ends June first—when Tommy's school gets out."

"June first?"

"Wait." He raised his palm. "Listen. Yes. June first. I start as a consultant and home game commentator for the Jefferson Jaguars on June fifteenth."

"What? The Jaguars?"

He nodded.

"Tommy and I are moving in here at the end of the school year. We'll probably come here weekends until then. I'm selling my apartment. This will be my new home."

Meg's mouth fell open.

"And I want you to quit your school and get a job here. And marry me. And live with us in Pine Grove." The words tumbled out in a rush. He took a breath.

"Leave New York?"

"We don't belong there. Those people at the World Series bash? I don't give a shit about them. And they don't care about me, either. It's just phony. I don't want that world anymore. I want what we had here. This is real. You're real. They're not."

"I agree."

"And your school? It sucks the life from you."

"I know. Harold has made this year horrible. I hate it there."

"Come live here, with me and Tommy."

"When, why did this happen?"

"After our talk, I realized that I'm a better father, and a better man when I'm with you. I like me more when we're together, in Pine Grove.

I figured, why not live here full time? It's gonna take a few months to get settled, and for the kids to finish up school. But we have time. What do you say?"

"It's not up to me alone. Charlie!" Meg called for her son. "How would you feel if we left New York, after the school year is over, and moved in here with Rusty and Tommy?"

"Live here all the time?"

"Yes. And go to school here."

"All right! When?"

"As soon as possible," Rusty put in.

"I gotta tell Tommy." Charlie ran off.

"You're going to do it?" Rusty asked.

She nodded.

Rusty whipped out a small black box from his pants' pocket. "Then we're engaged again?"

"I think you have to ask."

"Really?" He cocked an eyebrow.

"Really." She hid a smile behind her hand.

He dropped down on one knee. "Meg Gunderson, will you marry me, here in Pine Grove and live with me here forever?"

"I will."

Rusty slipped the ring back on her finger. "You're sure?"

"Never been more sure of anything in my life."

He took her in his arms and kissed her. His heartbeat soared. He sat back. "I'm so happy right now."

"Don't we have to set the table? Can I peek at the food? Something smells awfully good."

"Let's go."

Meg called the boys and gave them tasks. Soon the table was set and the wine was breathing. Rusty took her aside.

"I made some changes to the house."

"Changes?"

"It was kinda small. Since we had to put on a new roof, I created an attic and turned it into a playroom for the boys. There's more. Come on." He took her hand and led her through the house. They stopped at an empty room.

"I was going to ask you about this," Meg said. "A den?"

Rusty drew her close, draping his arm across her shoulders. He bent down to whisper.

"Don't tell the boys. But I thought, since we're such good parents, we might decide to have one more. One of our own. And it might even be a girl. So we'd need an extra bedroom."

Meg put her hands over her face and sobbed. Rusty's brows knitted. He stepped back and pulled her into his embrace. "What's wrong? We don't have to have another kid, if you don't want to."

"Oh, but I do. I do so much." He handed her his handkerchief. She mopped her face. "That's so sweet."

"Why the tears?"

"Because I'm so happy. I've been dreaming night after night about having a child with you."

"Oh, Meg." His eyes filled and he hugged her tight.

A buzzer sounded. They split apart.

"Turkey's ready." He rubbed his eyes.

"Oh boy! Thanksgiving turkey!" Came from the boys' room.

"Our first Thanksgiving." She sighed.

"First of at least fifty." Rusty beamed, took her hand, and headed for the kitchen.

Epilogue

Three weeks later

Meg pulled the short-sleeved pink cashmere sweater over her head.

"Let me do your makeup." Roberta sat on the edge of the new, king-sized bed in the master bedroom in Pine Grove.

"Okay." Meg ran a comb through her short hair.

"Put this around you," Roberta said, handing her friend a towel.

Meg sat while Roberta worked her magic with eyeliner, mascara, and highlighter.

"Not too much. I like the natural look."

"Yeah. But it can take a ton of makeup to get that."

Meg chuckled. The door burst open and Charlie blustered in.

"Mom, hurry up!"

"Charlie, bride's take time." Roberta picked up a small brush.

"Tell Rusty I'll be there in fifteen minutes."

"Fifteen minutes!" Charlie's eyes widened.

"Yes."

"Girls. They sure take a lot of time putting that crap on."

"Where did you hear the word crap?" Meg stared hard at him.

"Rusty said that you'd be okay with crap, but you wouldn't like it if I said shit."

Meg pushed away from Roberta. "Got that right."

"Tell them she'll be there soon, Charlie." Roberta shooed him away.

Meg plucked at her hair, then picked up her white suit jacket. She put it on and straightened her skirt.

"Where are the flowers?" Meg asked.

Roberta shrugged.

"They were in a box."

Roberta looked on the other side of the bed and found it on the floor. She opened it and handed Meg a nosegay of pink sweetheart roses.

"There's one in there for you, too." Meg put her flowers down on the bed. "And the veil?"

"On the bed. Let me do it." Roberta put her small bouquet of white flowers on the bed and picked up the white satin bow with tulle attached. She fastened it on Meg's head.

"Ready?" Roberta raised her eyebrows.

Meg smiled. "Ready."

They joined Charlie and picked their way across the icy path to the driveway. Fred waited in an SUV. He'd been running the car to keep the inside warm. Meg plopped down in the seat next to her son.

"You look so handsome in your suit." She grinned.

"Rusty's wearing a monkey suit."

"It's called a tuxedo," Meg corrected him.

"I like monkey suit better. Can I call this a monkey suit?"

"Why not?"

Meg looked out the window at the Christmas decorations in the windows of each house they passed. Lights on the outside, evergreen trees on front lawns sported different colored lights, or all white lights. Some flashed, others glowed steadily. Little Pine Grove had turned out all its finery for the Christmas holiday.

A bare tree stood in the house Meg and Rusty would share. Boxes of lights and decorations piled up beside the large fir. She couldn't wait to decorate it with Tommy, Rusty, and Charlie after the wedding dinner.

Fred drove carefully to Homer's, where the ceremony was scheduled to take place.

Meg had wanted a small ceremony at home, but Rusty had talked her into taking over Homer's and inviting the entire town. When they drove up, the lot was full, except for one parking space designated for the bride.

"Ready?" Fred asked, throwing the car into park and turning off the engine.

"Ready as I'll ever be."

"I'll tell them you're here and get the music started." Fred took Roberta's hand.

"Remember, I go down first. Fred will escort me. Then you and Charlie."

"I've done this once before, remember. I know how it goes." Meg stepped inside.

Within five minutes, Meg heard music. She and Charlie stood in the vestibule of Homer's Restaurant. She straightened his tie and then her jacket.

"Are you sure you want to do this, Charlie?"

"Walk you down the aisle?" He nodded.

"Why?"

"Dad would have wanted it."

Tears filled Meg's eyes. She pulled Rusty's handkerchief from her pocket and took a deep breath. "You're right. He probably would."

She smoothed his hair down and met his gaze. "You're okay with me marrying Rusty?"

"Yep."

"Sure?"

"Yep."

"Okay then. This doesn't mean we ever forget your father."

"Nope. I get it."

"Sometimes you're so grown up." She sighed. "I love you, Charlie."

"Love you, too, Mom. Ready?" Charlie offered his arm to his mother, then pushed the door open. Everyone stood up.

Chairs had been set up to create an aisle. Rusty in his monkey suit and Tommy, as best man, also in a monkey suit, stood by the fireplace. A judge in his black robes awaited next to the groom.

Meg and Charlie stepped slowly, in time to the music. Meg nodded to Laura Dailey, mopping her eyes, and her husband, Barney. There were many familiar faces. The coffee lady from Java the Hut, Jess and Stryker from the hotel, Giselle and Cal, neighbors, and Jory, who was covering the wedding for the Pine Grove Press and her husband, Trent.

When they reached Rusty, Charlie stepped back, placing his mother's hand in Rusty's.

"Thanks, Charlie."

The boy smiled.

Meg stepped closer to Rusty and the judge cleared his throat.

"We're gathered together to witness the union of this man and this woman in holy matrimony."

Meg didn't hear the rest of his speech. Her mind had zoomed back to the day she had wed John Gunderson. A mere twenty-two years old, she had been a nervous wreck. Looking back, she'd have to laugh. For all those nerves, the union had been a happy, if brief, one. Her heart squeezed for a moment.

As much as she loved Rusty, she still loved John, too. The memory of the incredible tension of her big wedding, compared to the small amount of stress for this one pleased her. She glanced into Rusty's eyes. He seemed so sure. No signs of nerves, no sweat on his brow, no fidgeting, no shifting his weight. He stood tall and straight, calmly, in one spot, listening to the judge.

Damn, he looked good. Confidence washed through her. As they made eye contact, he squeezed her hand and raised his eyebrows.

"You okay?" He interrupted the judge.

"Never better." She smiled.

"May I continue, Mr. Reisse?"

"Sorry. Sure. Yeah. Go ahead."

Finally, he got to the important part.

"Do you, Russell Reisse take Margaret Gunderson to be your lawfully wedded wife?"

She didn't hear the rest, only Rusty's resounding yes and the titter from the audience. Then it was her turn. At the pause, she agreed. Then came the ring exchange. Finally, the judge ran out of words and uttered the magical ones.

"You may kiss the bride."

Rusty took her in his arms for a long kiss. A few hoots from Barney and a couple of other men reached her ears. But, oh, it was so damn good to be in his arms again. After they drank their first glass of champagne and threw the bouquet, Barney Dailey came over to them.

"Tell me, Rusty. What made you finally make a play for Meg?" Barney sipped his beer.

"Your words, Barney."

"Me?" His eyebrows rose and he pointed to his chest.

"Yep. When you dared to me steal just one kiss. There couldn't be just one kiss with Meg. After one, I had to have more."

Barney chuckled. "You can name your firstborn after me."

Meg put in. "Rusty's right. Just one kiss and I was his." She raised her chin as he lowered his mouth to hers.

THE END

If you enjoyed this book, would you please leave a brief review. Thank you.

Books by Jean C. Joachim

<u>ECHOES OF THE HEART</u>
HEATHER & MIKE: THE ONE THAT GOT AWAY
SANDY & RAFE: SECOND PLACE HEART
LIZ & NICK: NO REGRETS
PAIGE & BILL: ONE FINE DAY
ANTHOLOGY
<u>HOCKEY</u>
THE FINAL SLAPSHOT
<u>BOTTOM OF THE NINTH</u>
DAN ALEXANDER, PITCHER
MATT JACKSON, CATCHER
JAKE LAWRENCE, THIRD BASEMAN
NAT OWEN, FIRST BASE
BOBBY HERNANDEZ, SECOND BASE
SKIP QUINCY, SHORT STOP
EXTRA INNINGS
<u>FIRST & TEN SERIES</u>
GRIFF MONTGOMERY, QUARTERBACK
BUDDY CARRUTHERS, WIDE RECEIVER
PETE SEBASTIAN, COACH
DEVON DRAKE, CORNERBACK
SLY "BULLHORN" BRODSKY, OFFENSIVE LINE
AL "TRUNK" MAHONEY, DEFENSIVE LINE
HARLEY BRENNAN, RUNNING BACK
OVERTIME, THE FINAL TOUCHDOWN

A KING'S CHRISTMAS
<u>THE MANHATTAN DINNER CLUB</u>
RESCUE MY HEART
SEDUCING HIS HEART
SHINE YOUR LOVE ON ME
TO LOVE OR NOT TO LOVE
<u>HOLLYWOOD HEARTS SERIES</u>
IF I LOVED YOU
RED CARPET ROMANCE
MEMORIES OF LOVE
MOVIE LOVERS
LOVE'S LAST CHANCE
LOVERS & LIARS
His Leading Lady (Series Starter)
<u>NOW AND FOREVER SERIES</u>
NOW AND FOREVER 1, A LOVE STORY
NOW AND FOREVER 2, THE BOOK OF DANNY
NOW AND FOREVER 3, BLIND LOVE
NOW AND FOREVER 4, THE RENOVATED HEART
NOW AND FOREVER 5, LOVE'S JOURNEY
NOW AND FOREVER, CALLIE'S STORY (prequel)
<u>MOONLIGHT SERIES</u>
SUNNY DAYS, MOONLIT NIGHTS
APRIL'S KISS IN THE MOONLIGHT
UNDER THE MIDNIGHT MOON
MOONLIGHT & ROSES (prequel)
<u>LOST & FOUND SERIES</u>
LOVE, LOST AND FOUND
DANGEROUS LOVE, LOST AND FOUND
<u>NEW YORK NIGHTS NOVELS</u>
THE MARRIAGE LIST
THE LOVE LIST

About the Author

Jean Joachim is a USA Today best-selling, award-winning, international romance fiction author, with books hitting the Amazon Top 100 list since 2012. She writes contemporary romance, which includes sports romance and romantic suspense.

Liz & Nick: One Fine Day won second place in the erotic romance category of the Oklahoma Romance Writers of America's 2018 International Digital Awards.

Dangerous Love Lost & Found, First Place winner in the 2015 Oklahoma Romance Writers of America, International Digital Award contest. *The Renovated Heart* won Best Novel of the Year from Love Romances Café. *Lovers & Liars* was a RomCon finalist in 2013. And *The Marriage List* tied for third place as Best Contemporary Romance from the Gulf Coast RWA.

To Love or Not to Love tied for second place in the 2014 New England Chapter of Romance Writers of America Reader's Choice contest.

She was chosen Author of the Year in 2012 by the New York City chapter of RWA.

Married and the mother of two sons, Jean lives in New York City. Early in the morning, you'll find her at her computer, writing, with a cup of tea, and a secret stash of black licorice.

Jean has 57 books, novellas and short stories published. Find them here:

http://www.jeanjoachimbooks.com. Chat with Jean in her Facebook group, JJ's Book Buddies. Join here: https://www.facebook.com/groups/489790604419710/